MYTH-TOUCHED

SHADOWS OF EIRELAND
BOOK TWO

JOANNA MACIEJEWSKA

Source France, 1 Av. Johannes Gutenberg, 78310 Maurepas, France.
compliance@lightningsource.fr

To families chosen.

CHAPTER ONE

In hindsight, I should have known that kneeling in front of a mythborn and suggesting he take his pants off would look wrong to any onlooker. On the other hand, neither Connor nor I could have predicted that someone would barge into his workshop at the very moment we were trying to test a new charm for his harness.

The sturdy web of leather and wire surrounded Connor's leg, holding various amulets and charms in place, and from what little I understood of its intricate design, it was meant to ease pain and allow him to walk. It felt only right that I helped him to improve the harness, as I was, at least indirectly, responsible for his disability. I thought that contact with his skin could help magic within the amulets and charms work better, thus the pants-off remark I threw.

Connor reacted to my enhancement ideas with a slight amusement, but he didn't protest trying things out. At times, I couldn't help wondering whether he did so to ease the guilt I felt whenever I remembered the circumstances that led to his injury, back when humanborn and mythborn were still at war.

He, of course, chose to remember only the good part of our first meeting, namely the fact I dragged him away from a giant's path, saving his life, but I couldn't forget what preceded it. It was a skirmish like any others in the war, so its details eluded me, and I might have not remembered the strike that would make me very personally responsible for his lame leg.

He never brought it up, though, as if my saving his life had erased all my prior deeds. Back then, if anyone had learned of it, I would have been branded a traitor. Now it had earned me the only friendly person in the mythborn-filled Court, a place I was stuck in for the past weeks, and his workshop had become a retreat from the Court politics and gossip, especially that hardly anyone ever visited it.

Well, at least until now.

I sprang to my feet at the sound of the door opening with more force than necessary and faced the scrutiny of a mythborn female whose expression made it clear that the old "this isn't what it looks like" response just wasn't going to cut it. She had red hair, thought more in the carrot department than in the fiery one, and skin similar to Connor's: peach, with slightly darker, marble-like veins marking it. Many of the mythborn had skin that bore resemblance to natural objects—stone, wood, sand, and so on, often in odd or fantastical hues, so it had to be a trait of their species. The amount of makeup covering the newcomer's face suggested she didn't consider her skin pretty.

"Clíodhna, have you met Kaja? She's a myth-touched learning our craft." Connor lifted from his chair, his moves stiff as the unbalanced harness immobilized his leg. "Kaja, this is my cousin, Clíodhna."

I envied his composure. He acted as if there was nothing improper about the situation, or perhaps he cared little of what others thought of him. During the past days, I'd caught glimpses of dismissal or pity other mythborn had for him, so I wasn't surprised he didn't bother trying to win anyone's approval. He stood confident, ignoring that the harness was forcing his body into an odd and likely uncomfortable position, and he stared at Clíodhna expectantly as if she was the one to explain herself.

Clíodhna glanced at me once more before focusing on Connor, and as soon as she opened her mouth, a wave of mythborn language slipped from her perfectly shaped—or rather perfectly outlined—lips. Nothing made it clearer that I wasn't invited to join the conversation than speaking language I hardly knew. Judging from the bits I caught, I wasn't missing anything important.

"Yes, I'll see you in the evening," Connor replied tiredly.

I considered it a courtesy that he insisted on using English, even if she didn't. All mythborn displayed uncanny linguistic skills, learning languages quickly, so she knew English at least as well as I did, if not better, considering we both were second-language speakers.

She opened her mouth, but Connor waved his hand.

"It's my leg that is incapacitated, not my mind," he said with clear ire. As all the mythborn I'd met, he was proud. "I can remember about a dinner with my relatives."

Clíodhna's lips arched, dissatisfaction lurking in the creases of her mouth, but she nodded. Then she left without even acknowledging me, and I was alone with Connor again.

"I apologize." Connor leaned over the table and picked up one of the amulets we'd removed from his harness before the incident. "Clíodhna's convinced that she's doing me a favor by dragging me to those family meals."

He reattached the amulet where it belonged and ran his

hand along his thigh and the magical harness, bringing my feeling of guilt back while he readjusted the charms and removed the newest addition. Words weren't necessary—I knew it didn't work the way we'd hoped for. So much for my brilliant ideas that were supposed to undo what I had possibly caused in one simple charm.

"We should get back to your lessons," he said.

His casual tone reminded me to not dwell on the past even if we both were haunted by it. After all, we weren't enemies anymore, not even because the war had ended. I was now what they called a myth-touched, a magically changed humanborn, and a member of the mythborn Court... Well, at least a nominal one. That meant we were on the same side.

Connor had never said it openly, but he made it clear that the quicker I made the transition from thinking like humanborn to behaving like a mythborn, the better. Until then, he suggested between the lines in quite an uneasy manner, as if he was forced to pass the message rather than believed in it, I was stuck within the old Collins Barracks building that used to house the Museum of Decorative Arts and History and currently was the seat of the mythborn side of the government.

With a sigh, I took the pile of parchments he offered. "I hope you don't expect me to match the finesse of your carvings." Memorizing a bunch of unfamiliar squiggles was a pain enough, and adding the mythborn equivalent of calligraphy to that tedious task wasn't on my list.

Connor smirked. "You *could* refine your skills a bit. You wouldn't ruin so many amulets if your etchings were more precise."

"I don't think improving my carving skills is what's going to convince Lady Eithne to let me out of here."

When I'd first emerged from the magical pool that saved me from death and made me into a myth-touched, the head of the Court insisted I stayed around for a while, as if going outside meant venturing into some sort of a savage land and not into a city that might still bear the marks of the past war but had already recovered enough to welcome tourists from abroad.

Lady Eithne wasn't even trying to make my stay sound like a suggestion, and having survived only because of her benevolence, I had little room for defiance. She let me write a short letter to Albert, likely to ensure that the Trinitians, or rather their leader himself, didn't go to war over the lack of news from me. But that was it when it came to the contact with the outside world, so as days passed, my patience was wearing thin.

I'd been spending most of my time in Connor's workshop, and even though his tutoring had immensely improved my skills of amulet, charm, and curse making, I had never intended to become a full-time artisan. When I first picked it up, it was mostly curiosity to see if the craft could help stabilize the chaotic magic that raged within me back then. I got better over time, creative with what little I knew, but learning it properly meant boring basics and simple tasks.

Connor sighed and shook his head. "Give the lady some time. Now her mind is focused on chasing down the other Snake agents."

"It's not like I want in on it," I replied with more bitterness than intended.

My last encounter with the Snake's servants was still fresh in my mind, including the memories of Emma's talons tearing into me and the magic poison eating away my body. Those images returned every other night in a fresh set of nightmares, spicing up the vast collection of bad dreams I already had.

"But she could say, 'Hey, Kaja, go for a walk, just be back before dinnertime,' and I swear I wouldn't be late," I added.

He gave me an apologetic glance, and I didn't press him. Whatever reasons Lady Eithne had for keeping me at the Court, he wasn't at liberty to discuss them, and the last thing I wanted was to make him feel guilty. He was kind enough to teach me and offer some distraction and companionship. Otherwise, stuck alone at the Court, I'd likely have gone insane.

"Why don't you take these to the garden?" he offered all of a sudden. "I wrote down the names of the runes in English for you, so you can study there and get some fresh air. Take a few days to learn them and relax. Being stuck in a workshop day after day doesn't do anyone any good."

I bit down the remark that he was spending even more time in said workshop than I did, and I snatched the papers in a desperate swipe. Even if going to the Court's so-called garden wasn't the same as going outside freely, I appreciated the thought. It didn't matter whether he really cared about my wellbeing or was simply tired with my growing frustration and low-key whining—his suggestion gave me a way out, and I needed it badly.

Otherwise I'd risk losing the only friendly mythborn I had around.

WHAT THE MYTHBORN called the garden, I considered a greenhouse. Located on the topmost floor of the building, it wasn't open to the outside weather. Instead, charms provided light imitating the sunshine Eireland always lacked anyway and produced a light summer breeze that carried scents of flowers and ripe fruit. Countless pots and flowerbeds took most of the space, and only narrow gravel paths led through the greenery. The mythborn architects had also removed parts of the roof, replacing it with tall windows—something I noticed back when I was only a visitor to the Court but never bothered to ponder, and even now they made little sense to me. One could look down into the courtyard, though I wasn't sure what for, since the empty cobblestoned square didn't offer anything worth watching.

I sat on the bench, pretending to study the runes, so that the few mythborn around would leave me alone. Not that many of them would stoop to a conversation with me anyway. Those who had the time to visit the garden midday were usually spoiled nobles, and I was hardly better than a humanborn in their eyes. In a way, not much changed in my relations with most of the Court mythborn since I'd become the myth-touched, except that instead of being able to go home whenever I'd had enough of their company, I was stuck here with those pricks.

Their hushed conversations reached my ears so clearly it was as if I was sitting next to them. The peculiar skill I'd acquired during my lifesaving ritual seemed to be growing stronger instead of waning, so at some point I had to learn how to control it. But listening in was more annoying than useful, as the meaning of their words escaped me more often than not. Many mythborn used primarily English and Irish, making the communication with everyone else easy, but some kept to their own language that after hundreds of years of separation hardly resembled the old Gaelic that they might have once shared with humans. I had to learn some of it if I wanted to get information they would be keeping from me otherwise, but at the same time I doubted any of the mythborn in the garden had anything meaningful to share. I suspected most of their conversations were gossip or some petty political games.

Yet I needed to hone my newly acquired skill. If I'd paid more attention to it, maybe I would have recognized the sound of footsteps stopping right outside the workshop and would have gotten up before Clíodhna made her entrance, sparing Connor and myself some embarrassment. I gritted my teeth, because all those "would haves" were children of my general frustration, and that feeling seemed to be an extremely fertile mother, spawning more and more unwanted thoughts.

Since I wanted a distraction to chase them away, I might as well see how well my new listening skill worked.

A mythborn walked past me, his gait rushed and uneven, so it would be easy to follow among other noise. With my eyes closed, I focused on the odd rhythm, doing my best to cling to it before it faded off in the distance. The conversations around me became clearer, and I even caught some that were carried in English, but the footsteps faded as they normally would.

Clearly, I sucked at that.

Determined to figure it out, this time I picked a mythborn sitting at a distance who was tapping his fingers against the wood of the bench. I couldn't tell whether it was a sign of impatience, or maybe he was tapping to a tune in his head, but it didn't matter. I needed something that I couldn't hear from where I was sitting—perhaps my skill picked up only on things that were too distant for my normal hearing.

In an instant, the buzz of many conversations around me became almost deafening, and it took a lot of my focus to tune them out. Still, I didn't catch a single sound of tapping... With all the mythborn talking as loud as if they stood beside me, I knew my peculiar skill was working, but for some reason, it wouldn't pick up anything but voices.

It seemed that the chaotic magic that once threatened my life after the ritual had become *very specific* magic. I wasn't going to complain, though. Hearing every single sound within who-knows-what radius would be cumbersome, while eavesdropping on conversations alone could be of immense value. I doubted that I'd learn anything useful from the Court's spoiled and bored nobles, but there were others around who exchanged secrets and orders, and the prospect of learning those was enticing. Even though, at the moment, it felt difficult and tiring, I hoped that with practice, it would become easier.

I looked down at the parchments. Now that I had more enticing things to explore, memorizing the runes felt even more like a pointless chore, but the sooner I was done with it, the sooner Eithne would run out of excuses to keep me at the Court. Well, I wanted to believe so, for the sake of my own sanity.

I paid little attention to the sounds of footsteps around me as mythborn strolled to the garden constantly, but when one stopped right in front of me, blocking what little light an overcast day was offering, I lifted my head and met Clíodhna's eyes. She grimaced ever so slightly when I didn't stand up.

"Anything I can help you with?" I took the initiative.

She looked me up and down. I'd seen this type of glare a long time ago, back when I was in high school. Back then, I also had been on the receiving end of it when the school's most popular girls would evaluate my clothes and makeup as insufficient to be socially acceptable, and then cross me off their party invites list. I didn't intend to dwell on the past, but the way Clíodhna carried herself, and the way she looked down at me, definitely brought a spoiled and entitled teenager to mind.

"Actually, yes," she replied in that tone that suggested I was being granted an ultimate privilege: an opportunity to be helpful to her. "I know what you're trying to do, and I won't allow your petty scheme to succeed."

I arched my eyebrow in polite interest. I doubted that Clíodhna was referring to my desire to get the heck out of the Court, so whatever plot she'd conjured, it had to be good.

"You're playing on my cousin's vulnerability," she continued, "but he's not going to fall for your charms. He knows you aren't worthy of him."

I almost burst out laughing. Sure, I liked Connor, and it seemed he reciprocated the sentiment, since he acted casually in my company, but I was certain the feelings on both sides were purely platonic. Having experienced what a real attraction to a mythborn was, especially with my inner magic's clear response to touch, I had no doubt that neither Connor nor I were interested in anything but friendship. I hoped I could explain that to the teen-like mythborn and send her on her way, wherever she was going next. Hopefully somewhere far from me.

But if I thought I'd get even a word in, I was wrong. Clíodhna was just getting started. "You think you can ensnare a mythborn from a good family just because he's a cripple—"

This time, I didn't let her finish. I jumped up from the bench and stood right in front of her face, any respect for personal space be damned. Mythborn didn't seem to care about it anyway, so they didn't get to complain.

Clíodhna took a step back, her mouth slightly open,

though words weren't flowing anymore, and her startled expression suggested she didn't expect me to react so strongly.

"He's not a cripple," I said. "He's a veteran who risked his life to ensure the privileges you're enjoying. If you can't see beyond his injury, if you can't see the hero he is, you're the one who's not worth his company."

Clíodhna's dumbfounded stare provided me a lot of satisfaction, and I didn't care whether I broke any protocols or etiquette. She deserved every bit of rudeness for what she'd said.

Her trembling lips and raging glare foretold the tantrum she was about to throw in response for my words. She opened her mouth, and I automatically tuned out the rant to come. I think she started with "you little," but at the same moment, my enhanced hearing picked up a commotion down in the courtyard. Guards were calling out, and even though I couldn't catch every word through the noise Clíodhna was producing, I caught the gist of the message: the Scáthanna returned.

Before I became a myth-touched, I worked with Eithne's elite squad for a while, and aside from Connor, they were the closest to friendly faces I had in the Court. I doubted they considered me a friend, but they cared enough to save my life when I was dying from magic poison... even if it might have been only at their teammate's insistence. If they were returning, perhaps they would have a few days off, and I could go talk to them... or at least spend some time with Riagán—a cheeky master archer whose interest in me, contrary to Connor's, was definitely a romantic one.

I snapped out of my thoughts, as the tone of everyone's voice carried concern and even fear, so I ignored my myth-born companion and rushed to the window.

Clíodhna shouted her displeasure at my turned back, but then curiosity got the better of her, and she joined me. Together, we watched the Scáthanna enter the courtyard, one by one... Only six of them.

With a blood-congealing feeling, I scanned their faces—ceannasaí Cathal led them, and then others followed with grim expressions. When I caught Riagán's gray hair as he walked in through the gate, I almost collapsed from relief, and the strength of that emotion surprised me. We might have "kind-of-sort-of" confessed having some feelings for each other, but with the little time we'd spent together, I didn't expect any deeper attachment to form.

The Scáthanna parted, with their ceannasaí heading toward the Court's main entrance, probably to report to Eithne, and the rest taking a turn toward their quarters. I ran their names against their faces before they disappeared in the doorway.

Laoise. Laoise was missing.

I pictured the black-haired scout, so skilled with her two knives she could put to shame some seasoned humanborn warriors, and I conjured all the reasons for her not to be around, from spying on someone to running a solo assignment, but from the Scáthanna's expressions and other mythborn's reactions, I knew none of them were true.

Laoise was dead.

I curled my fingers against my palms, fingernails digging deep into my skin as I tried to keep my own hands from shaking. Laoise was the closest to a friend I had among the squad, with my relationship with Riagán definitely more romantic in its nature, or at least she was the one I liked the most from the bunch. She was also as deadly and proficient as all the other squad members, so I couldn't even begin to imagine who or what could have bested her in a fight.

Clíodhna still stood beside me, her pretty face twisted in shock and disbelief. As far as I understood, the Scáthanna were almost a legend to many mythborn, and most of them likely considered the team unconquerable.

I bit my tongue before I treated her with some nasty comment. It didn't seem like a moment for payback.

"Your cousin made it back," I offered quietly. "He could have bled to death in the street or died by a giant's hand, but he made it back." I looked her in the eye. "When you get a chance, ask him how he got his leg injured, because this was also how he met me, and that's why we're friends. Maybe that will convince you I'm not after him."

I walked away before she could respond. I'd said all I had to say, and it wasn't my job to offer support or comfort to her. She could deal with her emotions on her own, but I hoped that at least she'd go and apologize to Connor.

The Scáthanna didn't seem in a mood to talk to anyone, and I didn't have anyone else to ask about Laoise, so I headed straight for my room. Tears were already gathering under my eyelids, ready to flow, and I didn't need some stuffed-up mythborn noble, one who had probably never experienced a loss of a companion, to witness them.

CHAPTER TWO

After a mostly sleepless night when I kept waking up at the slightest sound outside and at any voice speaking, near and far, I opened the door to Connor's workshop feeling the full weight of my tiredness.

Connor inspected me with concern, though he didn't look any better. I wouldn't be surprised if the news had triggered his nightmares as well. We never spoke about it, but we didn't have to. I knew that at times he slept as badly as I did, and I also knew why. The way he avoided any war-related topics suggested he felt as uncomfortable discussing the past as I did, and he wanted our first meeting to be just that: an event that brought us together.

"I see the news has reached you." His voice carried the same tiredness his body emanated.

"Not really," I grumbled. "I just saw them come back and figured out the rest."

He put away the piece of mythborn jewelry he was working on when I entered, likely some trivial amulet for one of the nobles. He must have chosen it for the simplicity of the task: enough to keep his mind busy without draining what little energy and motivation he had left after a night-mare-filled night.

"You should rest. Go for a walk in the gardens or try to get some sleep."

To my regret, he didn't mention anything about Laoise, and I wasn't sure whether it'd be tactful to ask. I'd been living with the mythborn for weeks, supposedly assimilating and all that bullshit, but I still knew very little of their customs. Maybe the lady was right keeping me at the Court, since I haven't learned everything I might need to know, but it wasn't like anyone was offering such lessons to me. It was almost as if they assumed I'd learn on my own by just being around them.

Nevertheless, things had changed now. I doubted Laoise's death was an accident with the threat from the Snake still out there, and it meant that peacetime activities should take a step back and make space for serious work.

"I don't want to rest," I said. "I want to learn whatever I should learn and be doing my job again."

I had no illusion that I could have prevented Laoise's death, but back before I became a myth-touched, I was a successful information broker, with many people bringing me news and gossip. Even earlier, during the war, I was a good scout. If I was out there, doing my job, my real job, I could have learned something of use, something that could have changed Laoise's odds, so being stuck at the Court grated on my nerves all the more.

"Then go to the gardens and study the runes I gave you. Come back when you memorized them all. Unless..." He paused, avoiding my eyes. "Unless you need to talk to some-one," he offered awkwardly.

"I'll be fine." I forced a more lighthearted tone. We both knew it was only a façade, but I would be damned if I burdened Connor, already struggling with his own traumas, with my fears and frustrations. "It's not the first time."

During the war, we often lost friends, squad mates, allies. I hushed the voice in my head trying to remind me the war was over. The Snake's agents still lurked in the dark, and instead of helping to track them down, I was playing a student to a mythborn craftsman. "Wasting time" wasn't even close to an accurate description of how I felt.

Connor didn't call me out on my lie. Neither he nor I could consider ourselves "fine" with so many war scars marking our bodies and minds alike, but at the same time, "fine" was relative. I wasn't much worse than I had already been, and Laoise's death would not be my breaking point.

"Go study the runes, Kaja," he said with sudden gentleness. "Focusing on a task should help."

I snorted but nodded and left. If I intended to torment myself with grim thoughts, at least I could keep Connor out of it. Maybe he had some better coping mechanisms, or maybe he didn't know the Scáthanna well enough to be too affected. Or, perhaps, he was in as bad state as I was but kept his composure for my sake. Leaving meant he could take the mask off and let his own emotions flow.

I made it through the corridors at a fast pace, hoping to look like someone who was too busy to stop for any reason. This time, the ambient magic of the building did nothing to soothe the turmoil in my thoughts. Perhaps Connor was right—I needed something to occupy my mind.

The garden seemed emptier than the previous day, and I welcomed the solitude. The last thing I needed was a hollow conversation with some mythborn who decided to kill their boredom by chatting with a lowly myth-touched. The greens had a soothing effect on my tired eyes, and the gentle aroma of flowers eased my tiredness. Outside, nature still struggled to wake up after a long and dark winter, and spring was still to come—even if the traditional calendar claimed it already happened on the first of February—so the evergreen and ever-blooming garden was one of the few benefits of being part of the Court. I inhaled and exhaled slowly, hoping to ease my tiredness. Maybe if I spent enough time here, I'd find some comfort or tranquility...

I slumped on the bench, not bothered to look presentable, and stared at the runes in front of me. If I knew they were my way out of the Court, I'd memorize them with the same dedication I had learned Trinitian signals during the war, but I had a hunch that lessons with Connor had nothing to do with my future. If anything, they felt like a way to delay any decisions and keep me from seeking confrontation. Which brought me to the only reasonable conclusion: if I wanted a change, I needed to go after it, and it meant finding a way to talk to Lady Eithne. She couldn't be busy forever, and she couldn't avoid me forever.

Out of the corner of my eye, I spotted the very subject of my thoughts strolling the narrow paths.

Even though I heard each stomp of the mythborn who rushed out of her away, their fancy shoes grating against the gravel as they nearly threw themselves into bushes and flowerbeds to ensure Lady Eithne had enough space to pass, I didn't catch a single one of her steps. With that quiet walk of hers, she could put a ninja to shame. Her dress, in a muted hue of navy that made me think of a stormy sea, was short enough to show the tips of her shoes, and Eithne was certainly walking, not floating. Yet, when the dress's fabric caught on a low-lying branch or two, I failed to catch any sound except for the branches quietly snapping back in their place.

She seemed to be searching, and when she spotted me,

her expression brightened. As she headed for me, my heart skipped a beat, flooded with hope that if she wanted to speak to me, maybe it meant changes, and maybe it would be a conversation instead of a confrontation I thought I'd have to stage.

Then, like a light breeze, Cathal walked past me, heading straight for Eithne with the confidence of a homing missile. She didn't seem pleased, and I wasn't either, because it meant I'd have to wait for my turn, but I could suffer my selfish impatience for a little longer. Whatever he needed from her was likely more important.

Besides, if they stayed in the garden, Cathal's presence was an opportunity: with my new skill, I could hear what they talked about and learn something useful. I relaxed on the bench, and while pretending to study the runes in front of me, I focused all my attention on the conversation about to take place. I couldn't help a glance, but I doubted it would look suspicious, seeing as everyone around was doing the same.

"My lady." Cathal bowed, though his voice carried hardly any respect.

"I didn't think you'd have time to enjoy a stroll in the garden." Eithne's response was equally cold.

I breathed out with relief—they were speaking in English. I took another glance in their direction as they settled on a bench surrounded by blooming bushes, but their body language didn't reveal any hostility like their voices did, and I couldn't figure out what was going on. I'd never known Cathal to speak so disrespectfully before.

In the past, he might have baited me with his harsh treatment, but he was never impolite. Besides, I was just a humanborn back then, so no one deserving any special treatment, while everyone around treated Eithne as if she was a goddess. I couldn't even begin to imagine what pushed him to such behavior, unless... Unless it had to do something with Laoise's death. My curiosity erupted like a science project gone wrong.

"I'm here because you were about to send her away under some pretense," he said bluntly. "This isn't what we'd agreed to."

"I intend to respect our agreement, but I believe this isn't the right time," Eithne replied softly, as if she chose to ignore his brash behavior. "She isn't ready yet, and I won't have her death on my conscience just because you insisted on rushing things."

"That's an excuse." I caught traces of frustration in Cathal's voice, though when I inspected his face in yet another quick peek at them, I found it as composed as usual. They were definitely keeping up their appearances for the benefit of all the other mythborn around.

I looked away before they caught me staring at them.

"If someone is to decide whether she's ready, it'd be me," Cathal added.

"Or her. Don't you think that if you ask so early, she might say no?"

"If it's a no, I'd rather hear it now, so I can make other arrangements. And if it's a yes, the sooner I hear it, the sooner I can make sure she's truly ready." He looked Eithne in the eye. "There used to be ten of us, my lady. If you wish us to perform at our best, you have to allow me to do what I consider the best for the Scáthanna."

As far as I could tell, neither of them looked in my direction even once, but I couldn't help but think their conversation had something to do with me. Silence followed, and I abandoned any attempts of pretending that I was studying the runes, instead openly watching them.

I wasn't the only one. Even if Eithne was trying to keep her face neutral, dissatisfaction still seeped through her expression, drawing the curious glances of other mythborn. Their speculating whispers didn't escape me. I almost chuckled at their theories. Most were convinced that Cathal was in trouble for whatever transpired with Laoise or for a failed mission.

"Even if it undermines my authority?" Eithne broke the silence first.

"Officially, you're yet to make a decision, my lady."

A trace of a grimace spoiled the corners of her perfect lips. "Fine. I'll make one favorable for you. But if she says no, you'll consider our agreement fulfilled. There won't be any more attempts."

Cathal turned his head, looking straight at me, and a blush spoiled my cheeks, as if they'd actually caught me eavesdropping. He couldn't know that I actually *was* eavesdropping, but it had to be clear by now that I was paying attention to their meeting.

"She won't say no," he said with confidence.

I shivered, because contrary to reason, in that very moment, it *did* feel like he knew I was listening.

Cathal rose from his seat and bowed. "If you don't need me anymore, my lady, I'll talk to her now. The sooner it's resolved, the better for everyone."

"Go." Eithne waved her hand. "And if she refuses, send her down to my office."

I didn't even try to pretend I was busy when he approached, and I moved to the side, offering him a seat beside me as soon as he stopped by my bench. He smirked at that but sat down.

"Kaja." This was all he offered in terms of a greeting, but

at least he used my name and sounded quite friendly. "How are you enjoying the Court life?"

I caught a hint of irony in his voice, as if he already knew what kind of reply he could expect.

I got straight to the point. "It's quiet and relaxing, but I can't wait to go back to doing my job."

He gave a polite nod as if acknowledging something trivial, but then his face changed, his features gaining the sharpness of someone who wasn't going to beat around the bush. Having had enough of games that seemed to haunt almost all conversations at the Court, I appreciated his approach.

"You're not going back to your old life," he said with blunt honesty. "The lady isn't going to let you. When you're finally allowed to leave the Court, you'll be sent out of Dublin, just like all other myth-touched."

It took me a moment to process his words. It wasn't that I didn't believe his claim. Somehow, under my skin, I'd suspected Eithne wasn't planning on letting me out anytime soon, but I wasn't expecting to be entirely cut off from my past.

I asked the only question I could. "Why?"

"The Court doesn't want you to meet with the Trinitians and your other friends and contacts," Cathal replied. "To reveal that we have a way to 'cure' the affliction, as many would see it. The ritual is only offered to the few the lady deems worthy, and no one here wants to see crowds at the gates demanding we make it available for everyone. The Court was already generous enough to share the affliction-stopping medicine with the humanborn."

I couldn't find a good answer to that. I understood their reasons, but I still felt cheated. Eithne had initially told me that I'd be staying at the Court for a couple of days, and then those days turned to weeks. Cathal's revelation made it clear that the weeks would soon become months unless I left Dublin—permanently, without a doubt.

"What now?" I asked.

He wouldn't have told me all that only to make me feel miserable. I already knew he had an offer to make, and now I understood his confidence in the conversation with Eithne. After such a reveal, I'd agree to almost anything he laid on the table, as long as he offered me a way out of the Court as well. My life plans didn't include living in the Court forever or moving to the countryside, away from the city I considered home.

"I'm sure you already know that the Scáthanna lost their scout," he replied in a more formal tone. "I'm willing to offer you that position if you agree to join us, not just work with us. This means you'll go through training I deem appropriate, and you'll take my orders without questioning them. But this also means that the lady doesn't get to decide what you do with your free time... or where you do it."

I couldn't help inspecting his face in search of deception. The Scáthanna were the mythborn's best, and even after the ritual's magic changed me, I had no illusions regarding my own capabilities. Being better than a humanborn wasn't much in comparison to them.

Cathal was looking at me, patient and stoic, as if giving me time to decide, but I didn't want to ponder all the possible implications of the choice I was about to make.

"How long will that training take?"

He huffed as if my question amused him, but his reply was serious: "I can't tell you for certain. But I can promise you that I won't be looking for excuses to make it any longer than necessary. I need a reliable scout, not a myth-touched playing one of us."

"Days? Weeks? Months?" I pressed. Though I trusted Cathal to keep his word, I needed some sort of a time frame.

He smirked. "I'm hoping you're desperate and determined enough to learn the minimum in under a month. Then additional training will be a matter of finding time for it."

I didn't need to consider his offer long. Sure, joining the Scáthanna meant much less freedom than I was used to, but more than I had now, or in the future that Eithne controlled for me. Besides, it wouldn't be much different from when I was working with them back when I was still a humanborn. Even if Cathal had to make a jab about my reluctance to follow orders, I always ended up doing what he and other Shadows wanted, the very way they wanted, so the only difference would be that I wouldn't get to play the last card and tell him to shove it where even molekind don't dig. But at the same time, that ship had already sailed when I chose to go through the ritual. Now mythborn got to decide what was going to happen to me, and the only say I had was who would be calling the shots.

Out of the two options, Cathal seemed an obvious choice.

"I'm in."

He didn't conceal his satisfaction, and I couldn't resist the thought that he was cherishing his victory over Eithne.

"I'll inform the lady of your choice. Collect your belongings from your room and meet me at our quarters." He stood up. The sudden amused expression he gave me made him look more personable than I'd ever seen him before. "Welcome to the Scáthanna, Kaja. I told you before we'd be working together again."

❧

I STOOD in the Scáthanna's quarters, holding my meager belongings: a few changes of mythborn outfits Eithne insisted I wore around the Court and the items I'd had with me on the day of the ritual, which comprised my old clothes, now awkwardly misfitting, and a bunch of assorted amulets and charms. Studying under Connor meant I added a few unfinished pieces to the last pile, but they still all fit in my bag.

Even though I had visited before on several occasions, I never ventured farther than their day room. I walked in, but it was empty. A long table stretched to the side, burdened with food, as always, and for a moment I imagined nobody ever cleaned it up. The idea of the Scáthanna eating week-old meals made me chuckle. Of course, servants must have ensured the meals were always fresh and ready, waiting and warmed by charmed plates, just like they did in the Court's main dining hall.

It was hardly a surprise that the squad didn't want to mingle with other mythborn who were mostly too boring and too formal in their behavior, and I expected the nobles were happy to not have Cathal's team around. Like Connor had told me during my first official evening at the Court, there were those who were entitled to be part of it, and those who Lady Eithne considered worthy of being its part.

"I see you'll be finally joining us for real." Lorcan entered the room before I had a chance to ponder whether I should sit down. "Come, I'll show you to your room."

It seemed that everyone except for me had already known what Cathal was planning—and it wasn't any news to them, if they even had a room picked out.

"I was told to wait here," I replied. The last thing I needed was to get on Cathal's bad side now that he could actually boss me around.

The Scáthanna's medic offered an approving smile, but then gestured for me to follow. "Ceannasaí isn't going to complain when you aren't wasting time."

He always came across as older than others, though of course, I had no idea how old he really was. With his blond hair and teal-hued skin that in the right light seemed to shimmer like water, he looked as ageless as any other myth-born. Perhaps it was his personality, one of a quiet and wise man, that brought the impression about.

I followed him through the narrow corridor, five doors on each side, and he opened the last one to the left. "This is yours. If you need anything, let one of the servants know. I'm sure at some point you'll want to collect things from your place, but until then, don't hesitate to ask for whatever you need."

I stepped inside. The room looked as impersonal as I'd expected—a bed, somewhat wider than the one in my old room, a desk with a chair, and a chest. No decorations nor embellishments adorned the furniture, and the walls were bare as well. The crystal window seemed to enhance the scant daylight coming in but didn't allow anyone to look in... or out, for that matter. Yet the empty space was plenty, considering the small room I was offered after the ritual, and I could fill it any way I wanted to. It couldn't compare to the size of my own apartment, but it was definitely an improvement.

"Cleansing area is this way," Lorcan said as soon as I dropped my belongings onto the bed.

We turned the corner and walked through the door into a larger area. To the side stood low shelves filled with towels and bathrobes, and then there was a row of showers. In the middle, there was a small pool or basin that seemed designed for soaking and relaxation. Steam rose from it, but not enough to fill the room. Opposite the showers, there were sinks and several doors that likely led to the toilets.

"They are charm-powered." Lorcan pointed at the showers. "Stand to the side of the water stream until you figure out the temperature charm." He gave me an assessing look. "And if you want solitude, I suggest coming here in the middle of the day. Very late evenings will work too."

"Thank you." I had to appreciate the advice, because joining the Scáthanna didn't mean I suddenly felt comfortable showering with them, even if the shower had curtains to allow some privacy. My thoughts drifted toward Riagán and showering with him, and all of a sudden, my cheeks burned.

"I figured you might not be used to our ways. Human-born seem odd in their need for... privacy." He must have interpreted my blush as embarrassment over the bathroom's setup, and I wasn't about to clarify it. "Come—ceannasaí should be back by now. I can show you the rest later. And if you have any questions, ask. Nobody's going to give you a hard time for not knowing things, and we all want you to learn everything as soon as you can."

We retraced our steps through the corridor and almost walked onto Cathal, who entered from the courtyard. Behind him, Sadb followed with a bewildered expression on her face.

"Ceannasaí, please! You have to reconsider!" She sounded desperate. "Faolan's going to be back soon, and I have to be out there—"

"Then you'll make sure you're done with your task as soon as possible," Cathal replied in that cold, authoritative manner I knew so well. He looked at me. "Kaja. Good. From tomorrow morning, Sadb will be training you in combat. All else can wait, but you have to be able to defend yourself.

Lorcan and I will be setting out in the evening, so until I'm back, you're reporting to her."

I turned to Sadb, but the words of greetings stuck in my throat like a fish bone. The expression she wore on her otherwise beautiful face could cut skin open, and for some reason, I was on the receiving end of it.

"You're starting at dawn," she barked. "Don't be late." She almost shouldered her way through, giving both Cathal and me a displeased glare.

I arched an eyebrow at him, but he smiled as if he'd expected such a reaction from her. "Sadb is the best among us. Take your lessons seriously. I hope to hear of your progress." Then he looked at Lorcan. "Be sure to pick up supplies before we set out. And get some rest."

"Yes, ceannasaí," Lorcan replied. As soon as Cathal walked away, he looked at me. "The training room is upstairs. You can get there through the stairway by the cleansing area. Don't be late and give Sadb reasons to punish you." With these words, he left me alone in the corridor.

I pondered my options and in the end headed for my new room. The list of runes was sticking out of my bag, so I picked it up with a sigh. Learning them had stopped being a priority, but since I had no other plans, they could at least fill the rest of my day. Anything seemed better than pondering the reasons for Sadb's reaction, and whether agreeing to Cathal's choice would get me the freedom I wanted.

CHAPTER THREE

When I climbed the narrow stairway to the next floor, muffling a yawn or two, I half expected Sadb to make me wait. I wouldn't put it past her after the previous day's display, but she was already in a spacious area that brought a dojo to mind. Charms embedded in the ceiling lit it evenly, and the wooden floor creaked gently under her feet as she performed a complicated routine with her training sword. I could only hope that she wasn't expecting me to match her proficiency with a blade. I was a scout, not a warrior.

"At least you aren't late," she said in place of a greeting. It was little consolation that she didn't sound too hostile. "Warm up and pick up a weapon you're comfortable with." She waved toward a blanket in the corner where lay multiple training weapons, mostly pieces of wood in various shapes and sizes.

I secretly breathed out with relief—she didn't insist we use something sharp.

I performed a short stretching routine. I hadn't done one since before the war, when I had the crazy idea that a sedentary job required an accompanying gym membership. I quickly learned that walking to work instead of taking an overcrowded Luas—as the local trams were called—provided me with all the exercise I needed, even if it was less pleasant than the gym when it rained. Then the war offered plenty of opportunities for some serious workouts, from running away from enemies to trying to kill said enemies before they killed you, but at the same time it left out such trivialities like limbering up. If you wanted to survive, you couldn't expect your opponents to wait till you were at your best.

Yet I was never the warrior type, and I never became one. I fought when I had to, but mostly I tried to avoid going hand to hand. When I could, I used curses we looted from our enemies, and I'd learned a thing or two about setting deadly traps. Taking on an opponent in a duel-like setting was the last thing I'd have ever considered. So as I approached the quite impressive display of training weapons, from short, knifelike ones to massive pole arms and broadswords, I hesitated.

Sadb approached, her sneer more than a tell that she knew I wasn't familiar, let alone comfortable, with most of the killing tools in front of me. "You could insist on a bow, and I'll gladly hand you over to Riagán. I'm sure he'll be happy to give you many long lessons."

I ignored the jab and shook my head. "I suck with bows." As much as I'd prefer to spend time with said archer, it wasn't the reasonable choice. "I'm not really much of a fighter..."

Sadb didn't wait for me to finish. "Laoise liked those, so maybe they'll suit you as well."

A strange tone reverberated in her voice as she spoke, like a mix of grief and longing, but I didn't have time to ponder it. She picked up two pieces of wood shaped into long knives, and the way she passed them to me was quite... expeditious. If my new body didn't have heightened reflexes, the weapons would have smacked me straight in the face.

The glance I got made it clear she was waiting for my complaint, but I knew better than to fall for her bait. Until Cathal returned, I reported to her, so I had to play by her rules, no matter how unhappy it might make me.

We moved to the middle of the room, and while I was still trying to figure out the correct grip on the knives and a proper stance, Sadb attacked.

I dodged her first four attacks, each time with growing desperation and more luck than skill, and then within the next three moves her wooden sword connected consecutively with my thigh, side, and elbow. The last strike sent a wave of pain that blinded me, and before I rolled away, I received two more painful hits to my back.

"I expected more from you." Sadb kept advancing, leaving me no time to get back on my feet, let alone prepare any defense.

I wasn't really sorry to disappoint her. Maybe if she didn't have expectations, her training would match my level.

"I'm not a fighter!" I shouted while making sure her next strike didn't reach me.

I didn't have enough breath and time to ask if we could start with the basics, and Sadb's focused face suggested that it would be pointless anyway.

"Then you better become one." It seemed that the ceaseless series of attacks didn't tire her at all. "Right now, you're not even worth the chance Cathal gave you."

Sadb kept me down on the ground, and all I could do was roll around and collect more hits as she stayed on me. With a stroke of luck, I blocked her attack with my knife, or rather with my poor fingers holding it. That break in her onslaught allowed me a kick, if you could call an uncoordinated leg jerk in her general direction a kick.

Sadb leaped away with enviable agility, but even though I failed to reach her with my clumsy riposte, at least I bought myself enough time to get back on my feet.

My body already hurt from multiple hits, and all I knew about fighting was telling me that I wasn't training—I was sparring. There wouldn't be anything wrong with it if the gap between me and my opponent wasn't so big that it could fit all the people who died in the war. And I wouldn't be surprised if there was some space left there too, just enough for Sadb's attitude.

"What the heck is wrong with you?" I let my frustration speak, even though my self-preservation instinct tried to veto it.

Sadb gave me a mocking smile. "Poor myth-touched who thinks she's special just because the lady found use for her. Did you think you get to wave a blade twice and call it done?" She lunged at me again.

I was ready, but with the unfamiliar weapons in my hands, I could do little to prevent her strikes, so in the end I gave up on defense. Sadb would keep hitting me no matter how hard I tried to block her.

All I could do was to reciprocate, though in much less coordinated style, so I took a swing, aiming more or less at her face.

"Finally, something!" she said.

Of course, she dodged my attempt with ease, rewarding me with another swat of her training sword. I tried again, silently tallying the bruises I'd collected so far. With Sadb unlikely to tire anytime soon, and with no end of this so-called training in sight, I could only hope I wouldn't end up with a broken bone.

❧

SADB MERCIFULLY LIMITED the training only to mornings, so I had afternoons to myself. With nothing else to do and nowhere to go, I lurked in the gardens, pretending I was away from the Court and studying the symbols from Connor. Even though cramming those seemingly random squiggles wasn't entertaining or relaxing, it was better than pondering my future.

One week of being "trained," and I abandoned hope Sadb would actually teach me something instead of creating Escher pictures with bruises on my skin.

Maybe she was waiting for some inner magic to activate within me and, in a swirl of stars and rainbows, transform me into a true warrioress, a full package including blood-lust and fighting instincts, but I found such an expectation unrealistic, even on an island filled with magic. Which meant that Sadb likely didn't have any goal other than to torture me indefinitely, or at least until I'd had enough. Not that I was ready to give her the satisfaction of my surrender.

"Kaja." Eithne approached, a benevolent smile on her face.

I might not have been paying too much attention to my surroundings, but I still should have caught the sound of her footsteps on the gravel when she got close enough. She truly had a stride of a ghost.

"It's nice to see you here," she added.

In an instant, her remark made me miss those blissful times when I was slowly dying from the affliction. Well, not that part, but the one where I was free from obligations to the Court in general and Eithne in particular.

If Sadb showed up that very moment demanding I resume my training immediately, I'd jump at the opportunity with a bright smile and let her meticulously beat me into a pulp, because even that was more appealing than Eithne's company, especially since the recent revelations. At least with Cathal and Sadb things were straightforward, while in the presence of the Court's lady I felt like I was dancing a jig on a minefield, and I wasn't too much of a performer.

"Lady Eithne." I forced myself to get up and offer a bow.

She sat down on the bench. I resisted using a childish excuse that I was just leaving and retook my place. Unless a miracle happened, I had to suffer through this conversation. I sensed the universe was sending me a message, because it seemed that whenever I wished for a distraction, things went from bad to worse.

Eithne regarded me with her emerald eyes, and a slight smile tweaked the corners of her lips, just enough to make me wonder if she was mocking me when she said, "You seem even more distrustful than you were *before* you joined the Court. I don't think I'd be wrong if I assumed it's your ceannasaí's doing. I see that he got what he wanted by any means necessary." Eithne shook her head gently, as if in disapproval.

"But was he wrong in what he said?" I threw her a challenging glare. Sure, after what Cathal had told me I hardly had any love for her left, but it wasn't like I had an abundance to begin with. "You've been deceiving me."

"Have I now?"

The arch of her eyebrows was a perfect expression of surprise, but I knew better than to trust it. Even before I'd taken her offer of the ritual, I knew she was a player, and I didn't expect that to change only because I was on her team now.

"Do you think that I could really hold you here forever or send you away from Baile Átha Cliath, from Dublin, if you really didn't want it?" she asked.

I almost laughed in her face. Of course she couldn't, unless she shackled me to a solid wall. At the same time, she was silently holding my life debt like a leash, so no shackles were necessary.

I wouldn't have any of her games. I went on the offensive instead. "So, it wouldn't be a problem, then, if I visited Trinity tomorrow? After my training, of course."

She pressed her lips in a narrow line, joviality gone from her face. "Shouldn't you be asking your ceannasaí instead? I'm sure you'll be quick to realize that since you've already agreed to become a member of his team, he has no reason to give you anything."

"Perhaps."

I still preferred to take my chances with Cathal. Contrary to Eithne, playing games wasn't on his agenda, and in the past he'd seemed honest and just with me, even when I kept things away from him. I still remembered that he showed understanding when his team discovered I carried a curse that could have killed anyone on his team if it activated at the wrong time.

"And what will you do then, Kaja?" Eithne's face became a mask of calm and friendliness once more. "When you finally learn you can't tell his truths and lies apart? Or when your ceannasaí sends you to your death without second thoughts?"

"That, Lady Eithne, would actually be something familiar and welcome."

Not only was I accustomed to being sent out like that, but it would also be nice to receive such orders without all the doubts and pondering that Albert attached to them. The leader of the Trinitians often allowed his personal feelings for me to cloud his judgment on whether I was the best person for the job, while Cathal would have no such sentiments. If I was to go, I was the best one for the task.

"It's more familiar than the Court's games," I added.

To my surprise, she smiled and nodded. "I'm not happy with how things turned out, beginning with your lone excursion into the northern part of Dublin that almost got you killed and ending at the Scáthanna's ceannasaí manipulating you for his own gains. But it might be that, in the end, you fit in the best with his team." She stood up. "Should you ever change your mind, come to me. I'm sure I could find you something more absorbing than charm crafting. Considering your past, I could see how you could speak with the Trinitians whenever the Court requires it, and I see no reason why you couldn't eventually become a point of contact for other factions across Baile Átha Cliath, and outside of it as well."

If she expected me to turn my back on Cathal at her mention of Trinity and offering what the mythborn likely considered a glowing career, she was in for a disappointment. I'd already had a taste of her promises leading nowhere, stuck indefinitely in excuses and delays. I also didn't expect myself to take on the role that she, for the better part, had kept for herself in the past. Before the threat of the Snake's agents' attacks, she was the one to speak to all the factions.

Yet it didn't seem wise to antagonize her, so I forced some appreciation into my voice when I said, "Thank you, Lady Eithne. It's good to know I have a choice."

Her eyebrow arched ever so slightly, as if she had a hard time holding her surprise at bay. I didn't care whether it was a genuine reaction to my courtesy, or whether she was questioning the truthfulness of my uncommon politeness. I didn't feel like playing more games with her.

In the end, she gained nothing. She didn't make me doubt Cathal, and she didn't convince me to come running back to her. What she did achieve was making me even more confident that I'd do anything to get the hell out of the Court and away from mythborn politics, because that was what the whole conversation had to be about. She didn't care about me. She wanted to get back at Cathal.

If I had to survive Sadb's kind of training to leave, so be it. Either the mythborn warrioress would finally deem me ready, or she'd make Cathal kick me out.

I smiled as Lady Eithne walked away, because if the latter happened, I'd see if she would really try to stop me when I walked out through the Court's main gate.

CHAPTER FOUR

Of course, my resolve to withstand Sadb's treatment was put to the test over the next few days. When she was in a better mood, she taunted me, mocking my skills, and when something irked her, we spent hours fighting in silence. All the same, not even once had she declared she was done with me, and I couldn't shake off the feeling that she had another reason for her mockery and torture, and it wasn't about making me miserable or forcing me to quit.

Yet she didn't seem inclined to share her motives with me, and she ignored any attempts at having a conversation.

I dragged my feet down the stairs after another unsuccessful try. Irked by the lack of progress and guidance, I matched my attitude with Sadb's and demanded she actually taught me something. It didn't go too well. The only thing I got to learn was that so far she had been going easy on me. I preferred not to imagine what the hard way of Sadb's teaching looked like, but I had a vague suspicion that her students rarely survived it.

After her short rant on how hopeless I was, she beat me

silly and left me on the floor, announcing the end of the training, even though she had a good three hours more of our usual allotted time to dish out additional punishment. I supposed it was some sort of achievement to make Sadb quit early.

I lay on the floor for a while, enjoying the stillness, but wood was hardly comfortable for my sore body, so I dragged myself up and headed for the showers, hoping no one would be around. I hadn't seen the others since the last time I spoke with Cathal, and I had no idea when they'd be back. They might have been back and out already, and I didn't notice, stuck in the endless cycle of training and trying to recover.

For a moment, I entertained myself with the thought that my ceannasaí would be interested in Sadb's teaching techniques, but I gave up on the idea. Even if he wouldn't be happy with my lack of progress and had a word with Sadb, he wouldn't be watching over her shoulder. I had a feeling that complaining would only make things worse between me and her. And judging by the exchange I'd witnessed on my first day, he also wouldn't let me train with someone else instead.

I clenched my fists as I took off the sweaty clothes and activated the heating charm. The water from the shower hit my aching body, bringing temporary relief. I stood in its stream for so long that half of the Court could have showered in that time, but I didn't care. If I had to suffer through Sadb's training, I could at least indulge in the comforts the Scáthanna enjoyed.

Back before the Magiclysm, hot water wasn't limitless. Heated overnight, when the electricity was cheaper, it sat in limited-size tanks that were supposed to hold enough to last throughout the day, but it always ran out a little bit too soon for my liking. In the Court, with charms heating up water as it flowed through the pipe, I didn't have to rush out of concern that I'd have to rinse the soap off in lukewarm water, so I took full advantage of it.

My muscles weren't any less sore when I left the shower, but at least I was warm and relaxed. Back at home, I'd have thrown several warmth charms into a bathtub and soaked in the water until my skin wrinkled, and that thought only made me miss my apartment more. Dipping in the common pool, where any other member of the Scáthanna could join me, wasn't going to cut it. I reached for a fresh robe, collected my dirty clothes, and headed to my room.

I wasn't fool enough to hope that Cathal would let me move back home once Sadb was done with me, but at least I would be able to get out of the Court. I needed my freedom. I needed it badly. Having lived alone for so long meant that the constant presence of others got under my skin...

Like when I turned the narrow corner and hit a myth-born who was just opening the door to a room. I moved out of the way, expecting that a comment about not paying attention would follow anyway.

"Kaja?" Riagán stood motionless, watching me.

The first word that came to my mind was *shit!*, and I swallowed it quickly before it made its debut in the conversation. I hadn't seen him since the day I joined the Court, and even though I still considered the memories we'd made pleasant, we'd never gotten to actually talk about what it meant, or whether it even meant anything.

He broke the silence first. "I thought you'd come."

A strange note in his voice suggested he was as uncertain on how to proceed as I was. I caught tiredness in it, too, which matched the dark circles under his eyes. His skin resembled dried-up mud even more than usual, and his shoulders slumped ever so slightly. He wore his uniform, crumpled and dirty and complete with all his gear, suggesting he had just returned from an assignment.

"It didn't seem like the right time," I mumbled.

In comparison to what he and the rest of Scáthanna must have been going through, my own problems seemed like the whining of a spoiled child, so I looked away, hiding my shame. I was pitying myself for the comfortable life I had and a little daily beating I had to suffer while Laoise was dead, and he had lost a team member... likely a friend.

"If you'd rather forget about what happened after the ritual, I understand," he whispered.

My eyes widened as I locked them on him. Without knowing more about how mythborn handled feelings for others and relationships, I couldn't figure out whether he was offering me a way out or trying to get one for himself. I took a deep breath and ignored the instincts that told me to take that chance to back out. If things were to work between us, I needed to be honest. And if he wanted out, he should have enough balls to say it openly.

"It's not that." Revealing my emotions felt worse than standing naked in front of him would. "You were all mourning your friend's death, and it felt like I'd be imposing myself if I sought your company." They also hadn't lingered at the Court, setting out almost immediately, but that was beside the point.

He looked at me puzzled. "Wasn't Laoise also your friend?"

I sighed. Mythborn didn't seem to comprehend the idea of things being "complicated." In a way, they were lucky that the Magiclysm had wiped out all the electricity and thus all of social media, because if they had to navigate through all the human dramas, flame wars, and relationship status changes, they'd never have had a chance to gain the upper hand in the war.

"Even if I considered her a friend, she was one of you, and I wasn't." I swallowed, searching for words. I didn't need to mention that I still thought of myself as a stranger among them, and Sadb's training methods and lack of communication weren't helping. "You shared memories and spilled blood, and it felt wrong to disturb it with my presence."

Riagán arched his eyebrow, but his expression had none of his usual playfulness—as if he was questioning my sincerity. "You still could have come... to me."

"Could I?" I met his gaze, unwavering. "We didn't really have a chance to talk about what happened and what it means. I'm not good at mythborn games." That wasn't the right word, and I cursed myself for using it, but Riagán didn't seem interested in picking on my slips. "I don't know how mythborn do romance, but humans don't usually mix it with grieving, so I waited."

He gave me a short nod, his face serious but not unfriendly. "You're here, and so am I, and we could talk now." He pointed at the opened door and took a step to the side. "If you want."

What I actually wanted was to drop on my own bed and drift into sleep before my aching body made me feel even more sorry for myself, but Riagán's unusual grimness stopped me from voicing my desires. If I did so, I'd miss the chance to talk to him. If he was only resupplying between missions, I'd have to wait days more for his return. Even tired and sore, I considered a quick solution a better option than endless postponing, so I entered his room.

The air inside seemed to carry the faint scent of camp-fire smoke and pine, as if it announced that I'd stepped into Riagán's domain... If one could call a room no bigger than mine, with the same meager furnishings—a simple bed, a desk, and a wooden chest—a domain. I expected the others to have at least some luxury items or keepsakes, but it seemed that the Scáthanna lived in a more private version of military barracks. The only thing of interest was the wooden display on the wall with three identical bows hanging on it. One looked more worn and used, suggesting the other two were backup weapons. On the desk lay fletching equipment. I didn't think Riagán charmed his own arrows, but he must have been making at least some of them.

He indicated for me to take the chair and then sat on the bed, tiredness once more showing in his moves.

Following an impulse, I sat beside him instead. If we were supposed to be working on some sort of a relationship, distance wouldn't help. He didn't move away, and I took it as a good sign.

"So, Kaja? I'd rather be doing other things in your company, but you wanted to talk." Riagán's teasing smile suggested what kind of activities he had in mind, though I couldn't help wondering whether he truly wanted it or simply made the remark to lighten the mood and put me at ease with behavior I was more familiar with.

Either way, as much as I felt tempted to taste his lips again and lose an evening in his caress, I needed some sort of foundation for our relationship first, whatever it was meant to be. Of course, "needing" was easier than putting it into words, but I had to try.

"Last time you were quick to act but didn't really explain much... I'm not sure what to expect or how to behave." Damn, it was difficult! I'd never thought I'd have to speak this openly in front of a mythborn, especially not the one I might like a bit more than I had planned to.

Riagán smiled but didn't offer any witty remarks. "What

would you like to expect? I'd be happy to make... long-term plans, but if you prefer to not get too involved, I'll respect that." When he looked at me, a hint of bitterness was on his face. "I'm not him, nor will I try to compete with him."

I found it hard not to grimace, but I did my best. No matter how many times I'd claim I'd moved on, my relationship with Albert seemed to haunt all the other ones, even those of a purely businesslike nature.

"I'm not looking for a replacement." My reply came across rather harsh even to myself, so I softened it with a smile. "And I'm not really interested in a casual acquaintance," I added with sincerity. Now that I had my life and hope back, I wanted something more solid, possibly with Riagán. "But building a real relationship takes time." I didn't mind a bit of intimacy, but it wasn't possible to instantly make it into something more, something that would last. I'd learned that the hard way the last time I tried.

He nodded, his serious expression contradicted by the gentle crease of his lips, as if my words sparked a smile. "Fair enough."

"What about Cathal?" I asked when I remembered that circumstances had changed since the last time we talked. "I don't doubt he already knows, but I'm a member of the Scáthanna now." Good intentions aside, having lovers on the team was like asking for trouble.

"As long as we both do our job, he doesn't care what happens between assignments. And he cares even less what others would say about us, if you're concerned about it."

His response sounded a bit too convenient, but in the end, he knew Cathal better than I did. "And what about you?" I asked. "I didn't have a chance to ask what you think about my being here." After all, I'd be doing Laoise's job, putting myself in the same kind of danger that had ultimately led to her death. If Albert was in Riagán's place... Oh, I'd hear an earful.

To my surprise, he brightened and his lips stretched into a grin. "I knew you'd be joining us long before you did. Cathal wouldn't have invested so much time in you if it was just an errand for the lady, and all her made-up delays irked him more than he was showing."

His comment shed some light on the conversation I'd eavesdropped on, and suggested that Cathal had either the balls or position strong enough to oppose Lady Eithne. No matter what Eithne wanted me to believe, joining the Scáthanna might really be a pathway to freedom instead of simply swapping rune-learning with Connor for painful lessons with Sadb.

"Besides, you can't be wrapped in pretty robes and stored away," Riagán added with a cunning smile. "I'm sure that you feel trapped here. I wouldn't be surprised if you were already devising some sort a curse to break a hole in the outer wall and escape."

I had to smirk at that. Ever since my conversation with Eithne, the thought of simply walking out of the Court and never returning had crossed my mind more than once. She indeed would have a hard time keeping me around unless she ordered me locked up, and *that*, Cathal would likely oppose.

But I still had some patience left, and I wanted to play by the rules, even if it wasn't exactly my style. Besides, to get up and leave meant being ungrateful for what she'd done for me and ignoring that I was, in a way, indebted to her. Not to mention that it didn't seem professional on my part to agree to Cathal's offer only to change my mind and disappear. Even if it was Eithne's ritual that had freed me of my affliction, I owed Cathal and his team a lot as well. After all, only their efforts had made it possible for me to survive long enough to even take Eithne's offer.

"You'll always be out there, putting yourself in danger," Riagán said, pulling me out of my thoughts, "so what happened to Laoise can happen to you." His smile dimmed and his eyes lost focus, as if he was picturing me in her place. "But now we're going to be on one team, watching each other's backs. And you won't go unprepared, since it's Sadb who will deem you ready."

I couldn't help groaning. His remark reminded me of all those painful "preparations" Sadb had had me go through. "I think she's going to kill me first. I'll never live up to her standards."

Riagán put his arm around me and pulled me closer. "You're complaining, Kaja. It's so humanborn of you." A familiar, playful tone had returned to his voice. "Instead, look at the final goal. When she's done training you, you'll be one of us."

"Which will be never."

If he thought that challenging my pride would make me stop complaining, he had it all wrong. Maybe if I wasn't all sore from Sadb's treatment, I would be willing to see some bright sides of the training, but with every part of me radiating pain, I stood firmly in the pessimist's corner.

"Both you and Sadb have things to work through. Until then, you'll likely be stuck with each other." He got up and searched through his desk drawer. "Here. This should help you heal after the training." He handed me a small pouch. "Sprinkle three pinches over your evening food, then a warm shower and an early night."

A few months earlier, I would have been cautious with a gift like that, but after all that had happened, I accepted it with gratitude and without any doubts.

"Of course, you could offer me some advice to speed things up." I couldn't resist the tease, though I suspected Riagán had told me as much as he could... or wanted. His remark still got me something to go on, especially when I remembered the scene Sadb had made on the day I joined the Scáthanna. There had to be more to Cathal's decision for Sadb to train me, and I had to find out what. I might be deceiving myself that the discovery was the key to my progress, but I wouldn't put it past my ceannasaí to have more goals than just ensuring I could fight.

Riagán sat back on the bed, this time much closer to me, and his scent teased me as I took a breath.

"Sleep with me tonight," he said gently.

I stiffened. It seemed the mythborn were much more open and much quicker when it came to relationships. Even though Riagán was attractive for a mythborn, and I hadn't had a lover for way too long, I'd really meant what I said about not rushing things. It seemed that he hadn't caught my remark of romance taking time, or maybe the mythborn really did do relationships differently.

"Just sleep, Kaja," he murmured tiredly, ignoring my sudden discomfort. "You have more training tomorrow, and I'm setting out again at dawn, but we could at least rest together."

"The bed looks awfully narrow." Yet I didn't move from my spot. Riagán's magic enveloped me, luring and comforting at the same time, and I liked the idea of "just sleeping" together. Perhaps he felt similar about it.

"You didn't complain sleeping on my lap," he whispered into my ear.

I remembered that one evening clearly. He'd come to talk to me and stayed for the evening playing my video game while I passed out, suffering the side effects of mythborn-made painkillers. The whole thing had turned out even more awkward when in the morning, rather unexpectedly and by accident, I got to learn I owed Riagán a life debt from the time of war.

"Because back then you cured my headache." I rested my head on his shoulders, appreciating the comfort of being close to someone... *with* someone. "If you can cure my bruises, I won't complain either."

He leaned over and pulled my shoes off. Then he slipped his own off and reached for the light charm on the wall, deactivating it and drowning the room in darkness. "I can't cure them, but I can make you forget... until morning." The kiss he gave me was definitely not of the "goodnight" type, deep and passionate. He embraced me tightly and shuffled us under the cover, clearly not bothered that he still had his clothes on, and I was in a bathrobe. On the other hand, for all I knew, the mythborn weren't aware such things as pajamas existed and didn't fancy sleeping naked.

"Just sleep?" I had to ask when he finally peeled away.

In the moonlight scantily getting through the crystal window, I could see his smile as he looked at me, maybe waiting for an invitation to more than "just sleeping." Then, without any reply, he guided my hand toward the headrest. Once my fingers brushed the wood, a sudden jolt of magic traveled through us, and a powerful sleep charm activated. I didn't fight to stay awake. I closed my eyes and allowed myself to drift off.

"Sleep well." Riagán curled beside me.

CHAPTER FIVE

I was not used to being idle. When I was an information broker, there was always something to do, a place to go, information to check out, or gossip to sort through. I also had to clean my place every now and then, do laundry, and food didn't make itself either. My life felt busy. Even if I had a quieter evening, I could sit down in front of a charm-powered TV and play a video game for a while.

Now, I had no job to do, and the Court's servants took care of cleaning, laundry, and food, so I found myself with more time on my hands than I ever had, and with much less to do. Unfortunately, unless I was willing to socialize with mythborn, my entertainment options were limited to trying out rune combinations on charms and amulets. The Court had a library, but of course their selection of works was all in their own language.

I sat at my desk, playing in equal parts with the piece of wood in front of me that I intended to make into a silence amulet and with my hearing skill. Jumping from one boring conversation to another felt like skipping channels on TV, and I couldn't get past a conundrum related to the arrangement of runes on my charm, so let my thoughts wander.

Riagán had been gone for a few days, and I missed his presence. That one evening with him made me realize that I was missing having someone to talk to, to simply enjoy time with.

After the war, I didn't have many friends around, with most of them succumbing to the affliction or leaving Eireland, but I still had acquaintances and business associates to keep in touch with, Albert and some veterans in Trinity to visit... I hadn't felt lonely or alienated.

In the Court, I hardly had anyone. I liked Connor, but didn't want to impose myself, especially as he had his own tasks, and my relationship with Sadb had little to do with talking or enjoyment.

"Ceannasaí." Sadb's voice sounded way closer than anything else.

I jerked even though I knew she wasn't in my room. Instincts, trained on pain, insisted I reacted anyway.

"How's her progress?" Cathal asked.

I didn't know he'd returned, but after all, even if Sadb knew when he was due back, she wouldn't have bothered to inform me.

"Physically, she's getting better," she replied, to my surprise. "But her mindset... At this pace, we'll be here for years."

I huffed. My mindset seemed like the least of the problems in this whole situation.

"What about *your* mindset? Are you sure you're trying hard enough?"

"I'm supposed to train her, not kill her," Sadb replied. "I can't tell her what she needs to figure out on her own, otherwise she'll just give us what we want for however long she needs to, and once she's through with the training, she'll be as useless as she is now."

I clenched my fists. So, Sadb expected me to figure out something but offered no guidance...

"Do you think Riagán was wrong about her? His judgment clouded?" Cathal asked.

"No, I trust him. I just can't figure her out." A pause followed, as if Sadb hesitated. "She almost died fighting that Léanmhar, and then barely survived the ritual. As far as I can tell, she's not scared, but... Perhaps she needs someone else to train her."

"You're the best among us."

Sadb grunted. "I know why you *really* made me train her, but it's time to face the truth, ceannasaí. She might need someone else."

"I don't want to hear it," Cathal replied, warning and tiredness clear in his voice. "You're not going back out until Kaja's ready, and she's not getting anyone else to train her. If I can't trust my team members to work through their issues, neither of them should be in the Scáthanna."

I caught a warning in his voice, as if he was telling her that either both of us were in the Scáthanna, or neither would be, but that didn't make sense... Sadb was already part of his team, a valued and skilled member, and I was not worth sacrificing her. If I was in Cathal's place, I'd sooner kick myself out than risk Sadb leaving.

But, to my surprise, she didn't question him. "Yes, ceannasaí," was all she said.

I heard footsteps in the corridor outside, suggesting they'd parted ways. Then knocking sounded at my door.

"Come in," I called. I stood up immediately as Cathal entered. "Ceannasaí."

He didn't say anything at first. His tired eyes took me in,

lingering on the bruises on my forearms. With my sleeves rolled up for work, they were on full display.

"I talked with Sadb about your training," he said. "I have no doubt you have similar thoughts about it." He walked in, closing the door behind him. "Do you think you would fare better with another team member teaching you?"

I hesitated. This sounded like a way to be free of the torture with Sadb, but having heard their conversation, I couldn't shake the feeling it was a test. "I would fare better with more guidance, regardless of whom it comes from." I chose a cautious reply. I didn't mind bruises if they meant I was learning something.

Cathal nodded. "You need to understand why you train, and why it is Sadb who's training you." He lifted his hand before I even got a chance to reply. "Think on it. The answer isn't for me."

As he left, I sat down on the bed. Both he and Sadb were clearly of a mindset that it was something I had to figure out on my own, so I went down the obvious path. I trained because I was told to. I trained to join the Scáthanna. I trained to be deemed ready, and to finally be able to leave the Court. The answers seemed so obvious... Then it dawned on me.

I didn't train to be able to kill.

So far, even when I tried to strike back during our training, it was because that was what I was supposed to do, and all I was trying to do was to keep her away. That was why Sadb was trying to make me hate her. She wanted me to find enough rage to truly *want* to hurt her, to find a way to beat her into the same bruised and sore pulp she was making me into.

I huffed, frustration resurfacing. She could have told me! We could have been done with the whole training already...

I immediately took that thought back.

This was exactly the mindset I'd had all along: do what's necessary to get it over with. She'd even told me in the beginning she was making me into a warrior, but I was too stuck in my own way to understand.

Laoise was a scout, but she wasn't any less proficient with weapons than any other member of her team. I still remembered than one evening when she faced an Afflicted, a humanborn warped by magic, without fear, knowing she had no chance to win on her own. All she could do was to buy me enough time to get away. Back then, I didn't run. I came to her aid.

The memory of my own battle with an Afflicted resurfaced. This time it was me who couldn't run, and I knew I was going to die, but I didn't give up. I fought as fiercely as I could... and then Riagán arrived. I survived against all odds, but only because I fought to the end.

This had to be what they were really seeking in their new team member. Sadb didn't want to lose time training someone who wouldn't put her heart into it, and I couldn't blame her. But now I had to find a way to convince her I understood while still fighting with my own nature, which told me I was no a warrior.

Maybe she could help me figure it out if I proved I was serious.

I rolled my sleeves down and put away the charm I was working on, then headed out. Now that I had a clear goal ahead of me, I knew just the mythborn who could help me achieve it.

~

I thought that with me out of the way, Connor would have gotten another apprentice by now, but when I entered his workshop, he was alone. All the better for me, because I didn't necessarily want any witnesses for what I was going to ask him, yet I couldn't help the anger growing. Connor was a fine craftsman and a fun mythborn to be around, and he shouldn't be shunned and isolated. I wouldn't be surprised if most of his brethren didn't know how to behave around him—something humans also often had a hard time figuring out when it came to disabled people.

"I need a favor," I said when he arched an eyebrow at my entry.

"I'm not sure whether I should be appalled by your lack of courtesy or appreciate your honesty," he replied with a smile, as if my non-mythborn ways were nothing but a source of amusement to him.

"I'd prefer the latter. More chances you'll grant me that favor."

He chuckled, and that reaction took years off his otherwise serious face. Before the war, he must have been a cheerful and easygoing mythborn... Except that, from what I understood, there was no "before the war" for mythborn. They came from the world where the only way of living was fighting against the Snake.

"So, what can a mere craftsman do for the member of the Scáthanna?" he asked lightheartedly.

"I'm hardly a member," I replied. "And I need a few curses. Nothing deadly... Just a few stun ones, and maybe a sleep charm..."

He narrowed his eyes at that, becoming serious. "Caitríona usually files requests on behalf of the Scáthanna to the Master of Crafts."

"Thus the favor."

He sighed. "Do I want to know what you need them for?"

"Training," I replied with sincerity.

"I suppose I better not ask if your ceannasaí knows about it." He gave me a sympathetic stare. "I take it said training isn't going too well?"

I shrugged. "Not how I expected, that's for sure."

"I was surprised when I heard Cathal chose her. I can't think of a worse possible person to teach you. And judging by the bruises on your forearms, she hates you more than I thought."

Instinctively, I tugged on my sleeves, even though they were already down. Connor had sharp eyes to catch glimpses of those bruises. "Why do you think she does?"

He threw me a curious glance, as if making sure I was really asking this question. "*I* wouldn't like you if you were replacing my lover on the team. And I'd hate that instead being out there, seeking revenge, I was stuck training you."

I gaped at him—oh, I did. "Sadb and Laoise...?"

That definitely made things clearer. Sadb's pleas to Cathal and his reason to keep her at the Court. Tasked with training me, she couldn't do something unreasonable like blindly charge too many enemies, or whatever else myth-born did to exact revenge and alleviate grief.

At the same time, I had to appreciate that she hadn't gone the obvious route, which was training me to the minimum standard as quickly as possible to free herself of me.

"It's nice to see that even though I'm stuck here, there is gossip I know and you don't." Connor snickered, clearly entertained by my dumbfounded expression. "If you decide to abandon your training, my doors are open. I've gotten used to having an apprentice, even a talentless one like you," he added with a clear tease.

"And about those curses...?" I gave him the nicest of my smiles.

"I don't have any, but I can make you a few." He put away the piece he was working on. "I could use some simpler task for a change."

Without hesitation, I took a seat beside him, like many times before. "If you show me what to do, I can help."

"Start with the standard pattern, just at the edges." He handed me a piece of leather.

"Wouldn't wood or metal be better?"

"I'm guessing you'd like them to look rather inconspicuous." Connor gave me a sly smile. "It might come as a surprise, but I did learn a thing or two from you. And even if your runes still look like a child's scratchings, you get the more important part of the craft, which is how to make them work together. I tinkered with the harness improvements you suggested some more, and they are faring well so far. Less pain, and my movement is more fluid."

"It's the least I could do," I replied. It was hard to take a compliment when helping him felt like a desperate attempt to make up for my own past deeds.

Connor's forehead furrowed, an expression I'd learned to read as dissatisfaction. "It wasn't you, Kaja."

I grimaced at that. "You wouldn't have told me so even if it *was* me."

His shameless smile was all the confirmation I needed, but then he became serious. "You don't need such knowledge anyway. If not for you, I'd be dead no matter who held the blade that got me. So, worst-case scenario, you've repaid for your deed already."

I could argue that his lame leg was hardly making it

even, but he had a point. I couldn't turn back time, and beating myself up over it didn't do either of us any good. "I'll be glad to repay you even more if you ever feel like tinkering with your harness again," I offered. "But not today."

"It'll be a while before I get to change anything." He pointed at my empty workspace, as I was still holding the leather he'd handed me. "So, have you discovered how to make invisibility charms, or are you actually going to work on something?"

I chuckled. Invisibility charms were our private joke ever since I'd asked him about them. "I made one yesterday, but I can't find it ever since I activated it," I replied dutifully, placing the leather on the table and reaching for tools.

The corner of his lip lifted slightly, though I doubted the joke actually amused him. Yet, through the short time I'd gotten work alongside him, it seemed like it was his way of appreciating the normalcy of my behavior, either as a myth-touched trying to fit in, or even—dared I think it?—a friend. After witnessing his interaction with Clíodhna, I had no doubt that he longed for that normalcy, even if it came from an oddball like me.

I sent him a playful grin. Even a good joke could get old, so it seemed to me like a good time to make another one. "Maybe when I finally find it, I should start working on a charm that'll let you fly. We wouldn't have to bother with your harness anymore."

A short, guttural laugh was my reward, and then Connor leaned over his table, giving all his focus to his work.

CHAPTER SIX

The next morning I got to the training area early, but Sadb was already there, swinging her training sword, and for a heartbeat I envisioned her having trained all day and night long. She showed no signs of fatigue, but I doubted I'd see any even if she had actually been practicing without a break. Her endurance wasn't only inhuman, it was... un-mythborn, if a term like that was ever to be coined.

I gave her a short nod and headed for the training weapons. As I expected, the very moment I picked them up, Sadb attacked, and I admired her composure. I could read frustration on her face, and with the insights Connor had shared with me, I also understood how unhappy she truly was babysitting me, but her moves were precise, as if she were practicing a mundane routine with no feelings attached. As much as I hated her beatings, I had to admit that she did hold her emotions at bay, and I never suffered anything more serious than bruises. If she really wanted to take her anger and frustration out on me, every single bone in my body would have been broken by now.

I rolled out of the way and went about my usual mix of somewhat successful dodges and entirely failed parries, easing into our daily routine. Throughout the several weeks of the so-called training, I'd learned some of Sadb's favorite strikes, and even though anticipating them was still hit or miss, quite literally, I'd gotten better at avoiding the heaviest attacks. Unfortunately, training still brought more pain than I'd have liked and less progress than I'd have hoped for.

"You're so *useless*," Sadb hissed. "At this pace, in ten years you might be a match for a beginner mythborn warrior. Maybe you should just do us all a favor and lie down and wait to die."

I ignored her teasing, just like I always did. It didn't seem like she was trying hard enough anyway. But when she attacked again, I intentionally failed to parry. Her training sword slid across my knuckles and down to my forearm, hitting a curse hidden under my sleeve. It activated upon contact, and I cherished the surprise on Sadb's face when magic exploded between us, sending us both flying. Stun curses were always nasty, but at least I was ready for the effect and regained my footing a second sooner than Sadb. The ringing in my ears was unbearable, but nothing the war hadn't gotten me used to, and, seeing an opening, I lunged forward.

Sadb didn't disappoint me. Before I got to her, she was already back on her feet, striking at me in a defensive manner.

I had to give her credit for realizing mid-move she was about to hit another curse, but as she diverted her wooden blade, I dove low and slammed my other forearm against her stomach. The curse activated on contact, and the short huff of pain she let out was satisfying. But instead of collapsing, as any decent target of a double-stun curse would, Sadb wavered on her legs and promptly dug her elbow into my exposed back.

"Shit," I muttered as I met the floor in a rather violent way.

I didn't even try to roll out of the way, and braced for a serious beating. This one I probably deserved for cheating, but to my surprise, Sadb took a step back.

"Finally something," she said. "Are you going to get up and fight on, or are you done?"

I got back onto my feet. "I don't have more curses," I confessed. "I expected you to be down by now."

Sadb snorted. "So what was your plan? Knock me out and flee?" I might have been fooling myself, but the tone of her voice seemed a notch friendlier than a moment ago.

I shook my head. "I wanted to talk."

What I really wanted was to take her down and maybe even get a few revenge hits while she lay defenseless, but I should have expected that she'd surprise me as much as I did her. Either way, this was still the opening I needed.

She gave me a slow, cautious nod, as if reluctantly agreeing that I'd earned the right to have a conversation.

A quiet voice at the back of my head kept repeating: *Don't mess this up, don't mess this up...* and I found myself at a loss for words. Yesterday, I'd boldly imagined myself not needing too many of them, counting on my plan to get the message across, so I hadn't prepared a speech. Now I was about to suffer the consequences.

"I need your help," I said in the end, "in figuring out how to be a warrior."

Sadb arched her eyebrow, and a rather sarcastic smile crept over her lips. I would bet she suspected I wanted an easy way out.

"I'm not one, and it's not in my nature to be one," I added.

"And therein lies the problem," Sadb replied coldly, "because I'm supposed to make you into a warrior."

"I know."

Something in my voice must have convinced her I was both serious and honest, because she looked at me with less contempt. "I suppose you can't change your nature," she said, softer than I expected, "but you could train yourself to ignore it to some extent."

"Will you help me?" I asked, almost holding my breath. If she said no, we'd likely be back where we started.

Sadb regarded me in silence for longer than I found comfortable, and I had to fight the need to fidget. Being alone in an empty training room made me feel like I was on display, evaluated and judged. In the end, I probably was, and it might be the first time Sadb actually did it rather than assuming I was hopeless.

"Why the sudden change of heart?" she asked.

I shrugged. "I finally figured what this training is about." I would not confess that I'd eavesdropped on her and Cathal. "I was too focused on what I wanted, on the goal, and never thought what was needed of me. Becoming a part of a team like that... It's new to me."

The closest I'd ever gotten to it might have been teams in corporate world before the war, but back then we didn't have to trust our lives to each other—just the deadlines. With people changing teams, jobs, and even countries, there wasn't much on which to build a deep trust like the one the Scáthanna shared.

"It sounds nice." Sadb was still watching me closely. "Like you figured out what the right things to say are."

"I'm not asking you to believe my words alone," I replied

without hesitation, "but I need help in becoming what you need me to become. I can promise I'll give it my best if you guide me, and if that turns out to be not enough, then we'll both know I'm not cut out for this, and you'll be done with me and go onward with your revenge..." I bit my tongue a moment too late.

I didn't even try to recover from my slip, because Sadb was already sneering. She was quick to put things together. "I see certain gossip reached even you."

"That's your personal matter," I replied. She could be sleeping with Eithne herself for all I cared. "But it tells me that you do care about training me properly. Otherwise you wouldn't have told Cathal the truth about how the training is going. Because you did, didn't you? He came asking if I needed someone else to train me." I figured I could imply I knew about it without revealing my strange skill.

Surprise flashed on her face. "You *chose* to be stuck with me."

"So did you," I replied. She could have told Cathal I was doing great and we would be done soon. And after I joined the team, I'd likely be dead before anyone realized that wasn't entirely true.

That seemed to hit the right spot. "Very well," she said. "If you will prove to me those weren't empty words, we'll get serious about training."

"How?" I asked before the sound of her words could even fade. She was giving me a chance, and I wasn't about to miss it.

She gave me a sly smile. "I'll give you a day to prepare. Make more toys or whatever you want." She looked around in thought. "Though nothing that would burn this place down. And tomorrow you're going to try to kill me."

I opened my mouth to protest, then closed it with a snap.

Contrary to what I might have thought, Sadb's request made sense. Even with my curses, she didn't expect me to win a one-on-one fight with her, and I doubted we would be using sharp blades, but it still could be a way to prove I was serious.

A day was hardly enough to make enough curses, so I would have to ask Connor for help. If he obliged, I had to find a way to repay him for all those favors.

"Deal."

THE TRAINING ROOM trembled when the stun curse activated upon my painful contact with the wall, face first. I couldn't see Sadb's expression, but I could swear she was snickering behind my back. We'd been sparring for a good half an hour, and even though the fight seemed a bit less one-sided than her usual beatings, as if she truly was giving me a chance to prove myself, I still had a hard time even shaking her composure.

She took a step back, letting me recuperate, and as I peeled myself off the wall, I tossed the next trinket, another contact-activated curse, feeling only mild guilt for abusing her courtesy. She was already learning my tricks, because she didn't try to swat at it, and instead dodged the threat swiftly.

I smirked, because the curse still activated as soon as it landed behind her. I'd made sure those things were more sensitive than car alarms in prewar Dublin—which, I could swear, activated when you even looked in the general direction of a vehicle. As a reward, I got to watch Sadb fly across the training room. Of course, she used the momentum to launch an attack at me, and I feigned a parry while using my free hand to flick another nasty surprise at her.

Sadb wavered and paused, giving me a chance to leap back and prepare another curse. Her eyes were barely open, but she was fighting off the sleep better than I had hoped. Once the fight was over, I had to ask her what kind of amulets she wore or what she did to raise her resistance to curses. I hoped her secret wasn't "getting hit with them repeatedly."

"You got a sleep charm. Smart." She yawned but otherwise seemed quite awake, making me question whether I was indeed as witty as she claimed. "It won't do you much good in a real fight."

I nodded. "In a real fight I could use something more lethal." Even though Sadb had made no specific provisions beyond fiery and destructive curses, I wasn't trying to actually kill her, so I'd limited myself to stun curses.

Sadb laughed and attacked once more. I threw the curse, and she lunged to the side so fast, I could barely follow her movement. Before I realized, she smashed into me with all her body weight. She might have the figure and looks of an ethereal creature, but her body was pure muscle, so I stumbled sideways.

"Got some of that sleep charm on yourself?" Sadb mocked, but without her usual viciousness. By her standards, she sounded almost caring and concerned.

I barely had time to recover, and threw my next curse blindly. I didn't even get close to her, and one well-placed kick sent me down to the floor.

"That's enough," she said. "You're starting to make mistakes."

I massaged my sore backside as she inspected me in thought. I could only hope it meant I'd passed her test.

"You rely on curses too much, but I can work with that," she said. "A few things surprised me, so you will focus on them. With your general lack of fighting skills, they'll have to keep you alive." She looked me in the eye. "But this also means that you'll have to get up close and personal with your opponents and go for the kill at the first chance. No heroics, no mercy, and no attempts of capturing anyone alive."

I hesitated, then nodded. I might not be a warrior, but my survival instincts were strong enough. I knew I didn't stand a chance against most opponents, so when I couldn't avoid fighting, I tried to end it as quickly as possible. The only difference would be that instead of fleeing when the opportunity presented itself, I'd actually have to kill my enemies. On the brighter side, Sadb was likely to equip me with all the skills I needed to do the deed.

She took a step forward, and—the last thing I expected —helped me back to my feet. "This also means killing your own."

It took me a moment to understand she was talking about the humanborn, and I looked away.

I'd never fully thought about what it meant to be on Cathal's team, to be one of "Eithne's elite killers," as Albert would likely put it. We had peace, and both mythborn and humanborn seemed interested in maintaining it, but it didn't mean that one day I wouldn't find myself opposite my former comrades. One thought of Albert being at the receiving end of my blade or curse, and I knew I'd have a hard time, even if my life depended on it.

I couldn't help thinking of what would happen if it wasn't *my* life that depended on Albert's death. Being part of the team meant others relied on my doing my job.

"You better train me so well, I'll react before I have time to think about it," I said somberly.

To my relief, Sadb seemed satisfied with my reply, even if she must have known that my sentimental approach to Trinitians could be hers or her teammates' undoing. "I hope that one day you're going to see us as you see them. Or as more."

She didn't say the word, but I understood anyway. I already had the strong notion that the Scáthanna weren't just a team. They were a family, and they chose carefully who they allowed to join.

At the same time, they didn't seem to expect their new addition to become one of them *just* because she'd joined, and it reminded me that I would have to work hard to build relationships with all of them. To learn from them and of them, to talk, and to joke... I didn't even know which of them could take a joke or what mythborn would considered funny. Connor seemed to enjoy some of my quips, but I could seldom tell whether it was politeness at my attempts or if he actually found them amusing.

Sadb gestured me to follow, and from the pile of training gear she picked one: a piece of wide, curved wood that reminded me of a short sickle, or perhaps an Egyptian khopesh, but the shapes didn't quite match. It had to be a mythborn design.

"This one is traditionally used alongside a saber, as an offhand weapon, but you'll use it as your main, drawing attention away from your throwing hand," she said. "It's less cumbersome than a sword and has slightly longer reach than a knife. At the same time, no one will take it seriously, so if you get proficient with it, you might have the upper hand." She demonstrated several moves, and the wooden blade flowed in her hand. "It can keep your opponent at a distance, lock his weapon while you throw a curse at him, or stop him from moving away."

She passed it to me, and I mimicked her moves. The weapon lay well in my grip, and I could see how it would work with my fighting style.

"Play around with it for the rest of the day, and make a list of charms and curses you think would be useful. For training, we'll use uncharmed items, so you don't have to make new ones every day." She became serious. "Do you trust Connor to help you with the task? I don't want to go through the Master of Crafts with that request."

"I don't want to get him in trouble," I said. "He already has a lot on his hands, and if he starts helping me, he might fall behind with his other tasks."

"You're thoughtful." She gave me a nod. "I'll deal with the Master of Crafts. I'm sure our charmed equipment and curses are overdue an inspection, and Connor seems like a perfect person to perform it."

For a split second, I wondered how Sadb was going to ensure things fell in place. Then I tried to imagine any mythborn trying to say no to her demands, no matter how specific they were. The only two who would not falter were Cathal and Lady Eithne.

"The three of us will discuss what you need, and even though Connor will make most of it, learn from him what you can. The ability to replace a curse or two in the field might save your life one day," she continued. "But other than that, tell no one what exactly you carry on you, not even Riagán or ceannasaí himself. The less others know of your style and toys, the more advantage you'll have in a fight."

"*You* will know." I couldn't resist a smile.

She looked at me with stoic grim, but I caught the

corner of her lip trembling. "Someone has to make sure that you don't kill yourself with your own arsenal before others get that chance."

I WALKED down the stairs from the training room no less sore than I had been in the past weeks, but definitely more satisfied. Sadb hadn't changed her approach of learning by doing, so we still sparred a lot, but she also taught me moves, proper stances, gave me ideas on how to leverage my budding fighting style, and called out my mistakes, offering advice on how to fix them. It finally felt like we were getting somewhere and that one day I could actually become skilled enough to truly count myself among the Scáthanna.

I was about to check up on Connor, who—encouraged by Sadb—had taken one of the empty rooms in the quarters as his temporary workshop, when I spotted a lone figure in the corridor. The mythborn was someone important, judging by his outfit and pompous expression.

Of course, he headed straight for me.

He said something in the mythborn language, tone demanding and unaccustomed to any disobedience, and then repeated it with clear ire when I didn't react.

I was about to ask him to switch to English when Sadb said, "I don't think it's proper to demand that the Scáthanna member fetches anyone for you, Master of Crafts."

She approached from behind and stopped beside me, virtually blocking the corridor if the mythborn tried to get any further.

"I wouldn't have to *ask* if I could find my subordinates where they're supposed to be," the Master of Crafts replied. "It's been three days since you stole Connor away from his work, and we have obligations to fulfill. He should be done with his task by now."

"He'll be done when I say he's done." Sadb stared at him with an open challenge.

The mythborn shrank for a heartbeat, then straightened his back, his face determined. "I'll not have you keeping my best craftsman occupied for a mere whim. Just because your—"

I saw where this was going, and cut him off before he could finish, because Sadb's expression had already hardened. "You might want to choose your next words carefully. Very carefully."

For a brief moment, I thought he was going to finish the sentence anyway, but he glanced at Sadb and swallowed. "I need Connor back by tomorrow morning," he said instead. "Any longer, and I'll complain to the lady herself."

He turned without gracing either of us with any courtesy or goodbye.

"I'd like to see that," muttered Sadb. "You should have let him finish. That self-important, worthless scum would have gotten what he deserved."

"And your being questioned about his murder would help us how?" I didn't know how mythborn did murder investigations, but I was willing to bet it wasn't a quick or simple process.

"Between the two of us, we could have told any story we wanted," Sadb replied. "And maybe Connor would get the Master of Crafts title, like he deserves."

"They wouldn't give it to a cripple," Connor said behind us. "Someone like me wouldn't fit into their perfect social circles."

We both turned. He was leaning against the doorframe to his temporary workshop, his expression serious. "I should have expected he'd come sooner or later. Master of Crafts doesn't like it when he loses control over us." He shrugged. "I'll finish what I can tonight, and you should be able to copy some of the simpler curses by yourself. I might manage to work on a few more in my spare time, so stop by in a few days."

I hesitated, finding no right words. Connor was doing me a favor, and it was getting him in trouble with his superior.

Some of my guilt must have shown on my face, because he sent me a smile. "Don't worry, Kaja. He can't do much to me, because if he goes too far, I'll leave. And if he lectures me too long for my liking, I'll start adjusting the charms on my harness. Reminding him of my injury always makes him uncomfortable, and he excuses himself from my company pleasantly quickly."

"Probably because he was too cowardly to pick up arms himself," Sadb commented with a sneer.

Connor shrugged. "The Court mythborn," he said in a tone that suggested those words explained everything. "I better get back to work, though. You'll need those curses." He disappeared back into the room.

I looked at the closed door in silence, fighting waves of frustration. It wasn't fair that he had to answer to some mythborn prick. It wasn't fair that he probably deserved that prick's title and position. It wasn't fair that he was stuck crafting charms for ungrateful nobles when he could be doing something more meaningful. And it wasn't fair that almost everyone at the Court looked down at him because of his past injury.

"I might be late for tomorrow's training," I said. The least I could do was to keep Connor company and help with the simpler tasks.

Sadb inspected me with curiosity. "You care. You cared about what he was going to say about Laoise too, didn't you?"

I had quite a few witty responses at the ready, but it wasn't the right time. I nodded and headed for Connor's door. Sadb didn't push, and I appreciated it. Caring wasn't really a thing I liked to advertise. War had taught me that it could put the very people I cared about in danger, and abandoning wartime habits was hard.

She headed off, and since Connor had left the door open, I entered the room.

"You know, for someone who feels immense guilt at the very sight of me, you sure seek my company often," Connor said, amused.

"How do you do it?" I asked. "Don't you ever get frustrated?"

He sent me a smile. "I used it all up in the first months, after..." He looked away. "I'd admit that back then I was cursing everything and everyone for my state, but you'd take it personally, so I won't. I was pitiful for a while. Then, because I still had to deal with all the problems that come with being alive, I put myself together and promised myself that I'd give no one the satisfaction of seeing me this way again."

He made it sound so easy and effortless, but it wasn't hard to imagine how much determination and discipline it required. I'd never asked Connor what his life was like before the war, but I suspected he never saw himself crafting amulets and curses for others. Yet he took the cards that life had dealt him and made it into a winning hand as much as he could.

"One day... One day someone will realize your value, and all those pitiful mythborn will be left gaping," I said, still wrapped in my own thoughts. If there was justice in the world, Connor likely deserved it more than many others.

Surprise flashed on his face, and for a moment he looked moved by my words. Then he arched his eyebrow, familiar playfulness and friendliness replacing the previous expression. "Are you here just for spiritual support, or are you actually going to help?"

I pulled up the spare chair and sat beside him. The desk was smaller than the tables in our workshop, so I ended up closer to him than I intended, but Connor didn't seem to mind. I picked up one of the unmarked wooden balls lying to the side.

"Standard curse base?" I asked, reaching for the appropriate tool.

He gave me a nod, and I leaned over my task. In the corner of my eye, I saw him smiling as he focused on his own work. There was something carefree and relaxed about his expression.

"You know..." he said, never turning his head to me. "You're the first friend I've had in a long time."

I might have limited knowledge of mythborn and their culture, but I knew Connor enough to be certain he didn't make such a confession lightly and without dropping his emotional barriers. I also felt he wouldn't appreciate my spoiling the moment with a reply, so I just sent him a warm smile and left it at that.

CHAPTER SEVEN

Dear Albert...

I groaned, staring at the blank paper in front of me.

Eithne had insisted I write another letter, as Trinity's representatives had yet again asked about me. Part of me wanted to ignore her request and let her handle the consequences. I was growing tired of finding new ways to deliver the same message over and over again: *I'm fine, but I don't know when I'll be able to visit.*

Yet I dutifully sat at the desk, because not writing to Albert meant he'd become more insistent. I wouldn't put it past him to accuse Eithne of holding me against my will. In a way, he'd be right, but for the sake of peace and correct relationships between the Court and Trinity, I had to put on a show.

I gave the paper a hateful glare. After three attempts at writing the words down, I figured I'd first put them together in my head. Not that any reassurances I could conjure sounded convincing enough, and from the letters I got from Albert, it had become clear that he already suspected I was dodging answers. No wonder, since it seemed to be the story of my relationship with him in recent times.

First, there was the secret of dealing with the Snake's agent, which I was helping the mythborn with, and then the real reasons for the lack of the promised visit to Trinity after I survived the ritual, even if this actually was because of Eithne's deception.

As if that wasn't enough, I couldn't tell him that I'd joined the Scáthanna and had been busy training under Sadb's tutelage for weeks.

At the thought of the mythborn female, I instinctively grabbed my training weapon and performed several simple moves with it. With Sadb's help, they had become a habit now, and I suspected that if she told me to sleep with my weapon, my hand would be spinning that bloody piece of wood while I dreamed of something pleasant. That thought, of course, led me to Riagán. He hadn't been around for two weeks, and if Sadb hadn't mentioned that Lorcan stopped by to resupply, reassuring her that the others were fine, I would have started worrying.

Then one glance at the empty sheet of paper reminded me I was supposed to be writing to my ex-lover, not fantasizing about a potential future one.

A knock at the door was like a death sentence's pardon, and I didn't even mind it was Sadb who poked her head in. Ever since I'd become serious about my training and worked hard to grow some killer instincts, she'd acted in a less spiteful manner, as if matching her effort with mine.

"You look miserable," she offered without compassion. "I thought making charms and curses made you happy."

"I wish I *was* making them," I replied. Connor was still making my arsenal when he had a moment, but with the Master of Crafts breathing down his neck, I had to do as much as I could to help. "Lady Eithne insisted I write to Albert."

"Again?" Sadb arched her eyebrows in genuine surprise. "Didn't you write to him, like... two weeks ago?"

"Ten days," I grumbled. "But it's only going to get worse. I'm guessing he already thinks that you keep me prisoner, or even that I'm dead. I'm going to run out of personal memories to mention to convince him it's actually me who's writing these letters."

Sadb rolled her eyes. She approached my desk and slid the empty page to the side. "He can wait. You should be either training or making your curses, because the longer you take, the longer we're both stuck in here, and the longer he'll have to wait to actually meet you."

"One afternoon writing letters is not going to change much," I replied. "But I have an idea of how to speed things up." I smiled when Sadb leaned closer. If we had anything in common, it was the growing desperation to get out. "When Riagán returns, I'll ask him to stop by my old apartment. I have quite a stash of curses and charms there, and I'm sure I could use most of them."

Sadb grinned. "Why wait for him? Get ready. We'll go now and make it part of the training."

She said it so casually, as if she were inviting me for a stroll in the Court's garden, not to venture outside, defying Eithne's veiled order. Of course, I couldn't help wondering if this was some sort of a test. Was I to politely refuse and remind her that I wasn't allowed out? And if I went with her, would Sadb rat me out to Cathal and Eithne?

There was only one way to find out.

Without hesitation, I stood up, grabbing my jacket and bag. Playing by Eithne's rules got me nothing, and I wasn't going against Cathal's orders, since he wanted me to listen to

Sadb. Undoubtedly, such rationalization could be my undoing, but her offer made me realize I'd reached the brink of desperation. I needed to get out of the Court, no matter the cost, even if it was only for one afternoon.

She looked me up and down. "You will stand out too much. These are the Court's clothes, and the Court mythborn don't usually wear pieces of humanborn outfits."

When I wasn't training with her, I wore Court-made tunics and wide pants. With the Court's corridors and rooms charmed to a pleasant temperature, I hardly needed anything else, but going outside meant facing elements, and out of the meager wardrobe I had, only my jacket would do —the same one I'd worn on the day of the ritual.

Exiting my room, she motioned for me to follow. "I'll lend you something."

Her quarters looked exactly like mine and Riagán's, though there were few ornaments on the wall that seemed personal. I didn't take Sadb for a sentimental one, but maybe it was Laoise who'd put them there...

I turned my head away. During the war, we usually didn't have time to grieve, and when we did, it mostly consisted of getting smashed on alcohol scavenged from the nearby "off-license," as the liquor stores were called.

Even if losing so many friends had desensitized me, I could still relate to her loss whenever I thought of my Ela. Sadb had lost a lover, and I—a sister. It didn't mean we grieved in a similar way, but the pain must be similar: like a drill burrowing into flesh and like salt on a fresh wound, and numbing at the same time, as if it could render the whole body and mind useless.

"Here, these should fit." Sadb threw the clothes straight at my face, and I failed to catch them. "Your reflexes should be better by now," she reprimanded me.

I nodded, not trying to find an excuse, as I'd rather not tell her I was thinking about Laoise. The clothes she offered me looked like a mythborn take on human fashion: brown boot-cut pants made from a fabric I didn't recognize, a v-neckline blouse in a pleasant olive hue, soft like pure cotton, and a poncho-style cover sewn from patches of soft leather.

"You can keep the bag." Sadb smirked as I headed back to my room. I still didn't feel comfortable undressing in front of her, even though at odd times we shared the shower area. "You'll look like some humanborn wannabe."

I chuckled at the joke.

Changing didn't take me long. Sadb was already waiting in the corridor, still in her gray uniform, but now with her twin swords strapped on. She handed me a sheath in a familiar, curved shape, but this wasn't a training weapon. The handle was secured with a leather strap, and the guard was metal.

"In case of any trouble," she said. "Unless I fall, stay with me. If I do, try to make it back here... or go to Trinity if the route to the Court is blocked. No one will expect one of us to run there for help."

I nodded and strapped the sheath to my belt, its weight unfamiliar against my hip. We were going no further than my apartment on the other side of the river, a forty-minute stroll if we really took it slow, mostly through safe areas, but I kept my mouth shut. Sadb was right to make contingency plans, even if it was the loss of Laoise that dictated them.

"We'll leave through the servants' door. I don't feel like checking how determined the lady is too keep you in here." She sent me a grin.

As soon as I nodded, she led me out of the Scáthanna quarters.

~

WHEN I FINALLY STEPPED OUTSIDE, *outside* of the Court, I was drunk with excitement. The air, supposedly the same as in the inner courtyard, had a distinct scent of freedom, and Dublin's gray buildings against the equally gray sky felt like the most beautiful sight ever. Yet I didn't stand and stare, instead rushing after Sadb. The sooner we got away from the Court, the less likely someone would notice I was on the wrong side of the building's walls. Even if Sadb took responsibility, being caught meant questions and lectures instead of enjoying my first-in-months outing.

We made it through the narrow streets at a good pace, down to the lazily flowing river, and the occasional mythborn loiterers didn't bother us. One glance at Sadb's uniform and her swords sufficed to convince them to seek trouble elsewhere. Having her around definitely had some good sides.

Sadb chose to cross one of the smaller bridges. Without a wince, she paid the toll for the two of us and even offered an amicable smile to the dwellers, as if she wanted to make sure we were all on good terms. Yet her eyes never ceased scanning our surroundings, and every now and then, when she reacted to an unexpected sound or other stimulus, her moves became sharper.

Her caution became contagious. I couldn't help glancing into the shaded areas of the side alleys or openings of the crumbling buildings as we climbed the uneven cobblestones of the narrow street leading away from the river. We were entering the mainly humanborn area, and that alone could put her on edge, but I allowed the familiarity of my surroundings to ease my tension. After long weeks of prisonlike life, I was finally going home, and I'd do anything to ensure fear wouldn't destroy that joy.

At the same time, I appreciated Sadb being on guard, as her vigilance allowed me my respite.

The early afternoon meant that the streets were moderately filled. Or empty, if I wanted to go by prewar standards, when the crowds in the city center sometimes made it hard to navigate. The Magiclysm had changed things, and some days, especially further away from Trinity and Temple Bar, Dublin could feel a bit like a ghost town.

Several passersby threw us curious glances, then went about their business. In the Liberties, my old neighborhood, everyone knew that if you sought trouble, it found you, so they were careful to not invite any by staring too long. On the other hand, the humanborn and the few mythborn in the area did their best to cooperate, so things rarely got out of hand.

My street looked exactly like when I'd walked through it the last time, on my way to the Court. The same half-ruined town houses and apartments, the same colorful paint on the doors, and even the same trash that wind rolled down the street and back in an endless cycle.

Wrapped up in recollections and fuzzy feelings, I almost missed the metallic song of a sword pulled out of its sheath, but conditioned by Sadb's training, my body caught up faster than my mind, and I spun around with my hand ready at the weapon. Yet I kept behind her. If it came to fighting, I'd only be in her way.

"She's not home. Leave." The molekind mythborn who stood not further than three steps from us stared Sadb down, unmoved by the blade pointed at him. The molekind were the hairiest mythborn, with their animal features only slightly less pronounced than the bridge dwellers. "You're as unwelcome here as them Trinity people."

He sounded familiar, so I stuck my head out from behind Sadb. "Paddy?"

The molekind squinted, suspicion clear on his face. "Kaja. You've... changed," he said, caution echoing within his voice—but no disapproval, as if he was fine with what I'd become but couldn't be sure if I was.

I breathed out with relief. When it came to meeting the locals, Paddy was the best possibility. He wasn't a friend, far from that—just a concerned neighbor who wanted to make sure that neither the Court's nor Trinity's politics would affect the Liberties and people living here. The last time we met, he'd promised to keep an eye on any troublemakers, and he was definitely staying true to his word if he didn't hesitate to confront Sadb.

"You said Trinitians were here?" Since Eithne wouldn't be happy if I discussed the Court's business with outsiders, I steered the discussion away from the topic of how I'd changed and why.

"Once or twice. Poked 'round a bit but were smarter than trying to enter your place." Paddy studied me with an expression that suggested he was deciding whether I was real or not. "Their archer was here, too." He pointed at Sadb. "Had keys."

"I sent him here," I lied quickly, concealing my surprise that Riagán had stopped by. "Listen, I need to pick up a few things but then will be gone for a while. Will you keep an eye out on things around here for me?"

"Sure, pet." Paddy's unkempt brown hair bobbed as he nodded. Then he turned away, his back a broad target for Sadb, and walked down the street so casually, it almost felt like a dare for her to strike.

Thankfully, she was smart enough not to give him an attitude back. She was the better fighter, no doubt about it, but these were the Liberties, and the molekind living around got along better with the local humanborn than with the mythborn from across the river. It made the neighborhood quite a unique pocket of a mixed community, but at the same time it meant that if she tried anything, everyone around might take it personally.

As soon as Sadb sheathed her weapon, throwing one last suspicious glare at Paddy's distant silhouette, I motioned at the building. "Let's go inside."

I felt an urge to hide. Paddy's mention of Trinitians had made me realize someone could tell them I was around, and I didn't want to speculate how Albert would react to the news that I'd strolled through my old neighborhood but failed to make a call at Trinity. On the other hand, if Paddy had trouble recognizing me, I might be safe... Well, safe enough. It didn't mean I wanted to test my luck, though. All of a sudden, our excursion seemed like a bad idea.

"We were all curious," Sadb said while I was unlocking the door. "How did Riagán manage to get your keys? He wasn't eager to share the details, though he claimed it was a fair deal."

"Fair enough, I suppose," I replied, likewise not very keen on divulging any details.

Not everybody had to know I owed him a life debt or three, and settling one of them came at the low price of allowing him entry to my home... Though back then, when I'd agreed to the deal, I wasn't expecting that the "one thing" he'd be taking from my apartment would be my keys. I almost smiled at the thought that allowing him to take them meant that even though I didn't know him well, I subconsciously already trusted him enough.

I let Sadb in and then entered as well. She didn't go down the narrow corridor, and when the door shut behind me, I found myself trapped between it and a very serious mythborn.

"Do you even like him?" she asked bluntly.

My only response was a dumbfounded stare. Sadb definitely came across as straightforward, a pleasant change from the Court mythborn, but we were merely civil with each other, and our relationship didn't go deeper than ensuring we weren't stuck at the Court anymore. One day, perhaps we would become true teammates and maybe even friends, but now I'd sooner discuss such a topic with Orla, though the humanborn bow mistress had an attitude that could outmatch Sadb's. Clearly, the saying "better the devil you know" had a grain of truth to it.

She turned away, unmoved by my lack of verbal communication. "I wouldn't have killed you for a no."

"And would you kill me for a yes?" I couldn't resist as I flicked the light on and we entered my living room.

"So it's a yes."

I left it at that, because I couldn't lie that I felt nothing toward Riagán or that I "only liked him."

Thankfully, Sadb didn't seem interested in drilling me. Instead, she took in my living room, and I did too, as things weren't exactly as I remembered. Sure, the furniture was all in the same place, but everything else looked... tidier. Last time I was leaving the apartment, I hadn't bothered with too much cleaning, save getting rid of perishables. With only the days to live I thought I had back then, it felt like a waste of time to tidy up that pile of old correspondence or put away dry dishes. Apparently, Riagán had not only visited my apartment but taken care of it as well.

"I'll go upstairs and grab what I need," I said. "It's warded, so don't come up uninvited."

"I remember."

Right. They were all there when I was dying from poisoned wounds, and Riagán was explaining to Cathal why I had to make it back home if they were to save me. Nobody could enter my den without my being present.

As I climbed the ladder hidden in my closet, I realized this wasn't true anymore. After all, in a moment of gratitude, I'd allowed Riagán to access it freely. In a way, with my wards altered to let him in and the spare set of keys in his possession, it had become his apartment as much as it was mine, whether I wanted it or not. Having made a promise that I wouldn't change the locks, I either had to accept it or move out... If I actually got to ever live in it again.

Upstairs, my den welcomed me with the familiar disarray of items otherwise known as "mess." Yet I could notice Riagán's hand around. My bed, always a pile of pillows, blankets, and duvets, was made, with the extra covers folded and stacked on the nightstand.

Thankfully, he hadn't touched my unfinished projects and tools, and he'd only partially organized the bits and bobs I used to make my trinkets, as if not wanting to mess up my own way of organizing things, so I didn't need much time to dig out extra curses and a few protective charms. I also packed my notebooks and a few unfinished pieces.

The next stop was my closet. I'd had enough of the Court's outfits and wanted some of my own clothes, though I had to pick the ones I hoped to fit and look acceptable on my new, mythborn-like physique.

To my surprise, my clothes weren't overflowing the laundry basket, the side effect of my being too busy, first chasing the Snake's agents and then almost dying from the affliction. Instead, they were hung or folded, and—most importantly—clean. The scent of laundry detergent hit my nostrils, and I couldn't decide what was more probable—Riagán hand-washing all my clothes or learning how to operate a charm-powered washing machine. Either way, if he killed a giant with one arrow, I wouldn't have been more impressed than I was staring at my wardrobe, all neat and tidy.

I had to appreciate the thought he'd put into all of it. He'd taken care of the cleaning and tidying, but other than that, he hadn't moved or reorganized anything, as if he wanted to make sure that my apartment was as "mine" as when I left it.

Burdened with two bags, I made my way down. Sadb was sitting on a chair, and it looked like she hadn't moved from there the whole time I was upstairs. It would be nice to offer her some tea and maybe even put a movie on, awing her with human technology like I did when I showed video games to Riagán, but I wasn't truly free yet. Pretending to be able to stay here for however long I wanted wouldn't make it real.

I gave my apartment a quick glance, regretting that I couldn't take my charmed TV and game console back to the Court. It would allow me to fill my afternoons with something other than staring at the mythborn runes or etching them into various objects. I could, though, make work more pleasant.

With that thought, I dove into the tiny kitchen and rummaged through my cupboards for various dry snacks I always had stashed. After a moment of hesitation, I reached for the bottle standing in the corner of the counter. Żubrówka, bison-grass vodka originally from Poland, had been a parting gift from my old teammate, before the affliction claimed him. I wasn't much of a drinker, and I'd never found an occasion good enough to open it, but perhaps I could find one some time in the future and share it with my new team. I carefully placed it in my bag.

"I've got what I need," I said, coming back to the living room. "Let's head back."

She stood up. "I expected you to stall."

"If Lady Eithne learns about it, we'll both be in trouble." Even if she didn't learn it from us, it would be enough for the Trinitians to get wind of it, and Albert would be very vocal about my not paying them a visit, which meant Eithne would hear about it too.

Sadb headed for the door, on her way casually taking one of my bags. I didn't protest, since it wasn't about how much I could carry but about ensuring we both were mobile if our way back turned out to be more adventurous than it should.

I locked the door, and we headed back down the familiar street.

The sun wasn't setting quite yet, but as it lowered toward the horizon, the gray sky began darkening. At least my neighborhood wasn't too bad, so I didn't expect any trouble, even after dusk. Shadows moved on the other end of the street, and I smiled at the thought that Paddy and his "fellas," as he put it, were keeping an eye out for troublemakers.

I wanted to enjoy the stroll back, probably the last one in a while, but as we walked away from the street, the sound of footsteps followed us, in the same rhythm our boots beat the cracked asphalt. I glanced back when we turned the corner but found nothing except for the familiar row of rundown buildings.

"We're being followed, aren't we?" Sadb asked in a hushed, calm voice.

"I can't see anyone. But I can... hear someone." I didn't even want to ponder how ridiculous it must have sounded. My unusual skill couldn't pick up anything but voice, and if there were footsteps, Sadb should have heard them too. At the same time, my instinct claimed I hadn't misheard it.

The confession earned me an arched eyebrow, but one of surprise, not mockery. Then she shook her head. "I won't risk checking it. We walk back as we were."

I couldn't argue with that. We weren't supposed to be outside of the Court in the first place, so whoever was following us couldn't have known we would be around. If we headed back, we likely wouldn't walk into an ambush, because nobody would have had time to prepare one, while trying to catch whoever had been tailing us could stir trouble neither of us wanted.

"This could be some local knacker who is too stupid to leave a member of the Scáthanna alone," I offered. "Some people around here think the Court should stick to their side of the river."

Her grim expression suggested she had other concerns, and I couldn't help wondering if she was thinking about Laoise. Even if her death couldn't have been Sadb's fault, it would come as no surprise if she felt guilty for what had happened to her lover. If I was to die too, this time clearly because of her decisions, that could be a blow worse than one dealt with a blade. I could relate to such mindset, but I kept my mouth shut. Scratching somebody's wounds open was hardly courteous, and the best thing I could do for her now was to get back to the Court alive.

We walked in silence, with the faint sound of footsteps behind us ever so persistent, like a reminder that Dublin still wasn't as safe a place as we hoped it'd someday become.

CHAPTER EIGHT

I never thought I'd be relieved at the sight of the four-story, rectangular building known in the past as Collins Barracks and after the Magiclysm as the Court. Even though our tail didn't follow us across the river, I still felt uneasy as we made it through the empty and quiet streets. Back in the war, it was those moments of stillness that foretold an ambush or other trouble.

Thankfully, this once, my instincts were wrong, and we made it back safely.

We entered the Court as we'd left it, through the servants' entrance, and made our way to the Scáthanna's quarters. I breathed out with relief. It seemed our little excursion had gone unnoticed... until it didn't.

"Ceannasaí was looking for you." Faolan strode through the courtyard, his broad-shouldered silhouette towering over us as he approached. "We're supposed to have a briefing."

Sadb nodded and headed inside, so I followed her, feeling Faolan's displeased glare piercing my back as he walked behind us. I had no trouble imagining he blamed me for whatever insubordination Sadb might have committed by allowing me to leave the Court, but it also could be some general animosity. Just because Riagán liked me and Cathal chose me, that didn't mean all team members were happy about it.

By now, I was quite certain Sadb didn't particularly care about me, and her anger stemmed from her not being able to pursue whatever revenge she was planning for Laoise's death. But others... Riagán aside, I'd never formed any closer relationships with any of them, save maybe for Laoise—dead now, so she didn't count.

We dropped off my bags, and Sadb motioned at the day room. If she was concerned with consequences for our trip, she didn't show it. We entered together.

Cathal stood in the middle, a soldier-like statue in waiting, and the rest of the team had taken seats around him. Caitríona and Riagán were at the long bench by the table, their backs against it, and every now and then they reached back to nibble on food.

Opposite to them, Faolan was already leaning against the wall, and in the corner, Lorcan was sitting on the floor, fidgeting with a small charm or other trinket. All of them had traces of mud and blood on their clothes, and tiredness was written on their faces, which meant Cathal had called for the meeting as soon as everyone arrived at the Court. I could only hope it was mere moments ago, not an hour or two.

The thought that Sadb and I had made them wait was not a pleasant one. Even if our commander seemed patient, I didn't peg him as a particularly forgiving mythborn.

I expected our ceannasaí to give us a lecture or at least a stern glare, but he only waved at us to join the rest. Sadb casually leaned against the wall beside Faolan, throwing him a grin, and I took the bench. I smothered my need for personal space and plopped down right beside Riagán. He sent me a smile but didn't say anything, his eyes—like all the others'—already fixed on Cathal.

"The Court's forces are preparing to take down the Snake's lair in the Botanical Gardens," he said. "We were called back because the lady wants us to aid them. Cait will coordinate setting up the curses, Riagán's going to lead their archer team, and Lorcan joins the medic team. Faolan, Sadb, and I will be on the standby with the operation's leader."

It seemed counterintuitive to break up a squad whose strength lay in perfect coordination and cooperation, which I'd seen firsthand more than once, but it wasn't my place to question decisions made, so I kept quiet.

"And Kaja?" Sadb asked.

Cathal gave me a long, evaluating stare, then looked back at her. "You tell me. Is she ready?"

I wish I could say I didn't hold my breath, but I did. If Sadb cherished the power she had over me in that moment, she didn't let me feel it.

"She can hold her own," she said.

Faolan openly snorted. "That's why you don't even give her a proper weapon?" He pointed at the blade at my side. "So eager to get her killed?"

Sadb didn't even turn to him. "She can hold her own." She was still looking at Cathal. "Up to you, ceannasaí."

"Let's see first if she can take a proper swing with that vegetable peeler you gave her." Faolan moved forward in a motion so smooth and effortless, it was almost as if the wall gently pushed him forward.

Sadb glanced at me with her eyebrow arched, though she must have known that unless Cathal forbade it, I'd accept the challenge. We both knew that I needed much more training, but she'd called it: I was good enough to go out in the field—just not as skilled and deadly as others—and I wouldn't give up on the chance to get out of the Court, this time officially.

As soon as I rose from the bench, the atmosphere in the room changed. Cathal took several steps back, leaving the middle empty, and others leaned forward with almost predatory glares. Even Lorcan looked up from his corner. If there was any entrance exam for admission to the Scáthanna, this had to be it: the Shadows were about to decide whether I was worth keeping around or a waste of time. I really hoped I'd live up to Sadb's confident declaration.

Faolan spread his arms when I approached. "I'll give you a free one and won't try to hit you." His tone was somewhere between taunt and mockery. "I bleed, you pass."

I expected deception and didn't fall for his relaxed posture. The moment I attacked, he'd be on me. I stood at a distance from him and pulled out my blade, flicking it in my hand back and forth, keeping Faolan on edge as he glanced every now and then to track its movement. I had to feint a strike to draw his attention away from my other hand... and the curse I'd slipped into it before I even got up from the bench.

Sadb was standing by the wall, and a slight smirk danced on her lips, because not only did she know that trick already—she'd helped me perfect it.

The sound of a slight shuffle behind me put me on alert, and my instincts, nurtured by war and honed by Sadb, reacted first. I squatted, half turning to keep an eye on what-ever threat was lurking behind me without losing sight of Faolan, and narrowly escaped an elbow strike to the back.

I didn't have time for surprised gawking at Riagán's

betrayal. Sadb's training, hammered into my body in so many painful ways, took over. I smacked him with the curse I was holding and rolled away.

Both Faolan—who attacked a second later—and Riagán went flying when the magic field expanded. One pounded against the wall like a swatted fly; the other landed on the table in a ruckus of cutlery and broken plates. The curse pushed on me too, but I was prepared for its effects, so I used the momentum to get away and jump back to my feet. Ready to act again, I scanned the mythborn in the room. Which one would attack next?

Nobody moved except for Riagán, who scrambled off the table, wiping food off his face and uniform.

Sadb broke the silence. "As I said, she can hold her own. But if you want to test her more, I suggest upstairs."

"That'll be enough," Cathal replied. "We have no need for a scout's skills this time, so Kaja, you'll join me and others." He looked around. "We're setting out at dawn, the day after tomorrow. Until then, you're free. Dismissed."

At his word, everyone stirred, and one by one they all left... All except for Riagán. "Faolan didn't think you'd hit me." He sent me a smile that had nothing to do with an apology for trying to backstab me or setting up the test in the first place.

"You're lucky I didn't pick something nastier," I teased.

"You wouldn't have. It would have affected you too." He approached, confident both in his words and moves. Then he enclosed me in his embrace, and the smells of pine and campfire smoke mixed with those of sweat, journey dirt, and the cranberry sauce that stained his uniform. "You owe me a shower," he whispered into my ear.

"You shouldn't have turned on me." I faked a pout.

Riagán laughed and held me tighter, his face close to

mine. I expected a kiss, but he seemed to be simply enjoying our closeness.

"Come, let's get cleaned up." I froze on the spot, and he laughed. "You don't have to wash with me." A smile lingered on his lips, and his eyes shone all of a sudden. "At least, not yet."

"I don't like... crowds." The idea of showering with Riagán aside, the mere thought of sharing the bath with all the other mythborn made me want to hide in my room until everyone fell asleep.

He tsked his disapproval. "You can't be one of us and remain so humanborn at the same time." He wrapped his arm around my waist. "Come. The Scáthanna do not hide in the face of danger."

I didn't remark that I was a scout, and scouts were to remain hidden while they... well, scouted. As he led me down the corridor, I fought off the urge to find an excuse. Even if I didn't like the idea, Riagán was right—I couldn't remain so humanborn in my ways if I wanted to find a place for myself at the Court, and I couldn't alienate myself from the mythborn who became my teammates and who would have my back when needed. And if they did things differently than humans did, I had to get over it.

We grabbed fresh clothes and headed for the showers.

WHEN WE ENTERED, Cathal and Cait were soaking in the common pool, both of them buck naked and unconcerned about it. I turned my head away, and Riagán nudged me, amused.

"You *should* stare." He didn't keep his voice down. "The

more you do, the sooner you'll get used to the sight—and bored."

"And what if she likes what she sees?" Cait called out from the pool, putting her wet blue hair behind her ear teasingly. Even from this distance, I could see a nasty bruise marking her clavicle and several old scars on her chest.

Riagán grinned at her. "Then I'll make sure she has something better in view," he replied with unwavering confidence.

Cait's laughter filled the chamber, and even Cathal snorted, which put me oddly at ease. They behaved so naturally, so casually... I mustered a smile and headed for the showers with Riagán accompanying me.

He hung his fresh clothes beside the towels and took his shirt off. Following his own advice, I shamelessly stared.

He had a wiry body, with muscles on his arms flexing right under his gray skin. The way his skin looked made me think of a stained-glass picture. The cracks in it resembled dried-up mud and marked his whole body like fractured frames, and lighter scars added to that strange mosaic. Strange but not unappealing—mythborn always looked a bit eerie and otherworldly, but in many cases, their physique was more alluring than repulsing—except for bridge dwellers that looked every bit as ugly as a mix of a frog and a troll would.

He stood in front of me motionless, as if allowing my inspection. The smile lingering on his face made it clear he noticed that I liked what I saw. With his pants off, he walked into the shower cabin and pulled the curtain closed, as if indicating he didn't expect me to reciprocate. In the past, when I was still a humanborn with unclear allegiances, he had always nudged me out of my comfort zone just enough to unnerve me or make me curious, never pushing too far, and I appreciated he hadn't changed his approach. If he tossed me straight into the deep waters instead, I'd likely run away in a panic.

I hesitated. Even alone with Sadb, I had been undressing in the shower, and for a heartbeat, I was ready to revert to my habits, but then I chased the discomfort away and took most of my clothes off. Only in my lingerie, I glanced toward the other mythborn, but Cait was already out of the water, drying with her back to me, and Cathal looked like he was dozing off in the pool... or maybe relaxing with his eyes closed. He didn't strike me as someone to ever put his guard down when he wasn't alone.

With no one looking, I did the bravest thing I had since facing the afflicted Emma on my own in a deadly fight: I sneaked into Riagán's cabin.

He was already naked, switching the water on. Hot droplets hit my skin, and he turned, surprise clear on his face.

Before I could say anything, he held me tight, pressing me against the cabin's wall and giving me a long, passionate kiss.

With the steam rising around us and his body on mine, I had a hard time keeping my thoughts straight, and they bounced frantically back and forth between desire and panic.

I wanted Riagán. I would be lying if I said I didn't. At the same time, the memory of my last serious relationship was engendering all kinds of fears of what would happen if we rushed things. I knew Riagán was not Albert, and we didn't have the same history and problems, but it didn't mean I couldn't mess things up again by not being patient.

I didn't want to accidentally ruin things between us. I didn't want it to become some casual acquaintance with sex added as a stress reliever or a pleasant pastime. But I was the one to get into his shower cabin, so I couldn't complain if things I didn't want came to pass.

Riagán moved his lips away from mine, but he still held me tight. He leaned his head over to my side.

"I'm sorry." His voice barely carried over the sound of water, though, contrary to his words, he didn't sound apologetic at all. "I wanted to get it in before you said we were just showering."

"Riagán…" I didn't even know how I was going to explain how I felt, and I'd be damned if I brought up Albert in a moment like that.

He put a finger on my lips. His eyes shone with desire, but something else as well. I dared not to call it love.

"I understand," he said. "I like what you said about building something that will last. I like that you want to be mine and that you want me to be yours." He glanced at me playfully. "And I like that you do brave things, like coming in here to make that happen."

I would never admit it to anyone, but this moment, my heart melted a little. *Just* a little. "You're perfect, you know?"

That might have been a bit far-fetched, and maybe I didn't know him enough yet to make such a claim, but his confident smile was my reward. I wanted to both take that smile away by kissing him back and watch it last forever. I didn't know how, but Riagán made everything seem easy.

"With that out of the way, shall we make our 'just showering' more pleasant?" He was already helping me out of my bra with the proficiency of someone who wasn't doing it for the first time.

I leaned forward and kissed him, while my hands shamelessly explored his body. I could already see that I was going to enjoy "just showering" with Riagán, and for a moment, as he took my cue and started his own exploration, I didn't care whether we went slow or fast, and where would we end up. All that mattered was his touching me in the gentlest and most possessive of ways while we kept kissing.

"My brave, myth-touched Kaja," he whispered as he reached for soap without breaking eye contact.

Part of me was still terrified at the thought that we were going to ruin everything. I hushed it. Relationships took time to build, but they also required creating intimacy along the way, and if we kept at a distance all the time, this could well fall apart. One way or another, I had to take a risk.

Riagán's hands back on me, soapy and finding every piece of my skin to lather, were making me certain he was worth that risk.

CHAPTER NINE

I was warm and surprisingly comfortable, given that Riagán held me tight, cocooning me with his own body so tightly that I couldn't shift around much. His embrace wasn't one of captivity, though. As if his confidence was magic itself, it emanated protection and peace. It felt like in his arms I could survive anything. The world around us could crumble in another massive Magiclysm, and I'd be still in Riagán's bed, sleeping safe and sound.

Half awake, I cherished that feeling.

It took a moment of that semi-lucid state for Cathal's voice calling my name to bring me back to reality.

Riagán's hand slid along my hip in a way that suggested our ceannasaí had woken him up as well. "Maybe he'll go away if he realizes you aren't there," Riagán muttered in my ear, his hand traveling along my skin in a gentle caress. "We were supposed to have a day off."

They all deserved one, but I had not been out on assignments for weeks, and even though Cathal hadn't excluded me from the day off, he deserved some of my time. With regret, I got out of the bed and threw Riagán's tunic on.

Untied, it hardly covered anything, but I didn't think Cathal would care.

He turned as soon as I opened the door, his face expressionless and giving no clue whether he was surprised to see me instead of Riagán poking out. He also didn't react to my skimpy outfit. Had Sadb been in his place, a snarky comment would have been a certainty.

He held out a gray pile of clothes. "You'll need these for tomorrow. Cait's making sure you'll have a few more sets and other necessary equipment, and Sadb should have your weapon ready by morn."

I stared at what I now recognized to be the Scáthanna's uniform. On top lay a black badge with their symbol, ribbons of smoke weaving into a sword. In the war, this had been the emblem of human's worst enemies... and it was about to become my own.

"I don't want to hear it, Kaja." The warning in Cathal's voice was clear.

So I took the uniform from him without any arguments, although I had some really good ones. Then I waited for him to walk away, closed the door, and presented them to Riagán.

"I shouldn't be wearing it yet. I'm not even half as good as you are," I said.

"That's a poor excuse." He sat up on the bed, his eyes skimming along my bare legs with a smile telling me he liked the view. "You should try it on instead."

"It's not an excuse. It's a valid point." I pouted but placed the badge on his desk and unfolded the clothes. They seemed roughly my size. "If somebody kills me while I'm wearing this, they get to gloat that they got one of the Scáthanna. If I die wearing as little as your badge, Cathal can always claim I was just a myth-touched liaison and never a true member of your team."

Riagán's expression hardened. "We aren't invincible." The way he said it, with sudden pain, made it clear he thought of Laoise. "But nobody ever took one of us down in a fair fight, so no one is likely to even try. If you die, it's going to be in some dirty trap, just…"

"Just like Laoise died," I finished for him. "No one told me what, exactly, happened, and asking Sadb seemed like the worst possible idea."

He became even more somber. "She'd have told you if you asked, but I'm sure she appreciates you didn't. Laoise was scouting and got ambushed on her way back to us. At least, that's what we could tell from the blood and curse marks. We took off as soon as her flare went up, but we didn't make it in time." His hands trembled in anger. "She took three with her, maybe more if their wounded didn't survive, and most of us wouldn't have done much better in her stead." He looked up and forced a smile. "So if Sadb thinks you're ready enough to go out as one of us, you won't bring the Scáthanna shame."

I nodded, finding no argument for that. I also wanted the topic to be gone. The mythborn, with all their disregard for personal space, seemed very private when it came to grieving.

The uniform was an exact copy of what Riagán and the others wore: comfortable trousers that reminded me of human military outfits, minus the camouflage pattern, and a long-sleeve shirt with a lacing tie in front. The belt had a lot of leather pouches attached and looked scabbard-ready.

The boots, though, drew my attention. Tight and made of leather, they slid onto my feet and calves with ease, fitting perfectly, like socks, and only upon a closer inspection did I discover they had been charmed. Soft and comfortable inside, they became hard and sturdy on the outside once I put them on, ensuring I wouldn't miss my own boots. The soles would protect my feet, and the rest made it perfect to deliver hard and painful kicks to unsuspecting opponents.

"For better protection out in the field, attach the soles." Riagán pointed at the last part of my outfit. "Without them, they're good for the Court, or for when you need to climb." He demonstrated on his own shoes, spiking my curiosity about the charms used to seamlessly bind two pieces of leather together. "Cait will give you a full rundown later." He handed me the shirt and pants. "Don't make me wait."

"I thought you'd prefer me without clothes," I teased.

He didn't take the bait, so I put my underwear and the uniform on. It fit quite well, considering no one had taken my measurements, and when I was done, Riagán got off the bed. His expression didn't have any of the usual playfulness as he reached for the badge and pinned it to my chest.

"The emblem... You should wear it around the Court, too. It'll make your life here a bit easier and remind some stuffed-up nobles that not only do you have the right to be here, but you're also one of us now."

I cringed. It sounded a lot like mythborn games, though I could see wisdom in his advice, too. Maybe the Master of Crafts would treat me differently if he knew I was a member of the Scáthanna. On the other hand, he didn't treat Sadb much better.

"Or I'll be seen as someone who's desperately trying to fit in. I don't have many problems anyway, because most of the mythborn do their best to ignore me."

"But some give you trouble, don't they?"

"Nothing more serious than glares of contempt." I shrugged and chuckled when one particular memory resurfaced. "Although Connor's cousin was convinced I was after him."

"Clíodhna?" Riagán grunted. "She's just jealous."

"Jealous?" I really needed to learn more about mythborn relationships, because I seemed to have been missing a lot. First, Riagán's feelings toward me, even if he wasn't the most forthcoming about them in the beginning, then Sadb and Laoise and their relationship. And now, it seemed, Clíodhna's emotional issues were about to follow.

"She's been in love with Connor ever since they were youngsters," Riagán said. "But then Connor, instead of trying to stay safe, like a well-born family member should, joined the fight." He sighed. "When he came back as what many around here would consider a cripple, nobody spoke of a union between them anymore, and Clíodhna's stuck between obedience to her family's looking for a better match and her feelings..." He brushed my cheek. "You have a good relationship with Connor, and he seems more comfortable around you than around many mythborn, even considering your complicated mutual past. It's something she can't get, the way she behaves now, and she likely can't even understand why Connor's different around you."

The reminder that Connor thought of me as good company—and a friend—made me all warm and fuzzy, but I looked at Riagán with a serious expression. "And are you jealous?" I might be blunt, but clearing some things up was a better idea than letting them fester.

The smile he gave me was one of pure confidence. "There's no mythborn I'm jealous of."

"No mythborn? What about humanborn?" I asked, even though I knew his answer. He didn't even have to mention Albert's name.

Riagán cringed and looked away. "I'm trying, but it's

going to take some time," he said with a hint of apology, as if he was in the wrong for being jealous. "When the lady got interested in you and ordered us to watch you when we weren't on other assignments, I got to see... a lot. The way you looked at each other, the time you spent together..." He put a finger on my lips before I could reply. "I was growing fascinated with you, and the reasonable thing would have been to ask Cathal to give me other tasks. Instead, I kept watching and tried to convince myself that I was building some idealized version of you in my head. That the real Kaja would be as annoying and petty as all other humanborn, and she'd hate me simply because of who she thought I was. That once we knew enough and stopped watching you, I'd get over it. And that even if I didn't, all I had to do was meet you in person and destroy the illusion I'd created." He gave me a soft smile. "When we finally met, I wasn't about to give in. I wanted to ruin whatever lie I believed in. Instead, I became even more curious."

I remembered our first meeting well, because his presence and subtle testing of my limits were quite unnerving back then, but he did save my life as well... and then asked for a kiss to repay that debt.

A humanborn kissing a mythborn was a dangerous thing because of the addictive magic it activated, and I could see how he had expected me to react badly to the request, maybe with some insults and bitchiness. That would surely be enough to ruin any fantasies he had. Except that I didn't respond as he thought I would. Instead, I kissed him, even if it was just a smooch on the cheek—mostly to get rid of the life debt and its possible consequences, and...

"And now I'm here, a myth-touched sleeping in your bed," I said in a teasing manner.

He shook his head impatiently. "You're affliction-free now. If you really wanted to go back to Trinity…"

I groaned at the very idea. "I want to visit, sure. To see my friends, Albert included, and tell them I'm fine, so they can stop worrying about me. That's it." I looked him in the eye. "I might feel trapped being stuck at the Court, but it doesn't mean I miss Trinity. And I don't miss Albert more than a friend I haven't seen for a while. So if you aren't jealous of Connor, you have no reason to be jealous of him."

Riagán snorted in response, and I caught a bitter note in it. He didn't have to point out that there was a vast sea of difference between the two friendships, since I'd never even thought of sleeping with Connor, but at least I'd managed to amuse Riagán.

"I like what we have," I offered in a soft whisper, looking straight at him so he could read the honesty in my eyes. "I like the thought of what more we could have."

He didn't reply, but the shadow of bitterness faded from his face. He pulled me into his embrace, closing his arms around me, and that was the one cage I welcomed.

IT TOOK Riagán a while to finally let me go, and when he did, we headed for the showers. I expected we'd take a long time there as well. Perhaps in mythborn culture, taking things slow meant making every single one of them last. Not that I minded building intimacy with him this way.

"You know"—Cait's voice sounded behind us before we reached the end of the corridor—"some of us would also like to spend some time with our new team member."

We both turned to face her.

Her expression was half playful and half reprimanding. She was smaller than Riagán but of the same lean build, and from the glimpses I'd gotten in the bathing area the previous evening, every part of her body was wiry muscle. Even though I had never seen her fight, I had no doubt she could last at least several rounds with Sadb. Likely—and I smirked at the thought—much longer than I did.

"I got toys!" She presented her hands, full of pouches and satchels, to me, before Riagán got a chance to say anything. "All yours if you can sneak away from a certain selfish mythborn."

Riagán grinned at her, and she stuck her tongue out at him in a childish and surprisingly humanlike way. "We'll make it quick," he promised.

I somehow sensed that the mythborn concept of "quick" could be as different as their concept of "slow," so I freed myself from his gentle embrace.

"Or I could go now, and we could make it slow later." I hated the idea that Cait would have to wait for me. I waved at her. "Come, you can show me everything in my room."

As we walked away, I glanced at Riagán. He was looking at me with a soft and pleased expression, as if the delay in spending more time together meant nothing in comparison to acting like a member of their team. I sent him a smile and closed the door behind me and Cait.

She was standing in the middle of my room, taking it in as if there was anything unusual or special about it. I hardly had any personal items, so I supposed it looked bare to her. Then she stirred and dumped everything she was carrying onto my bed.

"Sadb told me about a certain inspection Connor had done for us," she said casually. "And, as I understand, we need to stockpile some offensive curses, just in case. She told me to get as much as I can, and if the Master of Crafts complains..."

"Blame it on her," I guessed.

No one would be surprised that a woman who had lost her lover would become obsessed with making sure her team carried a sufficient—or even excessive—stock of offensive and defensive tools. All that to conceal that there would be only one person in need of all those trinkets.

"So, you know," I added.

Cait shrugged. "Only what I need to. She said that Connor will be discreetly supplying you with anything we can't get without raising questions. Whatever he gives you is none of my concern." She looked at me. "Others will guess sooner or later that you have more than just our usual stuff, but no one will pry. Everyone will understand that one overheard conversation or accidental joke in public could put you in mortal danger."

I nodded, solemn all of a sudden. It was easy to guess that Cait had Laoise in mind, and she likely wondered if there was anything they all could have done—or *not* done— to prevent her death.

"Show me what you've got for me," I said, hoping the topic change would lighten the mood. "Last time, all I got to see was some shriek-hunting gear and a couple of flares."

Cait took the way out I offered, and we spent an hour on the inventory, consisting of healing charms, protective amulets, and various potions.

"When you have time, you should acquaint yourself with how they smell and taste," she said while demonstrating comfortable slots for the potions in one of the pouches attached to my belt. "It's useful in the dark."

I dutifully uncorked the first one marked as "antidote." It had a strong scent of a chemical mixture, but there was something alcoholic in it as well. I ran my finger against the edge and stick it in my mouth. It tasted as foul as the scent suggested, but also... "There's something familiar about it." I couldn't pinpoint it.

Cait grinned. "It better be. When you were dying from the Léanmhar's claws, we poured everything we had into you."

This wasn't exactly the memory I wanted to recall, but it resurfaced anyway.

I was looking into a missing person for Albert, hoping to win some points with him that I desperately needed, and stumbled upon the Afflicted orchestrating bombings across Dublin. I didn't have a chance to win that fight, and I would have died if Riagán hadn't arrived. And later, the rest of the team. I was about to turn into the same monstrosity I had fought, but instead of killing me, they did their best to save me... Even if they couldn't undo what was happening to me, they bought me enough time to get the lifesaving ritual Eithne offered me.

"I never thanked any of you properly," I said.

Cait nudged me. "We were just making sure the scout Cathal set his eyes on didn't get away from us," she joked. "A myth-touched joining the Scáthanna already rubs some noble mythborn the wrong way, so inviting a Léanmhar to become one of us would have been out of question."

"Not to mention the anger management issues," I added, allowing her to pull me into a lighthearted conversation.

The Léanmhar were aggressive creatures who attacked everyone in their way indiscriminately... and efficiently. The one I'd faced—Emma—was different, but only up to a point. When threatened, she turned to rage instantly.

"And I bet Riagán prefers the way you look now," Cait said.

I glanced at her. There wasn't any malice in her voice, so I guessed that, just like Sadb, she was just concerned about where this relationship was going. If it took a turn that either Riagán or I wasn't expecting, it could cause issues within the team. I had a hunch that if I gave any hint that I didn't like his attention, others would pass the word to him.

"He'd better," I replied playfully. "I'm not primping myself to look like one of those Court mythborn for anyone, not even him."

Cait chuckled, clearly satisfied with my answer. "Come, let's wrap up the training. Riagán's patient only when it comes to stalking his targets, and he's probably already wondering what's taking us so long."

Riagán showed patience in many other situations, but I kept that thought to myself. Instead, I pointed to a familiar shapes. "Flares, right?"

Cait nodded. "Keep at least two on you at all times. Even at the Court."

"Better to have and not need than need and not have," I muttered in reply.

She seemed pleased I'd agreed with her, and she rolled out a piece of paper. "These are the colors of the team. Memorize them when you have a moment. For now, it's enough to know that anything with silver means the Scáthanna, but in the future it'll be best if you know each of them. Sometimes specific assignments mean you have to ignore some of them or only answer a particular one."

The paper contained multiple colorful patterns, each with a description in mythborn runes. Underneath, clean writing translated them into human—the names of the team members.

Cathal's flare was all silver. Everyone else had silver as their first color, followed by two more. Riagán's was black and brown. Sadb had yellow and red. Faolan's name was beside the brown and green one, and Lorcan got a mix of teal and black. When I got to Cait's, I couldn't help looking up. She grinned at me as if she'd expected such a reaction to a mix of pink and orange.

Then she got serious. "I'm sorry, I only now realized that no one had asked you if there were colors you preferred."

I looked down at the paper. The last spot was marked as "Kaja." First silver, like everyone else, then white and red. I couldn't help smiling.

"I see you did some serious research," I said. I wouldn't have expected the mythborn to fully comprehend the idea of different countries, and it definitely required effort to learn what the colors of the Polish national flag were. "They'll do. Thank you for putting thought into them."

She brightened as if my reaction really mattered to her. Aside from our short interaction before the shriek hunt, long before I became a myth-touched, I hadn't had the chance to get to know her better, but she seemed friendly and cheerful—a person who'd prefer to see other people happy as well.

I let her walk me through the rest of my equipment. The Scáthanna didn't wear armor that would slow them down or make noise, but their uniforms, as it turned out, had warded threads that offered some protection. I constrained my curiosity as to how mythborn craftsmen had managed to ward something so small as a thread. It had to wait until I could grill Connor about it. Even if he didn't share any secrets with me, it would be fun to make him come up with excuses to keep them away from me.

"Daydreaming about Riagán?" Cait teased. "If you paid attention instead, you could do things other than just dreaming."

I gave her a grin. The more comfortable I was with my team members' teasing, the more likely they would stop it, or at least tone it down. No matter how friendly Cait was, and how others never truly overstepped any boundaries in their interactions, I'd rather not have the whole team poking around my private life.

Though with the way they all—and now that also included me—lived so close together, privacy was not something I'd be getting in abundance, and I had to get used to it.

"Let's wrap it up, then," I said. "I think I know enough to not frantically look through my stuff if the need comes, and if I have any more questions, I know where to find you."

She gave me a knowing smile but obliged.

CHAPTER TEN

Cathal hadn't lied about setting out at dawn, and I muffled a yawn. I might not be a night owl, but I didn't count myself among early birds either.

We stood outside the Court as Lady Eithne's warriors marched out. Three squadrons passed us by, and it seemed like every single mythborn in those units glanced at me in a more or less open manner. Apparently, being the Scáthanna's new member and a myth-touched on top of that was a big deal, but to their possible regret, I didn't look like anything special.

Once all of them left, Cathal gave the signal, and we departed as well. We didn't follow the warriors down the now-crowded street. Instead, our ceannasaí chose another route, and it made me wonder whether the wait was a calculated delay to make sure everyone saw me. It would be like him to throw some kind of unvoiced "she's one of us—deal with it" message to the Court mythborn.

We made most of the way in silence, everyone focused and serious, so I kept my questions to myself. Sadb might have trained me to fight well enough, but I still needed everything else, including how they operated and what kind of signals they used. Even if we were only going there to stand to the side and look professional, I'd rather be ready when it turned out someone needed our help. For the same reason, I'd packed all the curses I had ready. Better to have and not need and all that. Still, I felt like Cathal should have pinned a "trainee" badge right under my team emblem.

I was walking at the end of the group beside Sadb, who still held the informal title of my babysitter, when Faolan fell in with us.

"Ever been to the gardens?" he asked.

"It was a long time ago."

Ever since the Magiclysm, the former Botanical Gardens had been one of the mythborn's most closely guarded secrets, and Trinity had only unreliable gossip about it. The whole area had suffered from the sudden outburst of magic when the mythborn returned to this world, distorting vegetation and even the nearby buildings. If any humans were caught within the magic burst's range, we'd never learned what had become of them.

During the war, I'd seen the gardens several times, safely from afar. The overgrown thicket loomed over the rooftops, stealing the meager daylight from the neighborhood, and we learned soon enough that the area was more dangerous than facing a shriek alone, so we kept clear.

After the ceasefire, when the negotiations started, the mythborn made it clear the Botanical Gardens were to remain off-limits for all humanborn, and no one objected too strongly. The area, heavily contaminated with magic, seemed like a yet another problem, and we had enough of our own to handle. If the mythborn wanted to take responsibility for that mess, Albert was happy to give it to them, especially as the north side of Dublin was primarily myth-born area anyway.

Of course, curiosity might have killed the cat, but it also was responsible for many other deaths throughout human history, and the ink on the peace treaty hadn't dried up yet when the first curious explorers decided to ignore the agreement made. The Court made it clear that they'd not allow any trespassers, and Trinity had silently agreed to let the mythborn deal with any nosy humanborn... or rather, with what was left of those thrill seekers. Which was, in short, not much, but with a lot of blood.

"If you get separated from us, don't try to find a way out on your own," Faolan said. "Get the flare up and keep away from other mythborn."

I couldn't help arching an eyebrow at the advice.

Faolan grinned. "Most of the gardens are a maze of thorns and beasts. Many of our kind are as clueless in there as any humanborn would be. They're more likely to draw danger to you than help you get out."

"Shouldn't I be helping them instead?" After all, I was now one of the Scáthanna.

"If they were foolish enough to go inside, they deserve their plight," Faolan replied immediately without even a hint of compassion.

"Unless the lady says otherwise," Sadb muttered.

By her displeased tone, I guessed that the team had been sent to the gardens more than once on a rescue mission, likely to get some curious and brazen Court mythborn of the noble persuasion out of trouble.

"Unless the lady says otherwise," Faolan agreed with a shrug.

We took a corner, and the wall of greenery rose before me, concealing the rest of the landscape. I stopped, half terrified and half in awe. The sight didn't match the memories I had of a well-kept, mostly open-space park with flowerbeds, blooming trees, rock gardens, ponds, and orangeries...

The hideous thicket ahead tore through my recollections with a slap of reality, and I found myself at loss for words to describe it. The closest I could think of was a hedge that had been left to grow unkempt for decades or even centuries. Yet it was more than a hedge. Thick branches poking out here and there suggested there were trees somewhere deeper in that sinister green mass, and thick vines threatened any passerby with thorns longer than my thumb. The worst part was that they seemed to be moving, slithering among the branches like a nest of snakes.

The rest of the Scáthanna stood silently as I took the view in. Not a single one of them smirked or snorted, and when I finally tore my eyes away, Cathal simply gestured us to keep going.

We ventured into the gardens through what looked like a living green tunnel. I sensed the distorted magic around. That kind of chaotic energy couldn't hurt me anymore, but it reminded me of the not-so-long-gone times when the magic affliction was eating my body away, threatening to turn me into a monster every passing moment. Every step through the tunnel brought uneasiness stemming from my old fears, but I did my best to conceal it. From the glances I got, I was certain my companions had a good idea how I felt, but I was supposed to be one of the Scáthanna now, so I could at least try to look the part.

Deeper into the gardens, the looming hedge dispersed some, revealing patches of gray sky above. The thicket grew irregularly, creating corridors and wider spaces between. Needless to say, nothing I saw matched the few memories I had of the place. I could as well be walking in another world, so eerie did everything feel.

We made good pace, and Cathal led us with confidence until we reached a large clearing in which squads of mythborn practiced drills.

"That looks... inconspicuous," I muttered. It wasn't exactly how I'd go about setting a trap.

Faolan smirked. "This is just a distraction, but it'll ensure our targets stay cooped up instead of wandering about. The actual ambush is being set more discreetly." He indicated a direction with a slight move of his chin. I couldn't see beyond the thicket, but Cait, Riagán, and Lorcan were already heading there, looking like three friends chatting on an aimless stroll.

Meanwhile, Cathal led Sadb, Faolan, and me toward a small hill where a group of mythborn circled a table. His stride was confident and slow enough to draw gazes, as if he wanted to make sure everybody paid attention to him and not to the three of his team members who wandered away.

"Good to see you, Aengus," Cathal said.

"Cathal, I'm glad you and your people made it." A tall, broad-shouldered mythborn stepped forward.

He wore a field uniform embroidered with several Celtic weaves that made him look more important than others. One day, I had to figure out whether mythborn had any command structure that resembled human military, and where Cathal was in that pecking order.

I wondered whether Aengus knew he was named after a prehistoric fortress to the west of Ireland. In a way, he resembled it too, with the hue of his skin being a mixture of steel blue, like the sea around the Aran Islands, and the light green of the grass that covered the ancient stones.

"As much as I welcome your expertise, I hope we won't

be needing it." The way Aengus said it made me think he didn't mean what he'd said about being glad for our presence here. I supposed it made sense. No leader would like someone else to mess around in his operation.

"I'm always happy to lend a hand." Cathal approached and acknowledged him with a nod while we kept several steps away. "If nothing else, it's a chance to introduce you to the newest addition to my team." He gestured at me to come closer. "This is Kaja."

I could swear the other mythborn was appalled at the sight of me, though his face showed only slight discontent. "A myth-touched, ceannasaí? One would think you lack fine mythborn sons and daughters to choose from."

With such a comment, I had no doubt that his choice to use English instead of mythborn language, which up until this very moment I'd considered a courtesy, was actually meant to ensure I received the insults directed at me. I doubted he expected me to break down crying and quit the Scáthanna on the spot, so he could have been venting his own opinions and being generous in sharing them with everyone who would or simply had to listen, Cathal and me included.

I gave him a blank stare. After all, he wasn't addressing me directly, so I could ignore his remarks and let Cathal deal with it the way he deemed appropriate.

"Indeed I do," Cathal replied casually. "I lost a scout and needed to replace her. Court-grown warriors don't have such experience, and the countryside mythborn lack the in-depth knowledge of this city I consider necessary. Now, assuming you're done forcing me to explain my decision, I'd like to know the status of the operation."

Contrary to my expectations of inviting Cathal to join the mythborn circling the strategy table, Aengus led him away. Having no else to do, I rejoined Sadb and Faolan. They looked casual, just like bored military personnel forced to tail their commander, but their eyes scanned the clearing with focus and caution.

Aengus and Cathal stopped some distance away, and I pretended I joined my companions in scanning the surroundings while I shamelessly eavesdropped. I'd spent some evenings honing my listening skill and had discovered that it could be very selective if I focused enough. Like a radio receiver, I picked up bits of conversations all around me, but I could tune in to them and pick the ones I wanted to hear. I still needed a bit of practice when it came to tuning my skill *out*, but the sleep charm allowed me deep sleep at night, and during the day, when I was distracted, all conversations were nothing more than a distant background noise.

"We have everything under control, so you can just sit down and relax." Aengus sounded quite passive-aggressive to me. "I don't need your people to charge in showing off and ruining everything. If the lady hadn't insisted, you wouldn't even be here."

"Status of the operation, Aengus." From this distance, Cathal seemed unmoved by the rant. "If, of course, you're done with your complaints."

Aengus's back was turned to me, so I could only assume the grimace on his face as he replied, "My squads are finishing setting up the explosive curses. Once they go off, the ambush teams will go in, finishing off any survivors, and the squads here will pick up whoever stumbles outside."

"I'd prefer to catch a few alive."

"My orders are to burn the Snake's nest to the ground, not to accommodate your whims, but if anyone lives long enough to surrender, you're welcome to have them inter-rogated."

"Thank you, Aengus. I appreciate it." The gratitude in Cathal's voice rang with honesty.

"Just promise me one thing. When she dies, you'll at least consider Diarmuid."

I didn't have to wonder who that "she" was, and it helped me to understand the reasons behind Aengus's animosity toward me.

"If she dies—and I don't expect it to be anytime soon—I'll be looking for another scout," Cathal replied. "Your son is a great fencer, but his skills wouldn't do him much good out in the field. Every time I sent him out, I'd be risking his blood on my hands. You're my friend, Aengus. I wouldn't be doing you a favor."

Aengus huffed, but he didn't reply. After a moment of silence, their conversation drifted away from the topic and they started discussing some boring Court affairs, stopping only when one of Aengus's adjutants approached with a report.

Faolan nudged me. "Dozing off?"

"Maybe she didn't get enough sleep last night," Sadb commented with a straight face.

I ignored the remark, convinced that if the two of them banded against me, I'd have no chance in a game of wits and snarky comments.

"Since we have nothing else to do, you could start learning the lay of the land." Faolan pulled a folded paper out of his belt pocket. "The map isn't very accurate, but it should be enough for you to find your way around. If cean-nasaí agrees, once we're done here, I'll give you a tour. It'd be a shame for our scout to know less than I do."

I nodded. "I hope you aren't planning to feed me to those monsters you mentioned earlier."

It was only a half joke. Even when I was just a human-born working with the Scáthanna, I had a feeling Faolan wasn't particularly fond of me, so I couldn't shake my suspicions he'd take his chance to get rid of me. Everyone would understand if a barely trained myth-touched had an unfortunate accident in a dangerous area like this. Faolan could easily claim I didn't follow his instructions or got cocky...

He gave me an assessing look. "You *would* make good bait."

Sadb gave him a firm nudge before he could add anything else. "The map?"

I expected some more teasing and banter, but instead, he unfolded the paper. The light breeze of the ever-present Irish wind was playing with it, so we all squatted down, holding it to the ground.

I stared at the scramble of random green and brown lines that he called a map with doubt, but if Faolan noticed my expression, he ignored it. The lesson of the gardens' topography began.

By the time Aengus's squads had finished setting their trap, I knew the surrounding area better than I could have expected. A few snarky comments aside, Faolan was determined to teach me everything, and I appreciated it. He might not like me, but since I was his team member, he made sure I learned as much as possible.

As soon as everything was ready, Cathal wrapped up his conversation with Aengus, and as they approached a viewpoint on top of the hill, he gestured for us to come over. Sadb and Faolan didn't even try to hide their boredom, pretending they didn't notice Cathal's displeased glares, and I somewhat shared their feelings. Not that I was eager to get some action, but it seemed we all could have been doing something more useful—or pleasant—than watching other mythborn doing their jobs. And though I wouldn't admit it out loud, I could use some more training. There was a difference between being able to hold my own and actually being as good as everyone else on the team. When it came to physical training, no one got that well trained in a month or two, no matter how much their body had magically changed, and I was no exception.

I could only hope that the whole affair would end quickly. The half-ruined building that used to be a green-house, partially covered with the vicious, thorny vines, wasn't big, so there couldn't be many people inside. Five squads, including the three that were performing the maneuvers serving as a smoke screen, and the Scáthanna on top of that seemed like overkill.

With nothing else to do, I engaged my listening skill, if nothing else, to test how far it reached.

"As soon as the charges go off, attack," a male voice with a mythborn accent said. "You're supposed to create as much commotion and chaos as possible, so the other group can approach unnoticed."

I must have tuned in to some mythborn squad leader, but the orders he was giving sounded odd and contradicted what I'd learned eavesdropping on Cathal, so I kept listening in case Aengus had misled my ceannasaí.

"I want the blue-haired mythborn female alive. Alive, understand? I don't want the same mess you made trying to get the last one."

My eyes widened as the meaning of the words sank in. This wasn't one of the friendly mythborn, and he was getting ready to spring his own trap while we were preparing ours.

Then it dawned on me. I knew a mythborn with vibrant blue hair.

"Cait!" I said with urgency. "Cait's in danger!" The cogs in my head were turning full speed, trying to conjure reasons good enough for Cathal to listen and act. "It's a trap!" Even to myself, I sounded ridiculous, announcing it in a peaceful clearing before the operation even started.

"What—"

Faolan didn't get to finish. The charges went off, and the area filled with the noise of activating curses. Then more sounds joined in: encouraging battle cries mixed with disturbing screeches. A mixed band of mythborn and the Afflicted stormed out of the thicket, and along with them trotted the ugliest creatures I'd ever seen. They moved on all fours, close to the ground like lizards, but the rest of their sleek bodies resembled oily leeches that had rolled in a lot of broken bones.

Stunned with the sudden outpour of noise, I was paralyzed, but my body adapted quickly, and within seconds my hearing was back to normal. Among the countless voices, I searched for the familiar one. I needed to know more. Anything that could point me his way or reveal something important of his plan.

"Take their leader down." His voice was almost drowned in another battle cry I involuntarily picked up.

I let my instincts react. "Get down!" I yelled to Cathal as I ducked.

I had no way of pulling him down if he resisted, but the desperation in my voice must have convinced him. He dropped to a squat the very moment an arrow whizzed through the air.

Except that it wasn't meant for him...

Aengus let out a short yell of pain and collapsed beside us, a shaft buried deep into his chest but not his heart. My yell, after all, might have saved his life. Or only postponed his death, if the wound was serious enough.

In a heartbeat, Cathal was beside him, and I followed. Sadb and Faolan were on my heels with their weapons already drawn.

"They're trying to get to Cait," I told Cathal. "She's their target, just like Laoise was."

Of course, I only had a scrap of an overheard conversation and my speculations as a proof, but it wasn't time for explanations anyway. We had little time to act, and even less to discuss the details.

To my surprise, he didn't ask any questions. He must have understood that it was better to get to Caitríona and find out she was fine than learn all too late that I was right and she was the target.

He pointed at Aengus. "Keep him alive until Lorcan arrives. Sadb, Faolan, with me." He fired a magical flare just above us, and they took off.

I scanned my surroundings, but three of Aengus's adjutants scattered when another arrow hit nearby, releasing a powerful explosive curse, so I couldn't count on their help.

The chaotic battle all around us grated on my wartime memories, and my scout instincts demanded I find a place to hide. But with Aengus wounded, moving him was out of the question. I stifled the creeping fear, instead letting the familiar coldness and detachment take over. It would keep my mind somewhat clear for the time being, even if I paid for it later with nightmares.

With no immediate danger to either of us, I knelt beside Aengus. I couldn't save everyone, and the order I got was clear: make sure he survived long enough for Lorcan to take care of him. Unless we became the target of another sniper or some nearby enemy unit spotted us, I shouldn't have too hard of a job.

And, of course, I shouldn't have thought so, as upon closer inspection, the arrow's shaft glowed with curses I didn't recognize, prophesying Aengus's encroaching demise.

In the back of my head I wondered whether Cathal had known what he was leaving me with, because I had no bloody idea. And—which came as no surprise—before I could figure out how to deal with the shaft, the curse activated.

Aengus let out a short scream as the shaft melted, spreading over his skin like acid or blue lava. Even without a closer look I knew it was going to go through his body if I didn't do something quick.

I fished out a healing charm and magic poison antidote, and my mind flashed back to the previous day, when Cait was explaining how they worked, which brought a nauseating wave of worry. Then I focused on the task. Thinking about her wouldn't help me save the mythborn in my care. I had to trust that the rest of the Scáthanna saw to her safety.

I uncorked the antidote, and he drank hastily but shook his head as a grimace of pain twisted his face. The antidote wasn't working. With no other options, I activated the healing charm over his wound. The effect was almost immediate, but instead of showing signs of relief, the mythborn writhed in pain. The liquid on his body stirred and moved like an amoeba. When its tendrils reached for the charm, I moved my hand away. It didn't stop, stretching upward. It acted like a living being... Perhaps there was a way to get it off Aengus's body. I guided it away, but as it crawled across the mythborn commander's skin, it aggravated his pain, so I stopped. I couldn't leave it on him, because with every passing second the blue liquid ate away his skin and flesh— but if I kept trying, I could cause fatal injuries anyway.

I moved the charm closer again, and the amoeba-curse contracted at first, stretching rapidly mere moments later. I didn't want to imagine what it would do if I let it touch me, but for now, it seemed drawn to the charm. Carefully and slowly, I let the tendrils touch it. When they connected, I moved the charm away, and the amoeba stretched even more, as if not willing to give up its hold on it but refusing to leave Aengus. The blue lava kept advancing on the leather the charm was made of, getting dangerously close to my fingers. Against my screaming instincts, I didn't let go... but as soon as the malicious thing peeled off Aengus's body, I tossed the charm away. The azure ribbon of the magic amoeba fluttered in the air, still attached to it, and then it disappeared in the grass. I could only hope it wasn't sentient and wouldn't come back.

Aengus sighed with relief, though if someone asked me, it was quite premature. The curse had left a gaping wound, skin and muscle eaten away as if by acid, and even though the bleeding wasn't intense, I had no doubt it would turn lethal if untreated.

With the healing charm gone, I had to resort to primitive methods, but ripping sturdy mythborn-made clothes seemed futile, especially if his outfit was made with the same special threads as our uniforms. He hissed as I poured the rest of the magic poison antidote onto his wound, but it seemed to help. With no other choice, I ripped off his embroidered epaulettes and bundled them over the bleeding.

"Commander Aengus!" One of his adjutants made his way back to us, his sword bloodied.

That reminded me that there was still a battle taking place all around us, and I cursed myself for not paying attention. In the past, in a situation like that, I would have had a whole squad watching my back while I administered first aid, and I'd foolishly allowed myself to revert to those old habits, ignoring that the situation had changed.

If that mythborn had been an enemy, I'd have been dead. Apparently, no matter your instincts, no matter the training, peace *did* make you soft... and stupid. No more. I was lucky to have survived that long, and now it was time to actively work on surviving.

"Get a medic here!" I demanded.

The mythborn turned, paused, and jerked when one of the creatures leaped at him. His arm, half raised in what must have been a last-second defense, slumped, and he lost his weapon. He let out a gurgle from his ripped throat as he collapsed to his knees, and then fell into the grass, face first.

I allowed myself a second of a foolish hope that the monster would wander off, but its beady green eyes locked on me. With one hand still applying pressure to Aengus's wound, I shifted my balance, and in unnervingly slow motion I reached for a curse pinned to my jacket.

"Save yourself," Aengus whispered as his gaze followed mine to the creature. He tried to replace my hand on the wound dressing with his own, but his moves were sluggish and the pressure he applied—weak.

I didn't reply. Cathal had given me an order, and I intended to carry it out.

The leech-lizard-whatever-the-hell-it-was crept closer, and I hoped it would leap. I had no idea how agile these things were, so if I attacked first, it could dodge. The best chance was to get it mid-flight if—only if—it leaped.

Of course, it didn't.

As it lunged forward, its round mouth revealing a set of thin, hooked teeth, I tossed the curse. The creature coiled, barely dodging it, but it didn't get away fast enough. My trinket activated upon contact with the ground. A fiery ball extended rapidly and sent the thing flying.

I lay flat on top of Aengus as the flames reached all too close to us. Fire wasn't the best choice, but I hadn't had time to be picky about which curse to use and even less time to actually use it. At least I'd hit the leech-thing with it and managed to not kill us in the process.

Too bad I hadn't killed it.

The creature howled in pain as it got back on its feet. At first, it didn't look like the fire had caused much damage to it, but when it approached, its moves were wobbly. It kept turning its head to the sides, and I stared at its scorched-blind eyes. It was sniffing the air, but the smoke must have dulled its senses. Nevertheless, it hobbled in our general direction.

I switched out the hand pressing on Aengus's wound and reached for my weapon. I struck with precision that I attributed to Sadb's training. The blade crushed the bony thorns protruding from the creature's head and buried itself deep in the soft tissue, as if the monster had no skeleton save for the external one. Magic truly created the oddest of things.

I pulled my weapon out of the carcass as another leech-zard approached. Fumbling a little, as it wasn't my usual throwing hand, I readied another curse.

I didn't get to use it.

From behind the creature, Lorcan came sprinting, his

sword unsheathed, striking anything in his way. Without slowing down, he grounded the creature that was about to lunge at me and Aengus and came to a sliding stop. I moved away as soon as he knelt by the mythborn.

"Keep an eye on those things," he said, and then focused on the wounded.

I moved the curse to my throwing hand, but no immediate targets presented themselves. Around us, the fighting was slowly dying out, and the enemies' retreat suggested that we had won. Yet I looked toward where the curses had gone off. With wind spreading smoke, I had little hope of seeing gray uniforms among the mythborn deluging the area, and I didn't want to risk missing a nearby threat by engaging my listening skill.

"Kaja!" Riagán called from the distance. His bow was at his back, his quiver empty, and he held a sword in his hand.

I waved at him, relieved.

His uniform bore marks of a fight, but he walked casually, which meant we weren't in danger anymore. As he got closer, fear and concern flashed on his face. "Are you hurt?"

I looked at my uniform, marked with many red stains. I must have gotten blood on me when I leaned over to protect Aengus from flames. "I'm fine." I stepped to the side, letting him see the wounded mythborn.

He nodded. "Where's Cathal? It's his flare."

I appreciated he remained professional instead of fussing over me. "He and the others were trying to get to Cait." I looked down the hill again, as if the smoke-concealed battlefield could provide any clues. "No news so far."

Riagán gave me a solemn nod. Despite there being no enemies around, he, like me, was constantly scanning our surroundings.

The wait was excruciating, so when familiar silhouettes emerged from the smoke, I breathed out with relief. Then I drew that breath back in. Cait wasn't with them.

"Caitríona?" Riagán asked, his voice trembling.

Cathal shook his head. "We didn't find her." He stopped Riagán with a gesture before the archer stood up. "We searched thoroughly." He briefly glanced at me before he looked at Lorcan and Aengus.

"I'll be fine," Aengus replied to the unvoiced question, his voice quiet but stronger than before. "Kaja did a good job keeping me alive." He smiled. "What I said earlier... You were right."

Cathal nodded to him, then looked at us. "Spread out. Gather the survivors and organize an orderly departure. We'll regroup at the gardens' entrance. No splitting. Faolan with Lorcan, Sadb with Riagán, Kaja stays here with me."

"Yes, ceannasaí," they said almost in unison.

As they departed, Cathal indicated I could relax, so I sat down nearby. He didn't join me. Instead, he stood on top of the hill and kept looking toward where we'd last seen Cait.

I didn't like the grim look on his face.

CHAPTER ELEVEN

Aengus's forces gathered at the gardens' entrance, many of them wounded, but the casualties were fewer than I expected, considering they fell into a well-executed ambush, and that alone spoke volumes about the mythborn's training.

Cathal was giving orders, organizing the return and making sure the injured were sent in the first group. As he gave instructions to the reinforcements arriving from the nearby garrison, he made sure they knew to be on the lookout for a blue-haired mythborn female in the Scáthanna's uniform, but otherwise he didn't mention Cait. Other team members tried to prompt him, but he waved them off, giving out minor tasks that kept them busy and away from him.

At the same time, he kept me by his side and didn't give me any orders, so I ended up shadowing him with no purpose and too much time to think. I replayed the events in my head, trying to figure out whether I could have done anything differently and finding no answers.

When we finally made it back to the Court, the

atmosphere was even grimmer, as if Cathal's silence affected everyone.

"Dismissed," he said when we reached our quarters. "Kaja, my office, now."

Others exchanged glances but said nothing, and the corridor emptied as they rushed off. I followed Cathal. He opened a door and gestured me in.

We walked into a moderately sized room. The only furniture was a desk set against the window and bookshelves. I glanced at them, curious. Most shelves were filled with mythborn-made scrolls, but I caught several book spines as well. I didn't have time to check what kind of human literature Cathal would be interested in before he closed the door and circled me.

"You have some explaining to do," he said coldly. "And I recommend you don't waste my time, because the Court's investigators are not going to be as understanding."

I swallowed and nodded. I couldn't blame him for the coldness, and I appreciated he made an effort to speak to me alone, even though eventually I'd have to reveal the truth to the rest of the Scáthanna too.

"How did you know about the trap?" he asked before I could put together any explanation. "Are you serving the Snake?"

The second question felt like a slap on my cheek, but I knew better than to counter with some witty response. He had the right to suspect me, and I offered the truth.

"Ever since the ritual, my hearing has changed. I can hear pieces of conversations, sometimes at great distances. I can't fully control it, but back in the gardens, I heard a mythborn giving orders. When I put together it was a trap within a trap, I tried to warn you, but it was too late."

Cathal's face was expressionless. "I expected more of you." He didn't have to say that he didn't believe me.

I couldn't blame him. After all, having such a skill sounded like a tall tale, and my being a spy who had a last-minute change of heart definitely sounded more plausible.

Before he took a step toward the door, I stopped him with a gesture. "You talked to Aengus about his son. He wanted Diarmuid to take my place when I die, and you refused." Even as I spoke, it was clear that I'd failed to convince him again, so I kept going, with yet another confession. "I also eavesdropped on you and Lady Eithne on the day you offered for me to join. You argued with her, because she wanted to send me away. And you told her I wouldn't say no."

Cathal said something, and it sounded like a question, but it wasn't in English. It didn't sound like Irish either. I looked at him, puzzled.

"I asked how long you've known our language," he said.

"I don't. You were speaking in English..." His expression told me they weren't. I spread my arms out. "I have no explanation. I understood what I heard."

Cathal looked as unconvinced as moments ago. "So how far does that hearing of yours reach?"

"I don't know." Undoubtedly, my own words were digging a grave for me, but at the same time, I had to tell the truth and only the truth if I wanted a chance at making him believe me. Even a little lie would bury me for good. "I haven't told anyone about it, and I haven't really tested it in any meaningful manner. It seems to fluctuate, like magic, and I've yet to learn how to control it."

In the silence that fell, Cathal looked me up and down. I had nothing else to offer, but my honesty might not be enough for him. Even I had a hard time believing the ritual had bestowed upon me such a strange skill, and it wasn't all just a delusion.

"I'd have preferred you confessed. You owe us that much for the trust we gave you." Cathal sighed and shook his head. "I could believe you don't serve the Snake willingly, and we could have helped you if you were honest."

"Test me." I almost cut him off, my desperation growing. "Write a message and send someone to read it out loud. I'll stay here and repeat it word for word."

Finally I saw some curiosity, and my hope fed on it like a desperate junkie.

"You said you can hardly control it and don't know how far it reaches." He kept watching me as if searching for any deception.

"I'll take my chances." I gave him a firm stare. "There's no other way I can prove I'm telling the truth."

Cathal didn't hesitate long. "Very well."

He walked over to the desk. When he started writing, I turned away to make it clear I wasn't trying to peek and cheat my way out of the test.

"How far?" he asked.

"Up to you, ceannasaí, though I might have trouble if you send your messenger outside of the Court." I had my heart in my throat, as even within the Court's boundaries, picking out a singular message could be difficult.

He nodded as he walked past me. "Wait here."

When he disappeared in the corridor, I tuned in to his footsteps. If I was to hear the message, I had to know who was the one to read it.

"Ceannasaí, what happened in the gardens?" Riagán's tormented voice filled me with pain. If Cathal didn't believe me, none of them would, including Riagán. "Faolan says Kaja betrayed us. Is there any truth to it?"

"I've yet to determine the truth. Meanwhile, I need you to do something for me. Go up to the topmost floor of the Court and say nothing on your way there, not even a word of greeting to anyone. Once you get there, read this note out loud. Then you're free."

The silence that followed must have meant that Riagán was processing the odd request. To my surprise, no questions followed, and all he said was, "Yes, ceannasaí." The Scáthanna's devotion to their leader was truly awe-inspiring.

Cathal returned shortly. "I gave it to Riagán," he told me.

I nodded in appreciation but didn't reply. It would take Riagán a while to reach the top floor, but I wanted to be ready. Cathal wouldn't give me another chance if I messed up, and my heart, beating hard and fast, was almost drowning all other conversations I started to pick up, but not enough of them.

We stood in silence, and at the same time, I was surrounded by noise. I had to filter out random conversations around the Court, and Faolan's angry exchange with Sadb about me. It stung to be called the Snake's whore and other scathing names. I tuned their voices out. If I was to avoid being branded a traitor forever, I had to keep my emotions at bay.

The wait dragged like a funeral procession, but in the end, I fished out Riagán's voice, precise and clear.

"The moon glistens under your nails as you scratch it off the midnight sky. Forever bound in magic, we will..." I stammered. There was something in the mythborn language, and I couldn't repeat it clearly, but I still tried. The jumble that came out of my throat didn't even resemble what I was supposed to say. My shoulders slumped. "I didn't catch the last part." If Cathal wanted to, he could say I'd failed, but I had to cling to hope that this was enough to convince him.

He finished the sentence, echoing the words Riagán said. "This expression doesn't have a translation. I guess the closest would be 'laying oneself on the altar of duty.' It's an old mythborn poem about sacrifice."

I couldn't help arching an eyebrow—not at his choice of the message, but the fact he dealt with poetry at all. He'd always seemed down to earth to me.

"All nobleborn learn it when they're young," he offered. "Not many care to understand it, though." He looked at me with a softer expression. "So how come my scout has a skill I wasn't aware of?"

I almost breathed out with relief, because his question meant he finally believed me—but at the same time, it flooded me with guilt. I hung my head in shame. This wasn't the first secret I'd kept from the Scáthanna. Back when I was only their humanborn liaison, I hadn't told them I carried a curse that would not only kill me but also anyone who touched me while it was active. At least then I had the excuse of not trusting my former enemies, but now... Now it was worse. After all, they'd allowed me to join their ranks, and I was supposed to be one of them.

The least I could do was to shoulder the consequences. I might have saved my life and reputation by making Cathal believe me, but I wouldn't be surprised if he decided to kick me out anyway. I deserved it.

"I should have told you," I said somberly. "Even if there was never a good time or I didn't take the skill seriously. I might not be a traitor, but I still betrayed your trust." I swallowed and looked him in the eye. "Telling you what I've heard won't make up for it, but please hear me out." At his short nod, I continued, "The mythborn who set up the trap wanted Cait alive. I think he also wanted Laoise captured, because he wasn't happy that she died in that ambush."

"So whoever he is, he's after us, and he wants information." Cathal rubbed his chin. "Did he say anything else?"

"I didn't hear much more." I wished I had something else to give him. "After he gave the order for Aengus to be shot, it got too erratic to hear anything."

"Would you recognize his voice if you heard it again?"

The memory of the mysterious mythborn's words was still clear in my head, and I had no doubt I'd recognize him. "I'll keep listening for him."

"Later. First we need to tell the others and learn as much as we can about how much you can do with your skill." He looked at me with grave seriousness. "To say that I'm disappointed at what happened would be putting it mildly, but your warning likely saved Aengus's life, and if he praised you regardless of his low opinion of the myth-touched, I'm sure you did good job afterward as well, so I'll give you one more chance. Yet, next time you display such distrust in the people who are supposed to become closer to you than your family, you won't be one of us anymore. Forming bonds might take time, but you have to be willing to do so in the first place."

"I understand. Thank you, ceannasaí." I deserved that lecture and probably much more.

His expression softened a notch. "Come, let's tell the others. Riagán's worried, and the rest should know before their suspicions get the better of them."

CATHAL GATHERED the rest of the Scáthanna in the day room, and it took me a good hour of explanations and tests for them to finally drop their suspicions. In the meantime, I learned that it didn't matter what language people spoke—I always heard it in English. In a way, I found it amusing, as I'd have expected to hear everything in Polish instead. Yet, even though it was my native language, I'd hardly used it since the Magiclysm. Before that, I'd get online with my family and friends back in my homeland or go out with several of my Polish friends, but war... war had changed things. And after it ended, not many Poles stuck around, so English became more familiar to me than my mother tongue. Maybe that was why the myth-touched magic was tuned to it instead of Polish.

After they finally believed me, the Scáthanna wanted to test the range of my skill, but Cathal made it clear that it would have to wait for another day.

"I apologize for what happened," I said in the end, standing in the middle of the room like I was front of a jury. "If I told you earlier, things could have gone differently."

Had I told them, I wouldn't have been playing at map-reading with Faolan back in the gardens. I'd have been listening instead. I could have learned of the trap soon enough to make a difference. Cait could have been safe.

"Don't go there," Lorcan said. "Learn from your mistakes and move on."

I swallowed hard. He was right, of course, but it was human nature to ponder such things endlessly, inviting misery and the feeling of guilt. Humans might have used the excuse of trying to learn from it, but the truth was that we rarely did, too focused on our feelings instead of lessons to carry away.

"So, what now, ceannasaí?" Faolan asked. He still threw me displeased glares, but he wasn't as hostile as when I'd first entered the room.

"We'll keep searching for Cait or any information that can lead us to her," Cathal replied. "But we're going to be careful. No wandering off on your own. Outside the Court, it's always going to be at least two of us. If he wants to weaken us or capture anyone else, Lorcan and Kaja are likely to be his next targets, so they leave the Court only with Faolan or Sadb, and only when necessary."

He shot me an apologetic glance, and after I'd already disappointed him so much, I appreciated he thought of what it meant for me. He'd promised me freedom, and instead he was practically grounding me. Yet I didn't feel angry or disappointed, and it had nothing to do with my guilt. The situation had changed, and he was right. Lorcan and I were the next most vulnerable squad members, so we were also probable targets. I dared not think that if that mythborn went after either of us, it would mean Cait was already dead.

"What about Kaja's skill?" Sadb asked. "The lady will insist on putting it to use."

Cathal sighed and looked each of them in the eye. Then he said, "We won't report this to the lady."

The Scáthanna stirred, clearly uneasy, but no one spoke.

"The trap in the Botanical Gardens suggests that the Snake still has spies at the Court. If they learn of Kaja's ability, we'll lose our advantage," he continued. Then he looked at me. "You aren't the only one who received an unusual skill after the ritual. Our magic seems to be affecting the humanborn in ways we can't understand and foresee, and the lady is concerned. She insists our scholars study each case in hopes of learning more."

"In the hope of reproducing the effects or controlling them," I said, unable to keep my bitterness at bay. "Because this is what the ritual is, isn't it? You experiment to discover all the ways magic can affect us, and sometimes we survive and become myth-touched."

The realization soured my mood, but, truth to be told, it changed little. As far as I knew, they only performed the ritual on those who willingly agreed to it, and Eithne hadn't hidden the risks from me, so I assumed she was upfront with others as well. And anyone who was in the same situation as I was—about to die of magical affliction or transform into a monster—would likely take that chance to live.

"Did you overhear that too?" Faolan grimaced.

"No. But it makes sense," I replied. "From a strategic point of view, the mythborn have no interest in finding the cure to the magic affliction. But if you could make the chosen humanborn into myth-touched, and if you could give them skills you consider useful, you'd be gaining the upper hand if the war breaks out again. You could also try to find a way to make the ritual stop whatever magic wakes up in us if you fear we'll turn on you."

"Does this upset you?" Cathal asked.

I shook my head and offered a smile. "I expected Lady Eithne had her reasons to offer the ritual to humanborn. Seeing as I'm alive and still myself instead of a warped, mindless monster, I consider the price worth it." It was the truth, but even to my ears it sounded like something I was *expected* to say. If I was to mend bridges, I had to do better than that. "In a way, learning about it is a relief. I can stop wondering what games she's playing. The thought she could actually be altruistic made me lose sleep some nights."

They all smiled—well, more or less—as if *that* was the kind of answer they'd expected from me.

"So, all set?" Cathal asked. "I know Cait is still out there, and she might still be alive. We'll do everything possible to find her, but I don't want to see any foolish heroics that would put more of you in danger. The enemy already has an advantage over us."

From the looks on the Scáthanna's faces, it was clear not a single one of them liked his words, but each nodded without hesitation.

"Get some rest now," Cathal said. "I need to talk to the lady and make her aware of the situation."

He left, and I waited for the rest of the Scáthanna follow him. The last thing I wanted was company of the very people whose trust I had failed, and who now knew that if I wanted, I could hear anything they were saying. Riagán lingered in the room as well.

"I want to apologize to you," he said once we were alone.

I stared at him with no understanding. The one who had to apologize, and keep apologizing probably till the end of her days, was me.

"Others might have thought you were a traitor, but I shouldn't have doubted you," he added uneasily. "You did well today. Aengus will live thanks to you."

I shook my head. "I would have done well if I'd told anyone about that skill. Maybe Cait would still be with us. Maybe—"

He put a finger on my lips, his expression solemn. "You aren't to blame any more than we are. We all knew that myth-touched sometimes developed unique skills, but no one bothered to explain anything to you. We were just eager to leave you with Sadb, giving her time to grieve and having you trained at the same time, and we took off. And even if no one else had bothered, *I* should have thought to tell you about it."

"But if I trusted you all more..." I argued.

"*If* you did," he agreed. "But you didn't. We've worked with you long enough to know it'd take you time to fully trust us, and... we allowed ourselves to blindly believe we had that time instead of helping you settle in quicker."

I still thought that Cathal was right, and I should have exercised more trust in my teammates, but Riagán clearly was blaming himself for the whole situation, for not helping me become part of the Scáthanna well enough, and to argue longer would mean I'd cause him pain for no other benefit than proving I was the one who had messed up—which was something I already knew and didn't need to convince anyone else of.

He hugged me. "You did well today. Aengus will live thanks to you," he repeated with force, "and even if you think your warning came late... Without you, we wouldn't even know what happened to Cait."

I knew I had to do better than just "well." I had to find a way to learn more about what happened to Cait, even if it meant listening in on every single boring conversation at the Court and beyond it.

"We'll find her," Riagán whispered, as if he knew what I was thinking about. Without letting me out of his embrace, he led me into the corridor and to his room. "But we both have to rest first."

I knew he was right. I knew it. It didn't make me feel any less guilty about the prospect of sleeping in his embrace while Cait was still out there and likely in grave danger.

CHAPTER TWELVE

In the morning, I knocked on the door to Cathal's office. After the previous day's events, I'd rather keep my head down, train with Sadb, and work on convincing everyone I was of value... but I didn't have the time for, or the luxury of, making up for my mistakes in a slow but comfortable way.

Cathal called out from the inside, an Irish or maybe a mythborn word. I hesitated, trying to figure out whether it meant an invitation, though I could hardly picture him telling anyone to leave him alone. I reached for the handle at the same moment the door opened.

Cathal arched his eyebrow and stepped to the side, letting me in.

"Ceannasaí, I have an idea that might help us find Cait," I said, getting straight to the point. "We will just need a personal item of hers... The more she used it or was attached to it, the better."

His brow furrowed. "We could find something in her quarters." He gestured for me to keep talking.

"I don't know if you're aware, but before I worked with you, I tracked down a terrorist for Albert and Lady Eithne. I managed to find him with a locating charm of my invention, something similar to blood-bound charms. I don't know how well it will work, but..."

"Riagán mentioned he had a similar charm made," Cathal said with caution.

He was clearly watching for my reaction, so I gave him a nod. I knew that Riagán had used it to find me back when I was on the brink of death after facing an Afflicted alone.

"He told you. Good. Take him to Cait's room, and he'll be able to help you pick something that might work. I recommend visiting Connor as well, as he was the one to help Riagán with his charm. Together, you two might come up with something better."

"Yes, ceannasaí," I replied, as I had already been hoping that Connor might help.

"If anyone complains about our keeping him busy, tell them to bring it up with me. *Especially* if it's the Master of Crafts himself," he added.

I nodded. Sadb must have told him about the self-important mythborn poking around, and I almost hoped I'd run into him today. It would be nice to know Cathal would put him in his place.

But I didn't waste time on wishful thinking and headed out. The sooner we got a working charm, the better our chance of finding Cait alive. Out of Cathal's office and to Riagán's door—he opened without delay. His face brightened, but as soon as he noticed my expression, he got serious as well.

"We need something that Cait was attached to or carried often," I said. "We're going to make a locating charm. Cathal knows."

Riagán understood in an instant and joined me in the corridor. "There should be a few things in her room."

It wasn't locked, just like any other room in the Scáthanna's quarters. Sometimes I wondered whether mythborn were even familiar with the concept of keys, but I had no doubt they protected the places they considered important. Personal rooms likely didn't qualify for any extra security... or privacy.

I hadn't been inside before, so I expected a similar setup to Riagán's and Sadb's quarters, but even though the furnishing was the same, the room was not. Cait was a hoarder. A tidy one, with everything on the shelves, walls, or in boxes stacked neatly against the wall, but a hoarder nonetheless. Even her bed had three extra pillows and a decorative blanket—"a throw," as the locals called it.

It made the room feel smaller but also cozier, like a place someone actually lived in, not just stopped in between missions to get some sleep and grab a change of clothes.

At the same time, it would make our search all the more difficult, because we had no way of knowing which of the many items she really cared about. To my surprise, Riagán confidently walked in, rummaging through her desk like someone who'd been inside before. He returned to me with two items in his hand: a small figurine of a horse carved in dark wood and a simple copper bracelet.

"Do I want to know how you know?" I asked, half amused. I'd never gotten the notion that there was something between Cait and Riagán, even long in the past, so I wasn't jealous.

"I know her story," he said simply, though a shadow that crossed his face suggested a rather dark memory. It made sense. One would not expect the Scáthanna to have led happy and joyful lives. "Are you going to ask Connor for help?"

I nodded. As a craftsman, he had more experience than I did, and as a mythborn, he had more knowledge, too. I was lucky to have made the locating charm that helped me find Jonas Byrne, but when it came to Cait's life, I'd rather not rely on luck.

"Let's go, then."

We walked outside and were headed to another entrance when I spotted Lady Eithne leaving the building through what I understood was its main door, two guards at her side.

Riagán sighed. "Good that the ceannasaí is not seeing it."

"Why?"

"He's not happy that the lady sets out into the city like that. She's always insisting on speaking to everyone herself, even the Trinitians, and refuses escort more proper for someone in her position. Ceannasaí doesn't like that she puts herself in danger."

I wasn't surprised he didn't approve, and from a strategic point of view, I agreed with him—even if, personally, I cared much less about what happened to Eithne. But I did remember she regularly visited Trinity, and if Albert or any of his officers had an idea she wasn't just a spokesperson for the Court... Sooner or later they would learn about it. In a way, it was a small miracle they didn't know already—unless, of course, Albert had known all along and just played oblivious for the sake of maintaining peace.

"I'm sure she has some powerful amulets and charms at her disposal." I sought any reassurance I could give honestly.

Riagán stopped and turned to me, serious all of a sudden. "You might not like her very much—and I can't blame you, given she wasn't upfront with you about what happens after the ritual—but she's the best leader the humanborn could hope the mythborn to have. Anyone else..." He swallowed. "Anyone else gets the power and we're back at war sooner than you think."

"That bad, eh?" If Eithne was the only guarantee of peace, the mythborn must *really* hate humanborn.

"No one would go breaking the treaty immediately," Riagán said quickly, "but there would be demands, tensions would rise... You know yourself how little is needed to reignite hostilities."

I nodded grimly. Even if the majority of the population preferred peace and coexistence—likely for no better reason than living their lives without any hassle—there were enough hateful, volatile, and plain violent groups on both sides to cause enough trouble to make others feel like war was the only choice.

And the Scáthanna, instead of trying to make a difference and preserve peace, were wrapped up in some mythborn's schemes or personal vendetta.

"Come, let's get to Connor." Riagán must have noticed my souring mood. "The sooner we find Cait and whoever took her, the quicker we will be able to focus on fixing Eireland's problems."

He made it sound so easy, though maintaining peace was anything but simple. Yet I still appreciated his reminding me that we could only tackle one thing at a time—Cait's life was in immediate danger, while peace would last on its own for at least a little longer. Eithne was still alive and trying to preserve it, and Albert wasn't interested in pushing his people into another draining conflict. There were other factions across Dublin and outside of it, but they neither had the resources nor the pull of the Court and Trinity.

We entered the building and crossed the now-familiar corridors. Before I joined the Scáthanna, I'd spent enough time going between Connor's workshop and my room, with the occasional visit to the dining hall and the roof garden, to know my way around, but I still let Riagán lead the way. Something about it reminded me of our first meeting.

He sent me a smile over his shoulder. Perhaps he was thinking about it too.

Connor was only mildly surprised when we entered his workshop. "Let me guess, she's of no use, so Cathal decided to return her."

I smiled at the joke, because he only allowed himself similar amusement in the company he enjoyed. Others usually got the professional but rather tepid treatment. On the other hand, neither Riagán nor I acted as if we didn't know how to behave in Connor's presence, nor threw uncomfortable glances at his harness.

"For a little while," Riagán replied. "We need another locating charm. An official request from our ceannasaí, and an urgent one." He put the two items we got from Cait's room on the worktable. "Kaja made a locating charm in the past, on her own, so she might be able to help you with your task."

"How urgent?" Connor asked.

Riagán looked him in the eye. "I'd be happy to be able to walk out of here with one ready."

Connor inspected both items. "I can make one quickly, possibly within half an hour if you're happy with a basic one. Then, with Kaja's help, I'll work on something more complex."

"Do it," Riagán said.

He leaned against the wall, getting himself comfortable for the wait, while I pulled a spare chair to the table, watching Connor's quick work. Even if he had no time to explain his process in detail, I could still learn something that would help us perfect the next charm.

MY EYES BURNED, and rubbing them felt like treating them with sandpaper.

"You should get some rest," Connor said, not lifting his head from his task.

He wasn't wrong. I should. "Same goes for you."

We'd been working on the locating charm a whole day, a whole night, and I believed we were closing in on noon the following day. It was mostly Connor's task, as he was better with the runes, but we discussed ideas, and I fetched us food from the dining hall, which Connor found particularly amusing. Perhaps delivering meals wasn't the most appropriate task for a Scáthanna member, but I was starting to learn that being part of the team meant no one would question me, no matter what I chose to do... save maybe for trying to assassinate Eithne.

"Soon. I think we're getting close," he replied.

I could relate to the determination that rang in his words. Riagán had taken the first charm as soon as Connor was done with it and headed out immediately. He returned much later to check on our progress and let us know something was blocking the charm's work. They were quite certain Cait was somewhere on the south side of Dublin, but nothing more, and that alone seemed odd. Our enemy was a mythborn, and though some lived across the river, if he wanted to blend in and keep a low profile, the north side would be a better choice. So, with the first charm's questionable effectiveness, we were both desperate to make the next one stronger.

A banging on the door got our heads turning.

"Keep working. I'll get it," I said as the sounds outside suggested someone with an attitude was about to enter. I hoped that the sight of a gray uniform might make the encounter smoother.

As soon as I opened the door, I knew there would be nothing smooth about it.

The Master of Crafts' expression hardened as soon as he recognized me—or rather my uniform, since he glanced down at it seconds before his eyes locked on mine. By some standards, he was likely handsome, in that otherworldly mythborn way, but his constant expression of displeasure, in addition to his slightly orange-hued skin, smooth like a polished stone, made his face look unfriendly and rather unpleasant.

"You're going to leave now, Master of Crafts," I said before his mouth finished opening. If I wanted to end this quickly, I had to take the initiative. "And before you're going to complain to the lady about it, be sure to speak with Ceannasaí Cathal. Connor has been requested for official Scáthanna business for however long we deem necessary. And after that, he'll be allowed to rest and recover before returning to work."

He grimaced, looking down at me. "You're Cathal's new mongrel, aren't you? You should learn how to behave when your betters are present."

"The term's myth-touched, Master of Crafts," I replied calmly.

Generally, I had little appreciation for a lack of creativity when it came to insults. If someone wanted to really hurt me with their words, they had to do much better than picking them at random. Bringing up my sister's death would probably work, as I always reacted emotionally, no matter how hard I tried… but that wasn't the kind of ammunition I'd hand over to this mythborn. "And if you have any complaints about my behavior, be sure to bring them up when you speak with Ceannasaí Cathal."

"You can be sure I will," the Master of Crafts said.

"Very well." I gave him my best smile. "If that's all, have a pleasant day." I shut the door in his face.

Thankfully, he was smart enough to not knock again, and soon enough, I heard his stomping footsteps fade as he walked away.

Behind me, Connor whistled quietly in awe, and I looked back at him in surprise. This must be the first time I'd heard a mythborn whistle.

"If I didn't know who you are," he said, "I'd have thought you were any other member of the Scáthanna."

"Sadb's training." I shrugged. "Besides, I don't care what unimportant matter the Master of Crafts wanted from you, because I'm sure it wasn't about giving you a promotion or a raise." I had to wonder if Connor would even understand the last remark, though mythborn had to have some sort of employment arrangements, and I was sure he understood the general sentiment. "Cait is missing, and I won't have him waste your time. I have no doubt that Cathal will see it the same way."

Perhaps later, in the privacy of Cathal's office, I would get a lecture about my choice of words and behavior, but the Master of Crafts would never learn of it. Cathal was both too protective of his team and too smart to give the Court mythborn any advantage.

"I think I'm done," Connor said all of a sudden. "If you

have a map, we can check if your improvement suggestions worked."

I fished the map from one of my utility pouches and spread it out in front of him. It didn't cover all the areas of the sprawling city, but it should give us some indication where to look. We could get a bigger map later.

Connor moved the wooden horse figurine, now marked with many mythborn symbols, over the cloth the map had been painted on, furrowing his brow. "It's south again." He lifted the charm and hovered it over the south side of Dublin again.

A bad feeling twisted my gut. "Something wrong?"

"The magic within the object... It's unsteady. Comes and goes in uneven waves." He once more moved the charm over the map. "I can tell she's definitely somewhere on the south side, and likely not far from the river, but—" He stopped abruptly and inspected the charm.

I waited, fear swelling within me.

"The charm's magic. It's gone," he whispered—the words I'd dreaded to hear. He looked at me with compassion. "Look... It might be something else. Even the previous locating charm wasn't working properly, so they might be keeping her somewhere with a lot of magic."

"But it still should be working," I argued, pushing the words got through my clenched throat.

"It should," he agreed grimly.

There was, of course, a chance that something had malfunctioned withing the charm's structure. Connor was a superb craftsman, but magic was not exactly physics, and my ideas and suggestions for improvements might have caused more trouble than we'd anticipated.

I looked at Connor and knew that he believed those explanations as much as I did, because there was a much simpler reason for the sudden lack of the charm's responsiveness. Its workings relied on the emotional link between the object made into the charm and the object's owner. If those emotions were gone, the magic would vanish as well, and there was only one reason I could think of to make them disappear so suddenly and so entirely.

"I'll let others know," I said. "And you should get some rest. You've gone above and beyond to help us."

He clenched his fists. "If I worked harder..."

I could relate to the feelings of guilt and helplessness, but Connor didn't deserve such a burden. "You did your best, and I was a witness to your efforts. No one would have expected more from you." I walked to the door.

"Kaja... It's unlikely, but it could have been some magic interference. If whoever has Cait keeps her within wards strong enough..."

I nodded. "We'll keep searching," I told him. "At least we know now that she's definitely somewhere on the south side of the river."

"Close to the city center, too," he added.

It did narrow the search area, but only if one chose not to remember it was still tens of streets and hundreds of buildings.

"Thank you," I said before leaving.

As much as I wanted to make sure Connor didn't drown himself in guilt, others had to know that the odds of finding Cait alive had just dropped to nearly zero.

THREE DAYS with no news of Cait dragged like a sermon. Cathal took Sadb, Faolan, and Riagán to chase down any clues they could find, and that left me and Lorcan at the

Court. In the morning, I trained, despite Sadb's absence. I could always use more muscle and stamina, and I practiced the moves with my weapon in the hopes of becoming less clumsy with it. Being clumsy could be a way to mislead my opponents, but only if I could control it, not just be it.

I spent afternoons with Lorcan, learning what he could teach me about mythborn field medicine and healing charms. I wasn't an expert by any stretch, but I'd had enough practice during the war to be bored with the basics, and we both knew I'd never become an actual medic, no matter how much time Lorcan could devote to making me into one. If I was to make a bet, Sadb had a better chance of turning me into a killing machine—even if it would likely take a few decades—than he had of training me to become a surgeon.

"I thought you'd be paying more attention to the charms," he said when I muffled another yawn.

I'd woken up early after a restless night, since even the sleep charm in my bed couldn't overpower my anxiety and worry about Cait. Training only helped so much to take my mind off her, and it made me even less rested.

We were sitting in the day room, so I took advantage of the ever-warm coffee, but even the Magiclysm didn't make it strong enough to be a miracle maker. It could keep me awake—that was all.

"There's not much to it, unless you're going to actually teach me how to make them," I replied honestly. "Back in the war, we used them whenever we found some."

"You would have to ask Connor or another crafter about it." He waved his hand in the door's general direction.

I almost considered nodding eagerly and rushing out, only to escape the tedious lesson, but Lorcan likely knew the truth. "He won't teach me."

"After that curse... you made, I'm surprised you haven't figured it out on your own yet." His teasing made him a bit more amicable.

Out of the bunch, Lorcan had always seemed the least prone to joking, or any joviality, so to see such behavior made me wonder whether he was making an effort to make me feel like a team member.

"Not for lack of trying," I replied with a slight grimace.

Back when Trinitians first got their hands on the healing charms, looting them from mythborn dead bodies, I did my best to copy their markings. Those imitations didn't work, though, and I believed my skills weren't good enough to reflect the intricacy of the mythborn craft. But as I got more adept at mimicking their runes and even started experimenting with my own combinations—my masterpiece being a curse that could kill even an Afflicted, the very one Lorcan referred to—it became clear that I was missing a part of the secret. Which wasn't unexpected, since mythborn had many surprises up their sleeve.

I still remembered that before the ritual the mythborn female made me into a living ward, and I hoped that one day someone could explain to me how that was even possible. From the little knowledge I had, magic had to be locked in an inanimate object and then channeled through it. The mythborn's inner magic and humanborn's inert magic only went as far as activating the objects. No one, not even mythborn, was capable of slinging fireballs or doing any other feats the fantasy books of yore described.

"I don't suppose you can tell me whether it's Lady Eithne's order or his own choice?" I asked, baiting Lorcan. I had long ago come to terms with the fact that some secrets would be kept from me, no matter how much I'd proven myself, but fishing for information couldn't hurt—at least

I'd learn whose decision it was. Besides, it was a better conversation topic than the use of healing charms.

He clicked his tongue in disapproval. "You should call her as we do, the lady. It seems to me that you're trying to be one of us and not be one of us at the same time." He cocked his head and regarded me with narrowed eyes. "Maybe that's why you don't get to learn the Court's secrets."

His half-amused tone suggested the reprimand wasn't serious, so I fired back in a similarly playful manner, "Shouldn't trust go both ways?"

"I'm teaching you about charms, am I not?"

I rolled my eyes. "You aren't showing me anything a random Trinitian wouldn't be able to tell me."

Lorcan leaned forward, and I could swear a sly smile stretched his lips ever so slightly. "And what if I told you that the flow of a healing charm's magic can be controlled? You can expel it all in an intense burst if you're hoping to seal a serious wound, or slow the healing down if you're trying to keep the severely wounded alive until help arrives."

With one sentence, he'd remedied my boredom and proven my last words wrong, but I gladly gave him that victory. "How?"

I expected more teasing, but Lorcan assumed the teacher's role again. "It takes a bit of practice, but you can learn it now, because you've become a myth-touched. Humanborn magic is too unstable to be of use, and most of your people hardly have enough to even activate charms." He paused, considering. "Think about it as letting your breath out. You can exhale slowly or get all the air out in a single strong blow." He picked up one of the healing charms he'd piled on the table. "Here, hold it."

When I reached for the wood disk covered with runes, he enclosed my hand in his. His touch was pleasant, and I almost gasped at the familiar mythborn magic sparking between our fingers. I fought the need to tear away from him in case he'd read it wrong. But since he was the one to initiate it, I assumed it was within the boundaries of proper behavior.

"Now you know why mythborn don't shake hands often," Lorcan said casually. "Don't worry, it'll pass in a moment. There's no attraction between us to make it last longer."

"That would explain why Sadb never warmed up to me despite all that time she spent beating me up," I offered in a lighthearted manner, hoping it'd conceal my discreet sigh of relief. "But if attraction is necessary, how come there are so many stories of the humanborn getting addicted to the mythborn?"

I didn't mention my own addiction. Even though I'd hardly been attracted to Riagán the first time I kissed him, I assumed something had clicked between us, especially as he was already interested in me. If nothing else, it could have been the adrenaline high of the life-threatening experience we'd shared moments before it.

"Humanborn magic usually isn't strong enough to counter that of a mythborn." Lorcan moved his hands away from mine. "And the more intimate the touch, the more likely it's going to trigger a reaction." He narrowed his eyes. "Are you asking for a particular reason? Riagán wasn't very forthcoming about what was going on between the two of you, and I was surprised ceannasaí allowed it, especially with the lady's clear order that he was supposed to keep away."

I shook my head with a smile. "You don't have to worry. He was walking the line very finely." I might have considered him slightly unnerving back then, but not even once had he crossed boundaries. Even the kiss I'd paid my life debt with was my choice, and he let me retreat and recover instead of trying to fuel my addiction. I doubted that back then he'd even expected that I'd actually kiss him.

"Sounds exactly like Riagán." Lorcan didn't conceal his disapproval.

"If you aren't happy with him, I can't even begin to imagine what you think about my being on the team," I said. As far as teammates went, I was worse than Riagán: less skilled, less of a team player, and much more distrustful, and Lorcan knew that already.

I couldn't read his expression, but I'd definitely failed to shake his composure with my blunt remark.

"You're not half bad for a former humanborn, and if Sadb says she trained you enough, I trust her. But I'm still waiting for you to become an actual myth-touched, and not a humanborn playing one."

Of course he had to bring that up. I couldn't say I wasn't clinging to my old identity a bit, but I'd also tried my best to embrace the new one. "Adapting takes time. A representative of a species who for the past few millennia was waging wars still using bows and swords should understand it."

Lorcan burst out in laughter and startled me, but his reaction seemed honest, as if my comment had genuinely amused him. "You're forgetting that we have magic too, but point taken." He became serious again. "At the same time, comments like that make your real nature apparent. At first glance, myth-touched aren't different from mythborn. If you were willing, you could easily pass as one of us instead of antagonizing many at the Court. The political situation is already difficult."

That remark was made to get my attention. "You aren't

talking about relations with Trinity and humanborn in general, are you?"

"The lady is facing pressure from the mythborn outside of the city. They aren't as open to the idea of coexistence and to creating myth-touched. Some would be happy for all humanborn to die of the affliction." He sighed. "Your being one of us complicates the matter more. Many of the noble-born see it as an affront."

"Aengus," I muttered.

"Among others." Lorcan looked at me. "It's something you should consider, but in the end, you're right about such things taking time. And if being humanborn-like makes you better at your job, ceannasaí won't complain, and neither will anyone else here." He held his hand out again. "So we better spend our time on teaching you something useful."

I let him hold me again, and his magic flowed through my arm as he activated the healing charm. Even if I couldn't fully comprehend what he was doing, I got to know how it was supposed to feel. I gave him a nod, and he let go of me.

I inspected the healing charm, now as dormant as if it had never been activated. "I'm not sure I can mimic what you did."

"Let's give you proper motivation, then." He unsheathed his knife and, before I could protest, slashed his forearm deeper than anyone would deem necessary for a test like that. "The intense burst first. Squeeze whatever magic's left in that charm as quickly as possible."

"Your teaching methods are even worse than Sadb's," I muttered, but held the charm tighter.

Previously, I'd been using charms like all humanborn did: a moment of focus to produce a magic impulse, and that was it. Some of them were meant to have an "off switch," so I knew how to stop the magic's flow, but I had never thought of consciously controlling it, and I also hadn't been in a state that would allow me similar precision, with my body being consumed by the affliction. The magic within me had been unstable and prone to chaotic changes. To keep it in check had been challenge enough.

The ritual had changed it, and now the magic within me was almost as rhythmic as a trance song in a club.

"If you don't hurry, I'll have a new scar," Lorcan prompted.

I didn't need his remark, feeling the pressure already, and I hardly controlled the magic within me when I activated the charm. Its flow was steady but slow, nowhere near what Lorcan had asked me to do. I focused and forced the charm to expel its magic at once, visualizing mentally squeezing it out of the object. The cut on Lorcan's forearm healed so quickly that the wound vanished as I watched.

He gave me a nod. "Not bad for the first time. Now let's see if you can slow the healing down. It's useful if you know the charms you have aren't going to be enough to heal the wounds and you're trying to keep someone alive until help arrives."

"I can see how it would help with heat charms as well, to make them work longer."

"I'm sure you'll discover many useful applications of this skill." He lifted his knife again.

I stopped him with a gesture. "I can practice without your wounding yourself again."

He waved as if brushing my concerns off, but with the knife in his hand, it looked more worrying than reassuring.

Thankfully, before he could slash his forearm again, the door to the day room opened and Faolan walked in like a last-minute savior. He glanced at Lorcan unmoved, as if his teammate holding a blade to his own limb was the most natural sight. Though it was more likely that he didn't even register the scene, as his face was tense.

"They found Cait," he said. "We're heading out as soon as you're ready."

He disappeared in the corridor as Lorcan and I looked at each other. The tone of Faolan's voice, that deep pain, told us everything we needed to know.

We weren't going on a rescue mission.

CHAPTER THIRTEEN

Caitríona's face was calm in death, marked by what looked like a slight smile of relief. It was the only piece of beauty left on her whole body, mutilated in so many ways that it hardly resembled a mythborn.

She was found on a street in Stoneybatter. This area consisted mostly of small, one- or two-story residential buildings squished together into rows along the streets. Before the war, it felt cramped and poor. Now it looked empty and derelict, and I doubted many people lived around there. The mythborn had better choices in the whole north side of Dublin that informally belonged to them, and the humanborn could move to the other side of the river, and further south, where there were many modern and spacious residential buildings and single-family houses in greener areas.

This meant that there would be no witnesses to help us discover what happened, and all we had to go on was Cait's body.

The extent of her wounds, some looking older and partially healed, made it clear she had been tortured for as long as she'd been missing, and our enemy just dumped her here like in a detective procedural from the pre-Magiclysm era. Yet this time it wasn't some extra actor hired to lie on the ground for the opening scene. It was someone close.

We all stood in silence, taking in the extent of her wounds. I was the only one crying, but no one made fun of it, as if my tears were also theirs. As if I was crying for everyone.

Lorcan knelt beside the body, his moves those of a professional, and I had a hard time reading any emotion on his face. "She died recently, but not from the wounds." He looked at Cathal. "She must have been hoping we'd find her, and only gave up when she couldn't trust herself anymore."

Sadb cursed in mythborn, and I glanced at Riagán, hoping for an explanation.

"Cait killed herself," he whispered, "likely when she couldn't endure the torture anymore. If she waited that long, she must have learned something important. Something worth suffering for."

I nodded, sniffling. I resisted the urge to wipe my runny nose against my sleeve. It didn't seem appropriate to treat my uniform this way—not when Cait died wearing hers.

"It seems that some of the damage was done after her death. Whoever took her wasn't happy she slipped away," Lorcan added. "I'd guess he used healing charms and special concoctions to keep her both alive and conscious through his torture."

I shivered at that. We'd failed her. No matter what Riagán said about her learning important information, I could picture Cait simply clinging to life because she knew we wouldn't stop until we found her. How gruesome her ordeal must have been for her to have given up on hope. At the same time, were I in her place, I might have done the same, because there was only so much suffering one could endure, and if Cait's captor was trying to force her to give up secrets, death was a way to win against him.

"Would these concoctions be hard to find or prepare? Would he need someone to brew them for him?" I asked.

It was a long shot, but we had to find this mythborn's connections, and after the ambush in the gardens, it was clear that he wasn't a lone wolf. People he used and people he compensated would eventually lead us to him, and they could be easier to find than our enemy himself. Even his name or description would be of help, because then we could cast our nets again, and thread by thread, we'd make it back to wherever he lurked.

Lorcan didn't look up from Cait's body as he replied, "It depends on how skilled he is and how much time he wants to devote to preparations. I could brew my own concoctions if I had to, but I think he's more interested in the torture itself."

His words gave me a shiver. Whoever this mysterious mythborn was, he wanted to get the Scáthanna alive. I assumed he sought some sort of information, or maybe leverage or compliance, but to realize that he could be a revenge-driven sadist... It meant Cait had had no chance from the very moment he took her.

"Make a list of ingredients, then, and the mixtures too," Cathal said. "Kaja?"

I shook my head. Ever since we got to the area, I'd been listening for the familiar voice, but the mythborn who'd orchestrated this either wasn't speaking or wasn't bothering to watch the Scáthanna mourn.

Cathal gave a short nod back, acknowledging my fruitless efforts. Even though we were alone, we didn't want to risk discussing my skill openly. It was the only advantage we had, and, if not today then some other time, it could lead us to our enemy.

"Lorcan, Riagán, take care of Cait. The rest are on guard duty," Cathal said. He glanced at me and hesitated. "Actually, Kaja, you should watch."

I followed the two mythborn. Lorcan rummaged through one of the pouches by his belt and fished out a small sachet. Standing over the body, he spread its contents. Silver powder floated in the air for a few heartbeats and then settled on Cait like myriad tiny stars... It didn't escape me that not a single speck fell anywhere else.

Riagán said something in mythborn language, his voice calm and melodic, and I recognized the rhythm of the poem that Cathal had made him read the other day. Without the help of my skill, I didn't understand him, but I recalled some of the words. *The moon glistens under your nails as you scratch it off the midnight sky...* There was beauty and sadness in his voice, and even though I couldn't understand the poetic imagery the mythborn used, its intention was clear. I had never seen any mythborn pray, and the notion of religion and gods, or one god, seemed foreign to them, but that poem seemed as close to a mourning prayer as they got. Cathal had told me that the poem was about sacrifice, so there couldn't be anything more fitting as a farewell for Cait.

When Riagán finished, Lorcan laid an igniting curse down, and Cait's body burst into silver flames. Within moments, she was immolated, and shining ash rose into the air, disturbed by gusts of the ever-present Irish wind.

"This is all we get. This will be all you'll get, too," Cathal said behind me, his voice serious. "There won't be humanborn funerals, and your friends won't be bringing flowers to a pile of dirt where your bones lie."

"I understand," I whispered.

As much as I might be attached to some aspects of my human nature and culture, I cared little for this one. In the war, many people had perished without a chance for a proper burial, my own sister included, so I'd marked their graves in my heart rather than on some plot of land. And if Cathal wanted to give me exactly what any other team member would get, it meant he truly considered me a part of the Scáthanna, even after what transpired with Cait and the ambush.

The earlier conversation with Lorcan came back to me, and I felt a new resolve to truly make an effort to deserve a place among this team.

Cathal regarded me in thought. He couldn't have known what I was thinking about, and he definitely hadn't gotten a chance to learn what I discussed with Lorcan, but my response or maybe my body language must have revealed something.

"When we return to the Court, and you've taken time to mourn, come and see me. There is something you need to know."

To my surprise, Lorcan looked at him over my shoulder and gave what looked like a nod of approval. I glanced at Riagán, but his absent-minded, slightly tormented expression suggested his mind was still on Cait, so I would get no hint from him.

Lorcan put his hand on my shoulder in a gesture I'd expect from a long friend, not a mythborn I barely knew. "Take your time, as much as you need. There's no rush anymore."

I wanted to disagree with him: even if Cait was dead and we couldn't help her anymore, we still had to hurry to find that cursed mythborn before he caused more damage. Even if the Scáthanna, now aware of his existence, could protect themselves better, it didn't mean a sadist with a twisted mind wouldn't go after someone else... We couldn't protect everyone in any way other than getting that bastard.

But, no matter my own feelings, I knew that they all needed time to process what happened. They had only recently lost one team member, and now another... It had to have hit them hard, and I would respect the time they needed. I'd mourn with them, because I might not have known Cait as well as they did, but I'd spent enough time with her to care.

"Let's go back," Cathal ordered us. "There's nothing left to do here."

As soon as we reached the Court, I threw Cathal a glance. He wanted to speak to me, and I preferred to get it out of the way. He caught it and nodded, so as soon as he dismissed the others, I followed him to his office. We entered, and I chased away my discomfort at the memory of my first visit here. I wasn't under suspicion anymore, but Cait's death could easily be pinned on me, and, truth to be told, I wouldn't object if he blamed me. My resolution to become a real member of the team included taking responsibility for whatever damage I'd caused, even if indirectly.

Cathal pulled out a chair and offered it to me before sitting on top of the desk. It had to be the most informal thing I'd seen him do so far, maybe except for soaking naked in a pool with Cait. Remembering her in that moment, smiling and so full of life, brought that feeling of a clot forming in my throat, and I drew the air in deep, almost in desperation, as if my own emotions were about to choke me to death.

"You're holding on better than I thought," he said.

"I saw my share in the war." I managed to keep my voice steady, though I didn't mean to play tougher than I was. He'd already seen me crying in the alley, but I doubted he'd invited me to his office so I could shed more tears. Besides, witnessing my own sister being crushed and eaten by a giant made all other horrors minor in comparison, and it also meant it was harder to truly shake me. I had no doubt that I'd dream of Cait next time nightmares snatched me, but I wasn't about to fall apart.

At least, I wanted to believe I wasn't.

He sighed and shook his head in reaction to a thought he didn't share. When he looked at me again, his expression was almost apologetic. As if I shouldn't be the one to shoulder all the guilt for what happened to Cait.

"This isn't how I imagined you joining us," he said. "I planned on Laoise teaching you, and you having enough time to learn how we do things. I thought you'd have time to really become a member of the team and bond with the others. Instead, we left you quite on your own, and you ended up not trusting us enough to share your knowledge. More so, when I made you the offer, I didn't know Laoise's death was a part of a bigger plot. Someone's after us, and for all I know, this might be revenge for something we did in the past. I have no right to ask you to pay for blood you haven't spilled."

He'd caught me unprepared. I hadn't been expecting a speech like that, and it took me a few seconds to reply. "You didn't trick me into joining. I knew what the Scáthanna do, and I knew that if I joined, I'd be a part of it."

Cathal smirked. His arched eyebrow suggested he was about to call me out on what he considered a bullshit response, and I couldn't blame him. My attitude back when I was still humanborn was not one of compliance.

"You went through the ritual because you wanted to live, and you joined us because I promised you your life back, or at least as much of it as possible." He held his hand up before I could say anything. "There's nothing wrong with that. We both knew what the other wanted— you didn't deceive me, and I didn't deceive you. But the situation has changed. Not only can I not keep my promise of giving you some freedom, if you stay, I'll be putting your life at risk. It's only right that I offer you a way out. I'll use all my influence to make sure the lady doesn't try to keep you away from your friends outside the Court. She can't keep the myth-touched a secret much longer anyway, and you would be valuable both dealing with Trinity and helping us in other... not-so-life-threatening ways. Nobody will think less of you if you decide to leave us."

"*I* will." I looked him in the eye. "Unless you're trying to get rid of me in some polite mythborn way, I'm not leaving."

He got off the desk, his expression dead serious. "You saw what happened to Cait. You could be next."

I didn't try to hide the fear that came with a cold shiver. The idea of being tortured to death was a dreadful one, and if I dwelt on it, it would feed my anxieties as much as the prospect of being eaten alive by a giant did. Yet such images had never held me back before. When I witnessed Ela's demise, I knew that I couldn't have done anything differently to save her life, so it wasn't my inaction that had caused my sister's death, but hers. I had promised myself I'd never freeze when life demanded action.

"If not me, then who? Lorcan? Or maybe Riagán?" I said. "I'm already haunted by the thought that I could have done more for Cait. I don't want to feel the same about more of my friends and companions." Calling the members of the Scáthanna "friends" might be a stretch, but that was what I wanted them to become.

"Very well." Cathal's expression softened a notch, as if I was his favorite daughter who'd just told him she got an A on a math test. "Do you recall what Riagán said about Cait? That she killed herself?" He waited for my nod. "We can all do it if we feel there's no other way out."

Without any warning, he undid his shirt's lacing and took it off. I didn't even try to pretend I wasn't staring. Back in the bathing chamber, from a distance, I hadn't seen the quite impressive collection of scars that marked his otherwise humanlike skin. Some resembled claw marks, or could have been caused by wide blades, while others spread over his skin similar to curse burns.

He waited patiently through my gaping, with no smirk spoiling his stonelike face, then pointed to his shoulder. On a path of remarkably unscathed skin there was a small tattoo: the Scáthanna symbol, with what looked like his name wreathed in fine mythborn writing beneath. I'd seen it before, on Riagán's shoulder, and I assumed it was a team tattoo or the mythborn equivalent of dog tags.

"This is a killing curse that no one can take from you," Cathal explained. "Even if your enemy was to remove your skin or burn it, the curse will stay on you, and you alone will be able to activate it. Lorcan can give you one and explain how it works." He put his shirt back on.

I got up and headed for the door. "Thank you, ceannasaí, for giving me a choice and allowing me to stay."

Cathal smiled, but it faded quickly. "I appreciate you making that choice. We need you."

He didn't have to explain why. Down two members already, their means of catching whoever was after them had become limited. I wasn't only good for my hearing skill. Even if I'd have to work to restore my net of informers after all that time I'd spent stuck at the Court, I still had reach in places no mythborn could get to. If someone out there was talking about what happened to Laoise or Cait, I'd know sooner or later. And if our enemy was buying ingredients or potions, I could track him down. With its former population decimated, and the new inhabitants distrustful, people in Eireland had become more private than they used to be, but they still talked, sharing news and gossip. And fewer faces on the streets also meant it was harder to melt into the crowd.

"Unless you need me for anything else, I'll see if Lorcan has time for me now."

He waved me off, so I left his office. Undoubtedly, even with all his composure, he needed time to grieve as well. Cait was one of his people, and he likely blamed himself for her death at least as much as I did.

Outside, Riagán was leaning against the wall, waiting for me, and I swallowed hard. I had to tell him that I was staying with the Scáthanna, and that I'd be putting myself in the very danger that had claimed Laoise and Cait's lives. While I was doing it because I wanted to make sure *he* stayed safe by helping to catch the mysterious mythborn, he probably wanted to protect me and would rather see me far away from danger. If I'd wanted to make things easier for him, I should have left.

"Lorcan's got the needles ready," he offered when I approached.

I stared at him dumbfounded, wondering whether he had been eavesdropping.

He gave me a small smile. "Your guilty expression is telling enough."

"Maybe I feel guilty because I'm abandoning you in a time of need?" I teased as we walked to the day room.

"You're a survivor, Kaja, but not a coward." He stopped all of a sudden and turned to me, pinning me to the wall. His face was close to mine, and his eyes were shining. "I like the idea that I'll have to save your life several times more," he whispered. "I can already think of ways I'm going to make you pay off your life debts." He slid his lips down my neck, teasing, but didn't do anything more.

"I better be careful, then. Your payment demands are always unnerving."

He beamed as if I'd given him a compliment. With reluctance, he moved away, and I resisted the desire to pull him back. Having witnessed him after Laoise's death, I saw through the mask of carelessness and good mood he was putting on. I had no doubt he would've preferred I left the Scáthanna, so that he'd know I was safe, but I appreciated he wasn't trying to smother me.

"Come, Lorcan's waiting." I gave him a gentle tug. "And when he's done, we'll honor our dead in a humanborn way."

He shot me a curious glance, but as we were already entering the day room, I responded only with a mysterious smile. Later, when my tattoo was done, I'd show him how, back in the war and after it, humanborn fighters drank to our fallen and to those still alive. I'd show him, and any other member of the Scáthanna who was willing to participate, because that bottle of Żubrówka I'd taken from my apartment was big enough to go around.

I WAS ALONE with Lorcan in the day room, my shirt undone and pulled down over my shoulder as he leaned over me with his needles. I caught a glance of approval when I didn't try to cover my quite exposed cleavage in any way—any other member of the Scáthanna wouldn't have bothered to do so, and I was showing willingness to adapt to their ways.

Before he started the work, he'd offered me a sleep charm, but I refused. Instead, I sent Riagán to fetch that bottle of Żubrówka from my room, some apple juice and cinnamon from the kitchens, and anyone from the team who wanted to join us drinking.

"It's going to take a while for the tattoo to heal," Lorcan said as he worked. "We can't use magic to speed it up, but mythborn can take as little as a few days, so you shouldn't be far behind."

"So, how does the curse work?"

Lorcan's needle was making its way through my skin, forcing an occasional hiss out of me.

"Once it's done, you'll have to activate it. Until you do, it's just markings on your skin. Touch it where your name is and, while activating it like you would any other curse, speak chosen words. Whatever you say at that time will become the trigger, so choose wisely."

"So I'll have to be able to speak if I want to kill myself," I said.

The choice of wording was important too... It couldn't be anything too common, because a casual exchange could kill me, but nothing so complex that I'd have a hard time remembering it.

"You have to be able to speak to give away secrets as well, so this shouldn't be an issue." Lorcan huffed. "That's why the curse is close to useless. Unless you choose death, it doesn't keep you from revealing anything." He looked at me, his eyes wise, and once again, I couldn't shake the feeling he was older than the others. "Torture isn't the only way to make people talk. There are other ways that will cause people to part with any secret in a blink."

He sounded jaded and bitter, so I didn't pry. Besides, he was right. No curse could act as one's conscience and make their choice for them. If I valued my life or wellbeing more than honor, friends, or whatever cause I was fighting for, I could give all that up just to save my skin instead of choosing death. Nevertheless, the curse was the ultimate way out if I wanted to die for what I chose to protect. With it, I wouldn't have to fear that pain and torture would break me, making me reveal any secrets.

Besides, having something that could kill me wasn't anything new. Back when I was waiting for the magic affliction to claim my body, I'd had a similar curse on me, though that one activated on its own and not by my choice. It could also be taken away or triggered by an unexpected magic explosion, so a voice-activated one seemed a wiser and safer choice.

Thinking about the curse I had made as my ultimate way out brought up the memory of how I used it to save Laoise's life, and my mood soured. Laoise was gone. At least she'd died quickly, and I imagined her body disappeared in the same beautiful cloud of silver as Cait's had. A small, insignificant comfort in the face of the fact that they were both dead.

When Riagán returned with Sadb in tow, the atmosphere in the day room resembled that of a funeral home, solemn and quiet. Grimly accurate, since we were to drink to our companions' deaths.

"Riagán said you're going to show us some humanborn customs." Sadb plopped down on the bench beside me, sounding hardly enthused about the prospect, but she mustered a lighter note as she asked, "Shouldn't you be learning ours instead?"

"It'll take me a while to even pronounce that poem properly, and even more to fully understand its meaning," I replied. As much as I was willing to learn it, I was realistic about mastering poetic sentences in a language that had very little in common with contemporary Irish. "Ever tried vodka?"

All the mythborn in the room grimaced as if on cue. I could almost picture them in some ruined off-license, standing in a circle, curious and excited, passing around a salvaged bottle of vodka... and learning that it wasn't some mystic nectar to be savored.

"An example of how alcohol shouldn't be made. It's strong but tastes horrible." Lorcan didn't raise his head from his work.

"We have veenya," Riagán added somewhat apologetically.

I smiled at that. Magical alcohol that adapted to the drinker's tastes was indeed something hard to compete with, but I hoped I could at least wipe away some of the bad impression of human alcohol.

"I can't move, so Riagán's going to mix it. Pour some into the glasses. I'd say about a finger's depth." From what I knew, alcohol affected mythborn more than humans. I suspected it had something to do with its magic-blocking properties, though it didn't seem to help humanborn with their magical affliction, as one would expect. Either way, I didn't want to get my new comrades drunk with the first glass. "Now fill it up with apple juice, mix it, and sprinkle some cinnamon on top." I cringed when he produced a cinnamon stick and used it to mix the liquid. "Just grind a little bit in."

There was something peculiar in watching a mythborn use his combat knife, a blade made of an unknown metal with a dark wood handle, on the cinnamon bark as he prepared a human cocktail from a country relatively far away.

"The first toast always goes to the fallen ones," I explained as he passed the glasses around. Back before the Magiclysm, the toasts used to be different, more cheerful and hopeful, but during the war, we drank to ease the pain, not to celebrate.

I lifted mine, and Sadb and Riagán followed, their gestures uncertain as they tried to mimic me. Lorcan refused with a shake of his head, still focused on tattooing me.

"Maybe later," he murmured.

Sadb dipped her lips in the cocktail. "That's a surprise. It doesn't taste half as bad as I expected. It's like..." She paused, looking for a comparison.

"Apple pie, if you're familiar with human baking," I said. "This is what we call it back in Poland." I didn't go into details explaining that this particular flavor was only achievable with this specific vodka, which took its name from the bison grass used to make it.

Riagán sipped his and nodded. "It's not too bad."

I grinned. "Drink up, then, because there are two more toasts coming."

"We have time. The tattoo's going to take at least an hour." As Riagán replied, his eyes slipped to my cleavage and bare shoulder, and he made it clear he was enjoying the sight—but at the same time, he couldn't fool me. Deep inside, he was suffering too.

Sadb passed me a platter with cold meats and cheese, and once I helped myself, careful not to move the shoulder Lorcan was working on, she placed it within my reach. We ate and drank slowly, talking little and about things of no importance, as if each of us was dealing with our own thoughts instead.

In a way, we did, processing Cait's death and other things. I couldn't help recalling the mysterious mythborn's voice, as if I wanted to make sure I wouldn't forget him, and Sadb must have been thinking of Laoise, because her beautiful face bore marks of deep pain. She wasn't trying to conceal it, so it was the first time I'd gotten to see how strong her love was—and the grief that came with it.

The alcohol was strong as well—stronger than I remembered, which meant my new, myth-touched body wasn't as resilient as a humanborn one. Not a beneficial trait, since my information-gathering job often relied on pub-crawling and drinking with strangers. But the tattoo I was getting sealed my future anyway. Even if I was going to utilize my contacts and get us the information we needed, the Scáthanna didn't need a full-time information broker. They needed a scout.

Two more toasts followed, to long life and to peace, but I didn't refill their glasses for them. Vodka and magic didn't mix well.

"There, done." Lorcan finally put his needle away. "Do you know what words you will activate it with?"

I shook my head. I hadn't given it much thought, and I

knew it had to be something I'd never say by accident... Something I wouldn't regret not being able to ever say again.

"Maybe that's for the better," he replied. "It won't do you any good if you're too drunk to remember what you said." With his grim voice, his joke fell flat. He lifted the last glass, still full and waiting for him, and took a cautious sip. "Indeed, not half as bad as most humanborn liquors. To you, Kaja, and your tattoo. May you never have to use it." He drank the rest of the cocktail like a real human, in three quick gulps, and then put the glass down without a word and headed for the door.

"What got into him?" Sadb's voice suggested at least partial inebriation, and I wondered how well she'd do in a fight when vodka had a hold on her. Of course, I wasn't fool enough to offer a sparring match. She likely could beat me silly even in her sleep.

I shrugged. "Likely the same that got into everyone else." After all, we were drinking to honor Cait's death—or to process it.

Sadb stared at her glass, swirling the cocktail inside as if she could see Laoise's face in the golden liquid. "You know, for an ex-humanborn, you aren't that bad. Ten years or so, and you'll truly be one of us."

"Give me five, and I'll make you all into proper human-born," I fired back with a grin.

"And then we'll all join Trinity and live happily ever after." She lifted her glass in a toast and took another sip. "I think I've had enough for the evening." She got up from the bench, her moves as fluid and controlled as if she hadn't drunk a drop of alcohol.

Cathal walked into the room, and for a second every-body froze, as if his presence meant more dire news. Sadb laughed first, maybe at our reaction, and it seemed to break whatever grim spell had befallen us.

"Came to drink with us, ceannasaí?" Sadb pointed at her half-finished glass.

"Maybe later," he replied. "I'm looking for Lorcan. He was supposed to do Kaja's tattoo."

"He's done and gone," Riagán said. "Judging by his mood, he's probably somewhere alone. His room?"

"Not there. I checked." Cathal shook his head, concern flashing on his face. "If you see him again, tell him to come to me in the morning." He walked over to Riagán and took his glass. He sniffed the cocktail as if he could tell its ingredients that way, then took a generous sip. "I thought alcohol was supposed to be drunk for pleasure, not as a punishment." He passed the glass back to Riagán, who continued to drink it, unmoved. I still couldn't tell if such free and open behavior was normal among the mythborn or if it was the result of the bond the Scáthanna shared. Seeing how stuffy the Court mythborn were, I was leaning toward the latter.

"It's an acquired taste," I said with a shrug. His reaction didn't upset me. I appreciated honesty, and out of the four who'd tried the cocktail, two seemed to enjoy it enough, so I considered it a win.

"One that I won't be acquiring." He poured himself some veenya instead. A full bottle of the magical alcohol always stood on the table, though from what I'd noticed, the Scáthanna rarely drank it during the meals. "To the fallen ones." Cathal lifted his cup. "To long life. And to peace."

I stared dumbfounded, listening to him recite a human-born toast, and he gave me a measured smile, like a reminder that I should always expect he had something up his sleeve. I could believe it. Cathal struck me as extremely cunning, and a great strategist. As he slowly drank his veenya, still every bit the composed and stoic leader of his team—my leader, *my ceannasaí*—I was immensely grateful that I'd ended up on his side. To have Cathal against me... I didn't even want to think about it.

Riagán moved closer and put his arm around me. I leaned against him, closing my eyes. The alcohol had a numbing effect, hushing both the magic within and grief, inviting sleep.

"Get her to bed," Cathal said gently as I was dozing off. "Tomorrow we'll plan our payback."

CHAPTER FOURTEEN

I was sitting in the day room, working on a simple curse, more to occupy my hands and eyes than from a need to make one. My main focus was eavesdropping on the conversations around the Court. None of them had provided anything useful, and the longer I tried, the more tired I was becoming—my skill had its limits and was putting a strain on me. I would be happy with that knowledge if I didn't need to work longer and further...

"You know that you aren't going to find him at the Court," Faolan said.

I lifted my head. He was sitting at the other end of the table, stretched against the wall and facing me as if his only task was watching me. And, in a way, it was. The rest of the Scáthanna had set out with Lorcan to check local alchemists, healers, and other suppliers in the hopes that one had come in contact with the mythborn we were searching for.

Before they left, I'd suggested I was fine on my own and quite secure at the Court, but Cathal would have none of it.

No member of the team was to be left on their own, so I was stuck with the mythborn on the team who liked me the least.

"I might find a clue," I muttered.

He let out a short laugh. "Or learn the newest gossip those self-important morons are occupying themselves with."

I shot him a nasty glare. He was distracting me while I could be doing something useful. "I'm trying to make good use of my skill."

"I'd say you're trying to avoid making conversation," he said bluntly, "by trying to *pretend* you're making good use of your skill."

I dropped the pretense of working on the curse. If one thing could be said about Faolan, it was that he wasn't a mythborn to beat around the bush, which seemed to be a common theme among the Scáthanna, and I matched his bluntness when I replied, "You don't like me. Don't you think it's enough that you're stuck here with me? I don't have to add to your torture."

He smiled as if he appreciated—or even enjoyed—my straightforward reply. "I don't dislike you. I'm just disappointed, I suppose. The way Riagán talked about you... I expected someone different," he said.

Right, likely someone other than yet another human-born with all her flaws. I might have become a myth-touched, but that change was purely physical. Magic did nothing to fix my not-so-vibrant and so very human personality.

"Riagán is..." I paused. Saying he was in love would make it sound like he was a fool who couldn't be reasonable because of his emotions. Saying that he was infatuated would belittle the care and feelings he had for me. "Riagán is Riagán," I said in the end.

Faolan gave me a nod. "Don't worry," he said with sudden seriousness. "I might not like you or your methods much, but I still remember that you did save Laoise's life."

"And I remember you helped save Albert from an assassin," I said for lack of a better reply.

Suddenly, it didn't matter that right after I'd saved Laoise, Faolan was fuming about the dangerous curse I used to carry on me, likely asking Cathal to get rid of me or worse, and his help with Albert was to make sure the assassin didn't fall in Trinity's hands so that they couldn't learn the Court's secrets... This was probably as close as we would get to saying "I got your back," at least for a while.

"So, did you learn any hot gossip?" he asked in an amused tone. "Anything no one else knows yet?"

I got the cue. The time for heartfelt conversations and confessions was over. He had reassured me that, his personal feelings aside, my presence on the team wasn't going to be a problem, and he was ready to move on.

"I don't think I can tell the hot and not-so-hot gossip apart," I replied. "All of it sounds utterly boring, and one piece of gossip sounds just like all the others."

He laughed and shifted in his seat, losing some of the demeanor of a guard on duty. "Whatever's repeated the most is likely the hottest at the moment." He rubbed his chin. "On the other hand, anything that only a few know of might be actually more valuable, even useful."

"Do you really think that knowing beforehand what the Court's newest scandal is will help us?"

He gave me an evaluating look. "You're the one who collected and traded information."

I rolled my eyes. "Information, not gossip."

But there was some truth in what he said. Being an information broker meant that I'd collected everything I could find, and my job was to tell the common gossip and useful tidbits apart... or even to track down the sources to confirm the validity of whatever information I had.

"So this is what the Scáthanna do instead of heeding the lady's call," said a mythborn female who walked into the room. "You clearly don't deserve the privileges bestowed upon you."

Both Faolan and I turned our heads at the newcomer, but while my expression was one of a polite interest—as always when I dealt with self-important mythborn— Faolan's was almost hostile.

The visitor was tall and well dressed, with her hair in a simple and tasteful updo, decorated with subtle jewelry. Everything about her spoke of power and confidence. She wasn't someone minor with an inflated ego but one of the important players in the Court.

"Well, aren't you going to respond?" she demanded.

"There wasn't any question," I muttered before Faolan could say something even more outrageous.

She looked me up and down, grimaced, and focused her attention back on Faolan. "Where's Cathal? I need to speak to him."

"Ceannasaí's out on an assignment. I'll inform him of your visit when he returns." His tone was hardly polite.

"You'll do more than that," the mythborn female replied. "You'll go and get him for me. Now."

Faolan didn't move, and I didn't expect him to. "I'll inform him of your visit when he returns," he repeated.

One thing I had to give the mythborn was that she didn't

react to his blunt remarks. Had Clíodhna been in her place, we'd have a full-blown tantrum on our hands. All our guest did was huff at Faolan and then turn to me.

"Maybe you're smarter than your companion," she said in a tone already suggesting she highly doubted it. "You're new. You could use a favor or two at the Court."

"We have orders," I replied dryly.

"Orders that require you to sit around and do nothing?"

"How I lead my team is none of your concern, Keeper of Flowers." Cathal walked into the day room.

I swear, his timing couldn't have been more perfect.

Behind him, in the corridor, stood the rest of the team, and I let out a discreet breath of relief: none of them were missing or wounded.

"It is when it clashes with the needs of the Court," the mythborn replied.

"That's for the lady to decide." Cathal stood unmoved. "Your request has already been received and will be dealt with when I deem it appropriate. Until then, I suppose the Court will have to do without their floral arrangements at dinners."

Faolan openly snorted, and I could swear I caught at least one snicker behind Cathal's back.

"Should I remind you, ceannasaí, that the Scáthanna serve the lady just like we all do?" the mythborn said. "Perhaps you've grown above your stature, allowing yourself to become lazy and vain. Judging by recent events..."

She didn't get to say anything more, as the atmosphere in the room and outside changed.

"Leave now," was all Cathal said.

If Faolan was hostile before, now he was on a verge of going in for the kill, and judging by Cathal's expression, his ceannasaí would not give an order to stand down. I couldn't blame either of them. A mythborn who likely had never experienced battle and bloodshed, who had never watched a companion die from wounds or a curse in the field, was on the brink of accusing them of growing sloppy and careless, insinuating that Laoise and Cait's deaths were our own fault.

"*Now*, Keeper of Flowers," Cathal added.

She huffed and rushed out of the room, brushing past Cathal and pushing between the rest of the team standing in the corridor. For the first time since she'd entered the room, she looked shaken. Perhaps even with her instinct dulled by the Court's decorum and her own position, she'd sensed how close she'd come to dying for as little as words spoken.

With her departure, we all relaxed, although Lorcan's stern expression told me that their excursion had brought no leads.

"Anything?" I asked anyway.

Lorcan shook his head. He took a piece of bread and a banana and headed for the corner of the room. Everything in his posture suggested he'd rather be left alone, so I didn't push.

"We checked all the local suppliers," Cathal said. "He might be getting his herbs and concoctions from the countryside. It would make sense if he's not from around here."

"Or he's not above getting what he needs from humanborn," I said. "We're assuming that because he's a mythborn, he would do business only with other mythborn. But in the ambush, we saw humanborn as well."

The others exchanged glances.

"This is how the Snake operates," Sadb remarked, saying what everybody was thinking. "This might not be personal after all."

"He's targeting the Scáthanna," Cathal pointed out, "and in past years, we've killed enough of his agents for it to be *very* personal. But I'll inform the lady nevertheless. If it's known that we're busy tracking the Snake's servant, it might help to curb the ridiculous requests for our assistance she's been getting lately. Most of those tasks could be handled well enough by local mythborn authorities."

"Could this be a part of the plot as well?" I asked. I knew the Scáthanna were the mythborn equivalent of a special unit, but aside from our hunt for the Snake back when I was still a humanborn, I knew little of what, exactly, they really did. "It seems to me that this Keeper of Flowers is convinced you are using the Court's resources for personal gain and reasons, and if more mythborn around here think this way, it's not going to win you any support, possibly making you more vulnerable."

Cathal looked at me in thought, considering the idea. "It wouldn't affect us, as all we need is the lady's favor." He rubbed his chin. "But it could damage *her* position."

I nodded. I hardly understood mythborn politics, but from what Lorcan had mentioned, the mythborn outside of Dublin weren't so keen on cooperating with humanborn. If Eithne's position among them weakened, we could be heading for another war, or at least a period of hostility and chaos, which would likely serve the Snake's interest well. Peace and cooperation made it harder to divide and conquer.

"Do you know many humanborn suppliers?" Cathal asked me. "Or anyone else we can ask?"

"I know a person who could help us, but I'm not sure he'll talk to any of you." Truth to be told, I wasn't even sure Max would talk to *me*, not with my changed physique and while wearing a gray uniform. "I'll have to go with you."

"Not alone?" Cathal asked with a friendly tease.

I threw him a grin. I wasn't stupid enough to go on my own all the way to O'Connell Bridge, giving whoever was hunting us plenty of opportunities for an ambush. "I'm sure he'll prefer a private conversation, but it doesn't mean I have to be out of sight, just out of an earshot."

Cathal nodded and looked around. "We'll go tomorrow, but there's no need to rise early. Be ready by noon."

Most of the Scáthanna left, and Faolan threw me a smirk on his way out.

"He wasn't too obnoxious, was he?" Riagán asked.

I shook my head. "No more than I'd expect of him." I looked at the door, but said mythborn was already gone. "In a way, I prefer him this way to his pretending he likes me." We didn't have to best friends or even like each other, as long as we could do our job and have each other's backs. After our conversation, I was certain Faolan would have mine, and I had no reason to not have his.

Riagán smiled. "You're truly becoming one of us."

"I'm trying," I replied.

Now all I needed was to become actually useful, and because of that, I really hoped that I'd find us some clues.

When I stepped into the day room shortly before noon, I wasn't wearing my uniform. Instead, I'd put on the clothes I'd worn at the Court, topping them up with my own jacket and bag. As peculiar as it was, I would have preferred my uniform, since I'd taken so much time to make sure all my curses were in the right spots, and I was already developing a healthy habit of reaching for them without looking.

Most of the team was already there, in full gear. To my

surprise, they didn't express any disapproval over how I looked.

Cathal walked in and looked me up and down. "I take it that your contact isn't fond of us?"

In fact, I wasn't sure. Max's loyalty was to money, and anyone who could pay was welcome in his shop, but I guessed that, for the same reason, he'd rather not be affiliated with any particular faction. He was much more likely to talk to me if I was just another customer.

I shrugged. "He's not particularly hateful, but you were enemies."

"A former Trinitian?" Lorcan asked as he walked in, clearly having caught the last bit of the conversation.

"No, he's not fond of them either," I replied honestly. In this case, it was simple: Albert wasn't fond of Max's line of business, so Max wasn't fond of Albert and anything related to him. Come to think of it, fondness in general wasn't Max's thing. "And he lives on this side of the river."

That got their attention. I could swear I saw relief on their faces. The prospect of meeting some veteran friend of mine deep in human territory must have been making them feel on edge already, but the prospect of possibly allowing Trinitians in on the team secrets would have been worse.

Cathal rolled the map out, and I pointed at the location. Riagán, looking over Cathal's shoulder, sent me a smile, as he must have recognized the place. This was where I'd gone to get an antidote for the side effects of my kissing him on a cheek. He knew of it because—as I learned later—he'd followed me back then to make sure I was fine.

Sadb walked in, the last team member we were waiting for, and Cathal gave the signal to leave.

I expected him to lead us straight south, to the river to make our way along its banks, but he chose a route east, through Arbour Hill and King Street. It was an area I didn't know all that well, even before the war. Far from the city center, it didn't have any fancy shopping centers or popular venues. Smithfield Square was an exception, with a line of modern apartments facing the old distillery of a world-famous whiskey brand, and some small eateries and services. But the rest? It felt more like Dublin's back room, where you didn't let tourists in and didn't venture into it if you weren't local... or at least familiar with the neighborhood.

My instincts rebelled against traversing those streets, even though there was nothing particularly dangerous about them. It had more to do with being so deep on the north side of Dublin. Humanborn simply didn't go there without a good reason, and I clearly was still thinking like one of them. I could blame it on Eithne, who'd kept me confined to the Court. Without regular outings, it was impossible to get rid of old habits and train new instincts. On the other hand, with someone hunting for the Scáthanna, no route could be safe anyway, so it was better to keep those old instincts on tap.

We traveled at a steady pace, with Cathal and Sadb in front, Faolan and Riagán in the back, and Lorcan and me in the middle—a loose formation that was meant to protect the most vulnerable of the team should an attack come. The day was bright enough, especially for early spring, so we didn't have to worry about anyone lurking in the shadows, but the ambush in the gardens had made it clear that our adversary wasn't afraid to act in daylight.

We were halfway there when Cathal took a turn southward, and it took me a moment to realize we were walking into Henry Street.

Before the war, I'd known the area well. It was a pedestrian-only street surrounded by two lines of four-story buildings, which before the war were the fronts of many posh and popular stores... and shopping centers. Downtown Dublin had kept a lot of its historic looks by putting its shopping centers and car parks inside the existing structures rather than demolishing them and building modern and soulless malls. People hadn't even shied away from repurposing an old church for a party venue, a popular one in its time. I liked that about Dublin.

But that was before magic returned to the world. Now, Henry Street looked different, and yet the same. The stores' windows didn't display wares anymore, no fashionable outfits or shoes. Instead, they had benches and tables and little nooks with shimmering water, strange stone sculptures and wooden arrangements, making the entrances look more like the lobbies of expensive hotels. And they likely served a similar purpose, since, from what I understood, Henry Street had become a residential area.

It came as no surprise that the mythborn nobles would favor a street that before the war had all the signs of luxury while at the same time boasting a historic look, though its buildings mostly didn't date back further than the previous century. But, on the other hand, I doubted most mythborn dove that deep into human history, even if it pertained to the very city in which they were living.

We drew quite a few glances, but the mythborn didn't stare, as if the gray uniforms imposed respect and distance, and the pace Cathal had set was fast enough to discourage any interactions. I doubted any of the Scáthanna were in a sociable mood anyway, and if they wanted company, I'd bet they wouldn't choose the self-important inhabitants of Henry Street. I'd seen enough at the Court to tell that they didn't play well with nobles.

We made it through Henry Street quickly. I regretted not having time to scout the adjacent streets and back alleys. I was curious whether mythborn had upgraded the whole area or, like humans before them, they'd only focused their efforts on the main street. In prewar times, taking one turn was enough to step out of the land of posh malls and popular brand stores into the realm of small shops and local business with all their tackiness and shoddiness out in the open.

Henry Street ended at the O'Connell Street, and the Scáthanna slowed down as we approached the Spire. Its official name was the Monument of Light or Spire of Dublin, but in my whole time in Ireland I'd never met a person who used either of those. "The Spire" sufficed. It wasn't hard to describe—a large spike of stainless steel reaching up into the sky, high above all the surrounding buildings—and it was even harder to miss. Because of that, it had been a popular meeting point, and at any time of day, crowds of tourists and locals had swarmed around it, waiting or searching for the person waiting for them.

The war had changed things.

The Spire stood alone, because most humanborn weren't keen on venturing to the north side of the city, and those few who still lived in the area, likely clinging to their past lives, had no reasons for meetups by the Spire. At least the mythborn had let it be.

I couldn't help glancing toward the river. Past O'Connell Bridge, it was a straight shot to Trinity, and I could swear I saw the edge of one of its buildings up the street. I quickly looked away. I might be missing my former comrades, but this wasn't the time for recollections... or visits. As much as I wanted to see Albert face to face for the first time since I'd become a myth-touched, I had enough on my plate already without the drama such a meeting could possibly create.

Lorcan must have caught that glance, because there was an unspoken question on his face as he looked at me. I had no idea what he wanted to know, but it was hardly the place for personal discussions. So I shook my head, not caring whether he read it as "no, I don't want to talk about it" or "no, I won't try to run away to Trinity." Both were true.

Where Henry Street ended, Talbot Street began. There was North Earl Street between them, but I doubted anyone, save maybe the people who lived there, remembered it. I'd always considered Talbot a poor stepsister of the street we'd just left. While Henry Street boasted posh stores, Talbot was home mostly to small and tacky businesses, and even its "mall," if one could call it that, was shabby.

After the war, not much changed, but the street became emptier. The train station at its east end no longer spat out masses of commuters to fill the street with crowds every time of the day, and it looked even more miserable.

Sometimes, I wondered whether history itself weighed on the street, and the image of a memorial stone at the end of the street resurfaced in my head. Before the war, during those few years I lived on the north side, I'd walked past it often. Like others, I was making my way from Connolly Station to my workplace deeper in the city center. I didn't think much of the bombing it commemorated, but even as an immigrant with a limited knowledge of Irish history, I knew of the Troubles. At the same time, I'd never taken time to study any of it properly.

Yet every time I walked past the memorial, even rushing to avoid being late for work, I felt that overwhelming sadness and thought of the lives lost.

Did it still stand there, a silent witness to the past strife?

But Cathal took a turn south, venturing into the smaller streets between Talbot and the river, so I abandoned my memories and focused on the present. So close to the unspoken border between the humanborn and mythborn domains, the Scáthanna became more cautious, old habits and new threats pressing together on their instincts. And Max, even though he lived on the north side, had chosen an abode close to the Liffey.

His shop came into view soon enough, the only somewhat well-kept building in the crumbling neighborhood, with the familiar sign saying "Max's."

As we approached, a mythborn was just leaving. One look at the Scáthanna's uniforms and she hurried away with a frightened expression. She likely thought she'd need to find another supplier for whatever Max was providing her.

Cathal glanced toward the shop. "We'll wait here. Try to stay close to the windows."

He didn't have to explain it. As unlikely as an ambush was, the deeper into the store I went, the more vulnerable I became, and I didn't like the idea of ending up as a madman's prisoner just because I was too far away for them to get to me in time.

I walked in, scanning the interior. Thankfully, there weren't more customers around.

Max kept the store mostly empty, save the huge counter and the floor-to-ceiling shelves behind it—quite a nice piece of work, too, considering they had been made postwar in a resource-deprived country. Whoever the craftsman was had made them look vintage and purposeful rather than like some Frankenstein's monster of furniture. The mismatched vials and pouches filling the shelves added to that vintage look, and I could almost believe I'd stepped back in time if not for the very contemporary—and very unkempt—outfit of the dark-haired man behind the counter, namely washed-off jeans and a worn hoodie.

I could swear Max had gotten even thinner since the last time I visited, and his eyes became even more sunken, surrounded by dark circles, suggesting he still ignored his body's need to sleep and replaced it with some wicked concoctions that kept him awake and sharp.

"Hey, Max," I said.

My friendly welcome earned me an intense glare. He took in my face and my clothes, and his expression made it clear he couldn't place my voice.

"Do I knov you?" he asked in his heavy German accent, and there was no friendliness in the question.

I approached the counter. "Last time I was here, I left a vial with you." With Max, it was better to get straight to the proof. Anyone could say they were Kaja. Only a few would know that I'd left a vial with the Court's remedy to the affliction with him.

He did a double take. "I see you came to tell me about some unexpected side effects," he replied with caution.

I still couldn't tell whether he believed me or not, and that wasn't safe. If Max decided I was an impostor, I wouldn't make it out of the store alive... Walking out on my own—yes, probably, but definitely already dead.

"The drug is safe," I said, "and I hope you managed to copy it already, because I gave the other vial to Trinity, and last time I checked, they were making good progress. What happened to me... I had an accident involving too much magic." Specifically, one that included being almost torn to pieces by an Afflicted, but I wasn't in a sharing mood. "The mythborn stabilized me, but, well, *that* had side effects."

His eyes shot toward the window and the Scáthanna waiting there. I was sure they weren't trying to look particularly menacing or intimidating, but they did watch the shop, and Max knew those gray uniforms.

"They're my escort." It wasn't exactly a lie, because out of the whole team, I was the most vulnerable. "And I'm here because I need your help." I fished out a piece of paper, taking for a good sign that Max hadn't told me to get the heck out yet. On the other hand, if he didn't believe my story, he was probably just waiting for a good opportunity to poison me. "Is there anyone who has been ordering these specific concoctions or the ingredients for them?"

For a heartbeat, I wondered if he would dare touch the paper, but his curiosity must have been stronger than his caution. Max scanned Lorcan's list in silence then looked at me.

"We will pay for any information you can provide. Or compensate you in some other way, if you prefer." I hadn't thought of discussing it with Cathal first, but I doubted he would be concerned about money or a favor that Max could ask in return for his help. With all of our lives at stake, it would be a small price to pay.

"I still haven't decided if I trust you," Max replied with a hint of coldness.

I should have expected it, and fished for something quick and easy to win his trust. Something that no one else could know. "Last time I was here, you also gave me a lecture about drinking while pregnant," I said.

That lecture had been attached to a magic-blocking antidote I asked for to get rid of yet another set of side effects, those related to kissing a mythborn. Anyone watching me back then could have guessed I would need an antidote, but no one but me could have heard the scolding that accompanied Max's concoction.

"I'll see what I can find." Max pushed the list back to me.

"But it vill take some time. Vill they be paying?" He pointed at the window with his chin.

"Yes, but you can send it to me at the Court. This way it will look like private correspondence, and it won't damage your reputation." And it should also keep him safe. "As you can see, I have a condition I'd rather not trust mythborn quacks with," I added in a lighter tone.

He looked me up and down again as he let out a dry chuckle. "I vouldn't either."

"I'll be going. I hope you can get me something." I sure did, no matter how much it would cost us.

As I left the store, I couldn't help monitoring my own body. No sweats, no sudden shortness of breath, no elevated heartbeat... Just because Max *acted* like he believed it was me, it didn't mean he actually did. But with no symptoms, I had to hope that I made it out of Max's alive.

Cathal gave me a concerned look, so I rushed to the other side of the narrow street where the Scáthanna were waiting.

"He'll reach out to me if he has anything," I said.

I doubted anyone was around to eavesdrop on us, but I preferred caution over confidence. So far, our enemy had proven much more resourceful and better informed than we anticipated, and I wasn't about to give up our potential advantage by blabbing about it in the open.

As we headed back, I kept listening. Max might care only about the money and his research, but as a longtime customer and a paying client, I enjoyed some privileges— one could say even an almost a friend-like status—though it didn't mean someone couldn't find a pressure point to make him talk. Normally, I'd call it paranoia, but if our enemy noticed that in the past few days the Scáthanna were visiting drug sellers and potion suppliers, he could have been watching Max's place.

I couldn't help a small smile at trying to imagine what kind of a blackmail could work on him. The skinny German guy might look like easy prey, but I knew he could hold his own, and I wasn't worried. I just hoped for a chance to catch someone working for our enemy.

Yet, even though I caught many conversations around, Max's distinct voice remained silent.

I was in the middle of my morning training with Sadb when I heard the door opening and caught movement in my peripheral vision. Quickly, I leaped to the side, putting distance between me and a possible new threat without even stopping to figure out who had entered.

Sadb gave me a nod of approval as she continued her methodical attacks on me with her usual lack of mercy. Our sparring had shifted to focus more on my hand-to-hand skills, though she still expected me to try tossing small objects at her. She just didn't bother acting as if they were real curses, and as much as I'd rather not, I had to agree with her decision. In a real fight, some of my opponents could ignore small objects as non-threatening or even withstand the magic I threw at them and continue their attack just like Sadb did, so I had to get used to it. Of course, it meant she was hitting me more often again, which, in turn, spoke volumes about how I needed said hand-to-hand training.

As Lorcan approached, Sadb gave a signal to stop, and I took the opportunity to bend over and catch a few deeper breaths. Sweat was dripping from my... well, everywhere, and my muscles were sore both from the training and her strikes.

"A message was delivered," Lorcan said. "It looks like it's from your alchemist. Cathal and others are waiting downstairs."

It sounded urgent, and I refrained from groaning. I could take a moment or two to rest.

"We'll be there shortly," Sadb responded, and when he left, she sent me a grin. "Let's wash off first. Neither of us looks presentable enough to leave the Court if you got us a lead."

I glanced at her sweat-free body, ideal skin unmarked by any redness, and her almost perfect ponytail bobbing behind her head. Yeah, not presentable enough... I nodded with appreciation, because even if she could skip the shower, I definitely couldn't.

"I'll be quick," I promised.

I still took my time putting the training gear away in perfect order. Sadb would likely take it personally if I mishandled her toys, and I would feel the literal brunt of her reaction during the next sparring.

I didn't dawdle in the showers, even though I longed to stay in the endless stream of hot water forever. I heard Sadb enter, shower, and leave, and that was my cue to get out as well. I stopped in my room only long enough to throw on a fresh uniform, then I headed for the day room. To my surprise, Sadb caught up with me, even though I'd expected her to already be inside. I nodded to her in appreciation— waiting for me was thoughtful of her. I wouldn't be the last one entering.

To my surprise, the package was waiting for me unopened: a small cardboard box wrapped in paper and tape that made me think of the prewar times when we actually had a formalized mail delivery system. The address, though, was in the new style, saying only "Kaja" and "the Court."

On the other hand, back in the "good old times," it was a common joke that if you sent a letter in Ireland with just the flakiest excuse for an address, it would still get delivered, as in the smaller towns everyone knew everyone else. On top of that, some streets had two different names, and there were some that had the same names... All that, combined with the lack of unified post codes, created chaos that seemed to have worked only on the goodwill of people within the system. But in the end, it worked, though in the years preceding the Magiclysm, post codes were just being introduced, suggesting that there was some room for improvement. Now, we were somewhat back to square one —or maybe even minus one.

Upon everyone's anticipating gazes, I opened the package.

The box contained a vial, sitting safely in a nest of torn and crumpled paper, and a folded note. The page was huge but contained only a few lines. "'I always wanted to try this out on a mythborn. I guess you're as close as I can get to it. Hope this helps with your problem,'" I read out loud. At the very bottom of the page was another line. "'P.S. You'll owe me for this one.'"

The team gave me perplexed stares. I reached for the vial and uncorked it. The strong scent of whiskey hit my nostrils immediately, and I smiled. I was quite certain he'd sent me the same antidote I asked him for the last time.

Riagán leaned over, stretching his arm, and I shook my head. "I wouldn't drink it if I were you." Deep in the corner of my mind, I could almost hear Max's disappointed groan. I had no doubt that he wouldn't pass on the opportunity to have a mythborn trying out his magic-blocking antidote. Any other time, I might have obliged his curiosity, but I wasn't about to experiment on the mythborn I had some feelings invested in.

"That's it?" Cathal asked, all businesslike, as if the contents of the package weren't a disappointment.

I looked at the note again. The page looked awfully large and empty for those few lines he wrote, and it wasn't like Max to waste time and space for a joke, especially considering the note at the very bottom. But it would be like him to use a joke to conceal a message, and he was a chemist... Though, if my guess was right, he hadn't used college-level knowledge for this one.

"I'll need a candle," I said, and, faced with confusion, I remembered that we were at the Court, where magic was more common. "Or a heat charm should do." I couldn't resist a hint of a mysterious smile. "You're about to witness magic that humans learn as children."

Faolan produced a charm at lighting speed, and as they all gathered around me, I activated it and moved it close to the paper. It didn't take long for the dark letters to appear on the page—an address. Underneath was one sentence: *The only place that ordered all items from the list.*

I glanced around. They all had that odd fascination on their faces, similar to when I showed a video game to Riagán.

"I thought humans didn't have any magic before we came," Lorcan said, and I could swear there was slight awe in his voice.

"We have science," I replied. As much as I'd have loved to tease them all a little longer, we had things to do. "It was written with lemon juice... or something with similar properties," I added as I remembered that Max had *almost* gotten his degree in chemistry, "and heat exposes it. Most kids—well, kids from my generation, anyway—played with it at least once, so Max could safely assume I'd figure it out."

"But a mythborn wouldn't know it." Cathal nodded.

Max might not hate the mythborn, but he likely didn't trust anyone at the Court, so he'd thought of concealing the message. He was taking some risk assuming I knew the trick with the invisible writing—but worst-case scenario, if I'd proven clueless, I would've written back or paid him another visit.

"We're setting out at dusk." Cathal looked at me. "All of us. Until then, you're free."

Everyone started leaving, and I shifted, uneasiness and adrenaline hitting me. Cathal was right to not split the team to have someone babysit me at the Court. I trusted Max's information, but Cathal had no reason to, so he preferred to have his best fighters with him in case this was a trap. At the same time, taking me along was hardly an advantage if he didn't intend to send me out scouting alone, which meant it would make sense to leave me at the Court. Even with the Snake's spies possibly lurking in its corners, it was enough to ask Connor to keep me company. Neither of us was a fighter, but we knew how to use curses. I'd be safe. Out in the field, with a possible trap about to spring, I was a liability and distraction.

But then... I was also good at information gathering, and my listening skill was of even more value. If we were stealthy enough, I could get us information and our enemies would be none the wiser.

I exhaled softly. It had been a while since I'd trusted making decisions to someone else.

Cathal knew what he was doing, and I didn't need to second-guess him. After all, contrary to Albert, he would do what was best for the whole team without being bogged down by personal feelings and attachments.

Only then did I realize Cathal had been watching me the whole time, likely because I was the only one who hadn't left the room immediately.

"Ceannasaí." I gave him a nod and headed for the door.

Before I left, I could swear I saw a flash of an amused smile on his face, as if he knew what went through my head.

CHAPTER FIFTEEN

When we left the Court, the sun was just setting, bleeding a mix of fierce reds and intense oranges onto the sky. It seemed to be a thing in Dublin: dull, often overcast days followed by spectacular though fleeting displays of nature's beauty in the evenings. Any other time, I'd stop to enjoy these passing moments of daylight, feasting my eyes on vibrant colors so different to Ireland's standard "gray and grayer," but this time I hardly took notice of the sunset. With the prospect of a fight, whether we would be setting an ambush or being the ones ambushed, my mind was in that singular focus that didn't allow any distractions.

I sensed tension in the team. The Scáthanna might act like always, composed and confident, but below that surface was a whole array of emotions. The anticipation of an upcoming battle, hope for finding our enemy, and desire of revenge for Laoise and Cait—I knew, because I felt them too.

It didn't help that we were heading northeast, deep into the mythborn side of Dublin—an area I'd known little about even before the Magiclysm—and Cathal led us some convoluted way to minimize the risk of an ambush en route.

While others scanned the dark alleys we passed by in search for danger, I kept listening. The area wasn't too populated, but it still took effort to filter out the noise of common mythborn going about their lives, and I had a hard time doing so while keeping up with the rest of the team.

Lorcan put his hand on my shoulder and shook his head. He didn't even have to say anything. With regret, I nodded and stopped listening. He was right. I was gambling my focus on a slim chance I'd hear something worthwhile.

The night was already upon us, and the narrow streets of the north side inexorably brought back the memories of my last venture into that area, but I chased away the images of claws slashing at me and Emma's hateful glare.

This time, I wasn't alone. I had my team members watching my back, I had a plethora of offensive curses, and —what could be most important—I had weeks of training with Sadb. Of course, she would probably laugh at the slightest suggestion that I was ready to take on an Afflicted on my own, and I'd agree with her, but what she'd taught me so far gave me an advantage I didn't have before.

Cathal gave a signal to stop in a narrow alley. "We should be close enough. I don't want to risk us splitting, so our recon will be limited. Kaja?"

I focused on my listening. The area wasn't populated, but I had no way of knowing which conversations were the important ones, so I listened to all of them. I'd eavesdropped like that back in the Court already, but the mythborn there were so steeped in politics and gossip, I didn't think much of it. This time... I was picking up on the casual conversations of common mythborn, and it felt like I was violating their privacy. Not that I caught any secrets, but they didn't need an audience for their friendly banter with their spouses, instructing their children, or sharing an evening meal with their families. I sifted through them as quickly as I could, tuning out the voices that belonged to them and putting more focus on the conversations that didn't sound casual.

The Scáthanna waited patiently, with Sadb and Faolan on two ends of the alley looking out for any trouble, but the night was quiet and peaceful, as if mocking the threat we felt looming over us.

"I can't tell how many people are inside. There isn't much conversation going on," I whispered. "Something about boxes being delivered to various spots in the city, but..." I hesitated. "Some of those voices have humanborn accents."

I knew that some mythborn strove to blend in with the human population, adapting their patterns of speech and accents to make them similar to human ones, but they most often chose from the variety of Irish accents, as if trying to point out that they had the right to be on the island just much as the Irish did. They also lived closer to the river, or even on the south bank, in areas like the Liberties that had a mixed population. These were the accents of foreigners, and so deep in the north parts of Dublin, it struck me as uncommon.

Cathal was about to ask a question, but I raised my hand to stop him as I caught a scrap of an interesting exchange I'd rather not miss. "One of them is leaving now," I said. "If we could snatch him..."

All it took was Cathal's glancing at Riagán, and he left, getting Sadb along the way. As they disappeared around the corner, Cathal placed himself halfway between the alley's exit and the spot where I was standing with Lorcan. Faolan also adjusted his position, moving closer to us.

I couldn't help a pang of envy. In the time it would take me to figure out what was going on, the others had already taken and enacted unspoken orders.

"You'll learn in time." Lorcan kept his voice low and offered me a comforting smile. "We've been doing this together for a long time now." He looked over his shoulder. "Faolan's the newest to the team, and even he joined before we arrived in this world."

I wanted to ask more about the team and other members, because from that one eavesdropped conversation Cathal had had with Eithne, I knew there were once ten of them. Which meant Cathal had gone a long time without replacing the fallen members, and only Laoise's death... No, that wasn't right. They'd been considering recruiting me even before that. Laoise's death just sped up everything.

"Thanks," I whispered. The time for questions would be later, when we were all safe, and the mythborn responsible for all the death and torture was dead. "Don't hesitate to point out anything I miss."

Sadb and Riagán were back, escorting a humanborn. He had blond hair, the sturdy frame of a man who worked physically for a living, and his eyes were watching us all very carefully. He wasn't resisting or screaming, likely warned already that either would result in his death.

As they got close, he focused on Cathal with an ugly sneer. "Do you know who are you messing with?" He must have identified him as the leader. "Order your people to let me go, or you'll regret it."

I arched an eyebrow at his cocky attitude in the face of six dangerous-looking strangers, but Cathal remained unmoved. "You'll tell us all you know about the building you just left and the people inside."

"You don't get to ask questions," the man blurted.

Sadb nudged him as she gave him a nasty smile that said, *Oh, but we do.* Under her glare, the man flinched and lost his confidence for the moment it took him to turn his eyes back to Cathal.

I kept to the side, trying to not draw attention. Reading people wasn't really my thing, but catching cues was. From his behavior I was certain he didn't recognize who the Scáthanna were, but even if he took us for a bunch of muggers, it also suggested he was confident in his buddies to back him up.

"So, who are we messing with?" I asked.

I could swear he gained even more confidence. "I work for Donovan. John Donovan."

To my surprise, everyone else cringed. Whoever this Donovan guy was, they'd had dealings with him in the past, and he must have been a real pain then.

"Donovan wouldn't give work to a humanborn," Cathal said.

I listened, curious. John Donovan could be the name of an Irishman, but it was anglicized, and mythborn usually preferred the Irish versions of such names, both in pronunciation and spelling. They rarely bothered with picking surnames, too. Whoever he was, John Donovan had to be an interesting mythborn.

The man glared at Cathal smugly. "He clearly did, didn't he? You're probably one of those mythies who believe that the MPF is some sort of evil organization out to get all humans."

I almost gasped. The Mythborn Protection Force was an organized group that formed late during the war, and when the peace between the mythborn and humanborn was signed, they did everything in their power to push us all back into war. If there was anything that would fit a description of an "evil organization out to get all humans," the MPF was definitely it.

"If you really work for Donovan, we're allies." Cathal pointed at his emblem. "And you can tell us what's going on inside."

"Go and ask him yourself," the man replied without even glancing at the Scáthanna symbol. "I've got a job to do."

Focused on the conversation and pondering the information about MPF, I almost missed a clue. Our captive had kept fidgeting slightly ever since he stood before Cathal. At first, I took it for trying to find a way out or concealing he wasn't as confident as he wanted to appear, but a repeated move of his shoulder caught my eye. He was, perhaps subconsciously, trying to protect something.

"His bag," I said.

Sadb snatched it immediately, cutting the strap with a swift move and pulling the bag away from the man. It looked like a simple messenger satchel from the times before the war, worn down and stained in places. Sadb passed it to me before resuming her guarding position beside the man, sword at the ready. As I opened the bag, he tensed, and for the first time since he'd entered the alley, something resemblant to fear flashed on his face.

Inside, there were shredded rags, and I put my hand in with caution until my fingers closed on a round metallic object. I couldn't see it yet, but I had a good idea of what it might be.

"Looks like the MPF is changing their allegiances." I demonstrated a small explosive device.

The others recognized it too. In the past months, we'd been finding them in the hideouts of the Snake's agents.

"I have the right to protect himself in these dangerous times!" the man protested.

None of the Scáthanna graced him with any response. Faolan knocked him out, and Riagán tied him up.

"Let's go," said Cathal as Faolan threw our captive over his shoulder with such ease, the man could have been a stuffed toy.

"This once, I'm looking forward to talking to Donovan," Lorcan muttered.

"Personal reasons?" I asked.

The Mythborn Protection Force was an organization that claimed to have the interests of all mythborn at heart, so I couldn't imagine how they could end up on opposite sides to the Scáthanna.

"The MPF is... a problem, a channel for the mythborn outside of Dublin to sow discord between us and human-born," Lorcan replied as we approached the building. "The lady has to tolerate them, but as time passes, they grow bolder."

I nodded as I looked at the device in my hand. Trinitians had always hated the MPF for its open acts of terrorism as the war was nearing an end, and subtler sabotage after we signed peace, and Albert was convinced that they had the quiet approval of the Court. Well, I'd be glad to tell him that he was wrong. Lady Eithne was trying to preserve peace and sought cooperation with humanborn, and she wouldn't encourage the MPF to act.

Yet, if I understood correctly what Lorcan had said, some mythborn outside of Dublin supported the organization, so Eithne couldn't openly speak against them without losing political power or social standing. I could see how the MPF was a major thorn in her backside.

And now, as if we didn't have enough problems already, they might be working for the Snake.

As we were closing on the building, Cathal glanced over his shoulder. "Behave," he threw in no particular direction. "They need to be the ones to attack first."

And then, as if mythborn had a different idea of what "behaving" meant, he kicked in the front door.

JOHN DONOVAN's name wasn't the only unique thing about him. He was a mythborn, but unlike any I'd seen before. His facial features and the short fur covering his skin made him look like a molekind, but his towering, bulky body resembled those of the bridge dwellers. I guessed it wasn't a good idea to ask him who his parents were, especially as we had just stormed into his place, Cathal leading us with all the confidence of someone who was exactly where he wanted to be.

As we strode through the wide walkway between piled-up crates, Sadb had already knocked out an overeager humanborn who came at her with a hurling stick. There were at least a dozen mythborn and humanborn around already, and more walked into view before we stopped in front of Donovan.

"Easy, lads," Donovan said while few more humanborn and mythborn grabbed improvised weapons. "This is the famous Ceannasaí Cathal and his fellas. I thought the Court would have taught you at least *some* manners. No need to break a perfectly good door just for show."

Cathal looked straight at him. "Save your words for the explaining you're going to do at the Court."

"Right back at youse all," Donovan replied with a grin, using the Irish collective "you." The way he carried himself had nothing of that cheap smugness of people with no real confidence. He stood there, in front of the Scáthanna's leader, and behaved like he could take him. "You barge in here—"

"Cut this garbage. The MPF is dealing with the Snake."

Donovan's lips stretched in an ugly grimace, as if that accusation hurt him. "And what proof do you have?" He glanced at me and the device I was still holding. "A little curse one of those pesky humanborn carried around?"

Cathal took a step closer. "Tell me what I want to know, and we can agree that's not much evidence," he said quietly. "I'll even ignore that the MPF employs humanborn now."

Donovan burst out with laughter. "Or else?"

"We take you and your lackeys back to the Court, and they'll decide whether there's enough evidence or not."

Donovan scoffed. "I'll be back here before you're done explaining yourself to the lady."

"You, maybe, but your henchmen are unlikely to be that lucky. And I assure you, the Scáthanna will be very interested in what your humanborn... *employees* have to say about the MPF."

This time, Donovan shifted with slight unease, but I stopped paying attention to him. Cathal had him covered and knew how to play him best. Donovan's reaction suggested his workers knew things they could reveal when properly persuaded. I had no doubt that the Court had the means to squeeze the truth out of almost anyone, and Donovan must have known that. Whether he decided to play nice with Cathal was another matter.

I switched to watching all the workers gathered in the area, searching for cues in their behavior. The mythborn were exchanging worried glances, suggesting they had secrets they'd rather not share with the Court, and in turn, their apprehension made humanborn fidgety.

"Easy, lads," Donovan said again. "Nobody wants bloodshed here, eh?"

The tension eased a notch, but I could bet that they wouldn't listen to him much longer. Sooner or later, one of them would snap, and others would follow, because there were only six of us, and even if some of them had heard of the Scáthanna, they likely thought it would be easy to overwhelm us with their sheer numbers.

Donovan looked at Cathal, his expression less challenging. "I know we'd both rather not have the Court involved, so I tell you what... Come back tomorrow, ceannasaí. In the meantime, I'll ask a few questions"—his eyes moved from face to face, and some of his associates shrank under his stern gaze—"and hand over anyone who shouldn't be here to you. You have my word."

Cathal shook his head. "Not when the Snake is involved."

Donovan grimaced. "You going as far as accusing me?"

"If I have to," Cathal replied with a stern expression.

Sadb turned casually, as if scanning the surroundings, and looked at me. Then, without moving her head, she glanced toward the darker part of the warehouse. I gave a slight nod and engaged my listening skill. I didn't expect to hear much if someone there was trying to keep quiet, but to my surprise, I immediately caught a scrap of a conversation.

"...Donovan will handle it," a woman whispered.

"And what if he doesn't?" a man—mythborn, judging by

the accent—replied in a hushed but argumentative way. "You have to go. Warn him."

"About what? There's no way they made the connection."

"They're here, aren't they? Talking about the Snake." Silence fell for a heartbeat. "Look, just go. Better to tell him too much than too little. You know how quick he is to punish anyone..."

"Ugh. You don't have to remind me." Disgust and fear rang in the woman's voice.

I couldn't be certain, of course, but the way she spoke about the man or mythborn they wanted to warn made me think of our enemy. It wasn't hard to imagine someone like him being cruel to everyone, including the people who were his allies or lackeys.

There wasn't time any for explanations, as the mythborn said, "Go!" but Sadb needed none. As my hand shot to my weapon, she was already darting between the crates, and I wasn't far behind.

"Hold!" Donovan called out, but it sounded like he was trying to keep his workers in place rather than stop us.

Soon enough, the sounds of fighting behind me followed, but I didn't pay attention to them.

"Get the woman!" I called to Sadb as she jumped on the male mythborn behind the crates.

Her target flinched, but the reaction was too slow to dodge Sadb's powerful strike. He was lucky she wasn't aiming to kill, and he only got a taste of her fist. One day, I'd figure out how she could have so much power in such a sleek body.

The mythborn thumped against the wall and slumped down while Sadb was already dashing out through the side door, cracked open enough to indicate where the woman must have gone.

I slowed down enough to drop a sleep curse on the unconscious mythborn. I didn't doubt Sadb's force, but if he came to while we were chasing the other target, he could slip away, and we'd lose a source of information.

When I got to the door, a wave of hot air reached me as an explosion tore through the small backyard. The flames died quickly, indicating a curse as the source, and I moved to the side, away from the door, frantically looking around. Sadb! Where was she?! My eyes adjusted to the darkness enough for me to catch a dark figure climbing onto the brick wall surrounding the yard.

I wouldn't make it across in time, so I threw a curse. It landed short of the target, but it didn't have to hit her—stun curses affected the area all around them. As soon as it made contact with the ground, it erupted with magic. The woman on the wall grunted as she let go and fell. The thump of her body hitting concrete was satisfying.

Movement to the side made me leap away, but it was Sadb rushing to the woman and delivering a nasty kick to her side. Even watching it made my own body hurt, though I was certain that Sadb had never used this kind of force on me. No such luck for the Snake's servant.

Sadb lifted the woman and delivered a punch to her face, and I suspected it was more of a statement than a real need to subdue her opponent. Thin smoke was rising from her uniform, and it emanated magic.

"Are you okay?" I asked.

It would be like Sadb to ignore some mortal wound just to get to her quarry.

"Just minor burns. She missed," Sadb replied. "Good job with the curse." She looked around, her eyes narrow and watchful, then pushed the woman toward me. "Let's get back inside. Keep an eye on her."

Dazed and beaten, the woman offered no resistance. As she wobbled, barely standing on her own, I did a quick search of her belongings in case she had more of those explosive curses. Instead, I found a very familiar medallion in her pocket... a three-headed snake triskelion.

If I was inclined toward any compassion or under-standing for the woman, it evaporated immediately, and I dragged her back into the building wishing she'd try to resist. My punches might not be as hard as Sadb's, but I had a lot of pent-up anger that would add some power to them.

The inside was quiet already, and hushed moans of pain indicated that whatever fight had taken place, it was finished. Sadb was dragging the unconscious mythborn we'd knocked out moments ago into the middle, where Cathal and Donovan stood in the exact spots I last saw them, save Cathal's hand on his sword. The rest... Many of Donovan's workers lay on the floor, dead or injured, and few pressed their backs against the crates with their hands up and eyes wide.

"You just *had* to make a bloody mess, didn't you?" Donovan asked angrily.

Cathal ignored his comment, and when he looked at me, I threw him the triskelion. His expression hardened as he demonstrated it to Donovan.

"Did you know?" he asked quietly.

"Of course he knew!" Sadb said before the mythborn could reply. "He has humanborn working for him, and they deal with Snake-made curses." She came closer, her sword raised to strike.

All Cathal said was her name, and she froze before the

blade fell, but she didn't move back. I sensed that one wrong word could be Donovan's undoing.

"Does it really matter, ceannasaí?" Faolan took a step closer. "Dead people don't get to tell their side of the story."

I swallowed. I had little compassion for the woman who carried the Snake's symbol and her co-conspirator, and I likely could get over killing Donovan, but if we wanted no witnesses, everyone in the warehouse would have to die. They were all members of the MPF, but it didn't mean they all had taken lives or tried to actively sabotage peace.

"Dead people don't get to confirm your story either," Donovan said calmly.

Sadb's fist, the one holding the blade, tightened.

"Lorcan, fire the flare and alert the Court's guards," Cathal said. "Everyone here will be searched and questioned by them." He looked around. "Anyone who tries to sneak away will die."

"Fair enough," Donovan muttered, but he didn't seem displeased.

"And while we wait, you *will* answer my questions," Cathal added coldly.

Sadb grimaced, and only under Cathal's stern glare did she step away from Donovan. Our ceannasaí led Donovan away, and they engaged in a private conversation. I wanted to eavesdrop on the details, but it was hard to pay attention to their making arrangements, like blaming the dead humanborn on starting this whole mess, when I had to help Sadb with our prisoners.

She was tying their hands behind their backs while I was shamelessly searching through their pockets. I found no clues on the unconscious mythborn, except for another triskelion. One would have to wonder why the Snake's servants insisted on carrying the one thing that could reveal them as enemies, but on the other hand, they had to have something to identify each other. After all, no sane mythborn or humanborn would go about openly saying, "Hey, I serve the Snake, and I'm looking for my buddies."

I glanced back at Cathal and Donovan.

"He'll wriggle out of it again, cursed weasel!" Sadb said, displeased. "We're going to suffer the consequences of going after him either way, but if we killed him, this would have been the last time."

Faolan passed us with a grunt that must have been an agreement, because his expression, as he looked back at where Cathal and the other mythborn stood, was hardly friendly. To say that Donovan wasn't popular among the Scáthanna was the understatement of the year.

Lorcan returned inside, and we were all left with nothing to do except stare at our prisoners. The atmosphere was still heavy, though no one dared to look at us challengingly... or at all, as a matter of fact.

Riagán and Faolan were pulling the dead to the side while Lorcan administered some first aid to those wounded, most likely for no other reason than ensuring our sources of information survived. Sadb was guarding our two main suspects, so I took it upon myself to search the dead. No reason to wait for the Court's guards.

I found a few more triskelia, but nothing that could give us a clue whether these people knew our enemy. This whole thing was starting to feel like a fiasco, and we couldn't even seek comfort in having taken down an MPF unit, because as Sadb said, they'd likely be back in the street and causing problems again soon enough.

The shouts outside drew everyone's attention. Faolan stepped out to greet the arriving guards and explain the situation to them. As soon as he finished, Cathal approached us.

"We take our two prisoners and go. Donovan has every-thing covered here."

He gave a signal, and we headed out.

SOME TWO OR three streets down, Cathal ordered us all into a narrow alley. "Kaja with Sadb, Riagán with Faolan," he said. "Prisoners here, with me and Lorcan. Donovan said she's the one who brought requests from a buyer he'd never met. Including a list of very specific alchemical mixtures."

As I followed Sadb to the one of the exits of the alley, she said gravely, "You better not listen to this one. It won't be pretty."

We positioned ourselves at the edge of the wall, close enough to the main street to see if anyone approached, but still hidden within the alley's deep shadows, and I tried hard not to think that behind me an interrogation was about to happen.

I understood Cathal's rush. If the word of what had happened at Donovan's reached our enemy, he could ensure we didn't find him. The sooner we got information from this woman, the better chance we had of getting him.

Yet it didn't mean I felt at ease. If she didn't speak, Cathal would have to resort to threats or even worse—torture. I shivered. Of course, in the war, atrocities had happened, and I wasn't oblivious that sometimes information was extracted in questionable ways, but I'd chosen not to ask Albert about details. It was enough to know he was uneasy about it and used it as a last resort only. Still, he did allow torture when it was necessary, and *I* allowed myself to forget about it, focusing on my scouting missions instead.

"Perhaps I should listen," I whispered. "I shouldn't pretend this isn't a part of what we have to do sometimes."

War was dirty, and when the enemy didn't play by any civilized rules, it got even nastier. I had no doubt we were still at war. The mythborn had battled against the Snake back in their world and brought that fight over here. Humans just weren't aware of it until recently.

I hoped that when all was done, we'd still had some of humanity—or "mythborn-ity," perhaps—left in us to enjoy the victory and true peace.

Sadb gave me a surprised look. "What we do... is rarely pretty. You, too, will end up doing things that you'll regret for years to come, but nobody expects you to throw away your... heart," she said with an unexpected softness. "We knew accepting a humanborn... a myth-touched in our ranks would mean having someone who thinks in different ways. You've come a long way toward being one of us already. You don't have to rush it."

I swallowed. "Don't I? It seems to me we have little time... for anything."

Behind me, I caught the sound of slapping and a quiet but aggressive conversation, and I looked at Sadb with sudden understanding. "You're trying to distract me so that I don't listen."

She sent me grin. "Since we're not back at the Court, I can't beat you silly and make you forget about everything else for the time being, so talk is all I have. And I'd rather see you sheltered for a little longer than broken and hating yourself. We need you, your contacts, and your skills. We need you sharp-minded."

The thought that the Scáthanna cared about doing the right thing rather than being the truly heartless killers all the humanborn perceived them to be was comforting. Though, on the other hand, I didn't like the idea that the people who were becoming my teammates, or even my family, carried the burdens of all their past deeds while protecting me from the same pain. But as they carried theirs, I had to carry mine for the good of the team: to pretend a little longer that nasty things weren't happening when I wasn't looking closely enough, so that I could focus on helping to find our enemy.

Unfortunately, the sudden noise behind us was hard to ignore.

The woman screamed, but not in pain, more out of desperation... and determination, perhaps? It was only one word, and it sounded Irish, though its meaning escaped me. Involuntarily, I looked over my shoulder just in time to see Cathal and Lorcan scuffle away, both cursing heavily. The woman sat against the wall, her body limp and her face frozen in a scream.

I cursed too, abandoning Sadb and moving closer to them. "Did I miss something on her?" The idea that I might have put everyone in danger because I hadn't been more thorough with my search brought immediate guilt.

Lorcan shook his head. "Likely a killing curse. I'm not surprised some of the Snake's followers use them too."

The woman must have been more than just a pawn. Only a devoted fanatic would give up her life like that.

All three of looked at our second prisoner. The scream must have awoken the mythborn, because he was sitting on the ground, staring wide-eyed at the woman's body. His lips trembled, and his hastened breathing suggested a storm of thoughts and emotions.

I squatted down. "You don't want to do it," I said softly. "You don't have to. We just need a few answers."

He gave me a bitter smile. "You don't know him," he replied quietly. "You don't understand."

I understood all too well, because I'd never forget Cait's mutilated body, and the conversation I'd eavesdropped on suggested our enemy used torture indiscriminately on everyone. "We can protect—"

I didn't get to finish, but I doubted my words would have changed anything. The mythborn's lips pressed into a thin line, his jaw tightening in determination, and then he whispered a word. He faded in an instant, from a living being to a dead body within a breath.

"They're afraid of him," I said. "I think he treats them as badly as he treats his enemies."

Lorcan sighed. "If they all carry the death curse, it'll be hard to make anyone talk." He didn't have to mention that finding another clue would likely be more challenging.

"And those who will be willing to talk likely won't know anything important," Cathal said grimly. "Let's head back."

We fell into formation. Our pace was slower, as if failure weighed down our steps. Riagán, who was guarding the rear with Faolan, caught up to me, and Lorcan fell back without a word. We walked in silence, though from the glances Riagán kept throwing me, I sensed he'd rather talk. There was unease in his expression, as if he wasn't sure how the evening had affected me.

I sent him a weak smile and came closer, allowing my shoulder to brush against his. I hoped he'd know that nothing about what happened had changed my mind about him—and about being part of the Scáthanna.

CHAPTER SIXTEEN

The morning after our unfortunate meeting with Donovan, all of the Scáthanna flocked into the day room. Even Lorcan, whom I'd pegged as the least social of the bunch, was there, sitting on the floor in the corner, preoccupied with some scroll but present none-theless. Cathal was nearby, looking through some notes of his own, and Sadb and Faolan were playing some mythborn game whose rules eluded me. All I could tell was that it involved fruit and knives.

Riagán and I were sitting on a bench, me leaning against his chest as I looked through various charms and let my mind wander. The atmosphere was lighter than I'd expected after the failure and disappointment of the previous night, as if being together eased everyone's mood. There were darker and grimmer undertones to it, sure, but nothing akin to despair. Despite setbacks, the Scáthanna weren't defeated.

A mythborn walked into the room, her faint smile apolo-getic. She wore the outfit of the Court's servants. "Ceannasaí Cathal, the lady requests your presence in her office."

She curtsied and left without waiting for a response. I didn't think she had to, since at the Court, no one in their right mind would refuse Eithne or make her wait. I had a feeling that Cathal enjoyed some freedom in that regard, but I doubted he'd use that privilege without a good reason.

He stood up, gathered his documents, and left.

Everyone in the room looked at me expectantly. I had a good idea what they wanted.

"You can't be serious," I said.

"Better to know than not know," Faolan said. "So you're going to be doing it for the good of the team."

"Don't you think Cathal will tell us afterward?" I asked.

It wasn't that I hadn't eavesdropped on him and Eithne before, but now he *knew* that I could. It felt like I was already caught, even though I hadn't even started yet.

"Normally, yes, but..." Sadb shrugged. "You never know when it comes to him and the lady."

There was a story there, I could tell. "We have time before he gets there," I said. "And if I'm getting in trouble because you all are nosy, I might as well get something in return."

"Back in the other world," Riagán said, "the lady's family estate was besieged by the Snake's servants. They were well fortified, one of the few places that could hold off indefinitely... But they didn't."

I nodded grimly. Betrayal was the Snake's tool of trade, and I'd seen enough in our world to know there was always a way to turn someone, be it with promises or threats.

"Everyone else thought the place was lost, and those who didn't turn to the Snake had been killed. Back then we had to abandon so many places that one more made little difference, though losing a fortress like that one surely hurt everyone's pride," Riagán continued. "Ceannasaí took a small group of seasoned warriors and infiltrated it. From what I've been told, they killed many of the Snake's servants and all of the traitors who had caused the fall of the lady's family. He found and rescued one survivor."

"Eithne," I whispered.

"She wasn't our lady back then. Just a scared young mythborn who'd managed to hide and survive in a fortress full of enemies," Lorcan added, not even looking up from his scroll. "Everyone expected a union between them, and it would be one for the storybooks. Instead, he went on to form the Scáthanna with nine of his initial companions, and she... she engaged in politics, and despite her young age, she gained power and influence."

I looked at each of them. "Any of you?"

Sadb shook her head. "No, it was a long time ago. But Lorcan joined a few years after."

So, out of the original ten, only Cathal remained. I couldn't even imagine the burden of loss he must be carrying with him. His decisions meant life or death for his companions, and I had no doubt that he blamed himself for every single loss, no matter whether he could have prevented it or not. Albert was the same, but he had the whole of Trinity to lead, so not every death touched him personally. Cathal fought alongside his companions and had likely seen more than one of them perish.

"Now you see why we wonder what's really being said when they're alone." Faolan grinned. "Everyone's hoping for a secret romance or at least heartfelt confessions."

I rolled my eyes. Their last conversation I'd eavesdropped on wasn't all that exciting. On the other hand, they were in the garden with many mythborn watching their every gesture. With the Scáthanna members' story filling the blanks of Cathal and Eithne's past, I could see where all that curiosity was coming from. I would not admit it out loud, but it was slightly contagious, especially as I did have the means to learn something.

"Fine," I said. "I'll listen in."

I made myself comfortable, resting my head against Riagán's chest, and he murmured his approval into my ear. Then I closed my eyes.

The Court was familiar grounds to me now. I knew many of the voices well enough to tune them out immediately, and I lingered on those I didn't recognize, moving on only when I got enough of their conversation to know it was not of importance. I almost snickered at the thought that many Court mythborn, maybe including Faolan, with his taste for gossip, would consider some of those conversations crucial. To me, as long as they weren't discussing anything threatening, they could keep their petty secrets and play their political games.

It took a few minutes more before I caught Cathal, but when he spoke, his voice stood out like a beacon. "My lady, you asked to see me," he said.

"Come in," Eithne replied.

There was silence between them for a while, likely Cathal closing the door. Eithne didn't invite him to sit down, but she might have made a gesture to indicate the chair.

"Out of all the mythborn out there, did you have to go after Donovan?" She sounded tired.

"These were unfortunate circumstances," Cathal replied, "but all was settled with Donovan."

"Oh, yes, he confirmed your story about some foolish humanborn attacking you and making a mess," Eithne replied. "But that hardly explains why all of his workers were brought in for questioning, and he was to be held as well. Or why you've been seen departing with two prisoners that had never made it to the Court. Many questions were asked, and some mythborn raised concerns about your private investigation going too far."

"We found proof of the Snake's involvement—"

"I know," Eithne interrupted him impatiently. "But the way it was handled... You put me in a difficult position, ceannasaí."

I almost huffed my disapproval. Even in a private conversation, with no one—well, at least to her knowledge—listening, she was still using his title rather than his name.

"I apologize, my lady. It wasn't my intention."

"Some question whether the Scáthanna still obey my word."

"And that goes along with raising doubts whether you're fit to lead," he said with bitter irony. "They'll cling to any reason to have your influence and authority limited."

"I can't afford to lose a step. The situation's becoming more and more tense, and the mythborn outside Baile Átha Cliath aren't happy with our efforts to maintain peace and cooperation. If they see any weakness or an opening..."

The way she put it, combined with the tone of her voice —it sounded quite dire. Perhaps I should make more effort to eavesdrop on mythborn in the Court. If I found anything she would be able to use against her political opponents, this could tip the scales of power in her favor, and Cathal wouldn't have to reveal how he'd obtained the information.

"As much as I understand that your team has its own struggles, I need to show you still obey my word. I'm going to grant the Keeper of Flowers' request," Eithne said. "You will investigate the shriek sightings."

"I'd rather be of use to you, my lady, than run errands for a mythborn who can't make do without a few extra flowers."

"Do not speak so dismissively about our people's

customs, no matter how trivial you consider them. They were what made us survive all those years when the Snake's forces were closing on us." Anger rang in Eithne's voice.

Cathal's response was so quiet, I almost missed it. "Or they were what made us lose that war."

"If you have something to say, speak up." Apparently, Eithne had missed it, and it was likely for the better. She wouldn't like his response.

"We might be walking into a trap," Cathal said. I wasn't surprised he chose not to voice his other thought louder.

"Then take only the strongest warriors with you," Eithne replied. "If you're concerned about Kaja... I have enough guards to spare a few, or, if you prefer, I can officially request her presence by my side. I'm sure it's time I tapped into the vast knowledge your new scout has about Trinity and its leader."

I swallowed hard. I was almost, *almost* certain she was mentioning it only as an official excuse that would keep me safe at the Court, but Eithne was a player who used all the resources she had at her disposal. At some point, it wouldn't be an excuse but a goal.

"Thank you for the offer, my lady, but the Scáthanna watch over their own. Lorcan still has a lot to teach her, so this will be a good opportunity for them to catch up on some lessons." There was a slight pause. Perhaps he was getting up from his seat. "As for your request... The Scáthanna will set out immediately. I would appreciate if you kept the news of our departure quiet for a while. No need to give our enemy more opportunities for foul play."

"I will. And I appreciate your willingness to help, ceannasaí."

"All is for my lady."

The way he said it... I couldn't help thinking there was

deep caring in his voice. Perhaps something more? I hated the idea that Cathal was in love with Eithne and she didn't reciprocate his affection. This one thing, I decided, I wouldn't share with the rest of the team. Whatever his feelings were, they deserved some privacy.

I quickly relayed the gist of the conversation to the others. They made no interruptions, listening carefully to what I was saying, though I couldn't help feeling that they were slightly disappointed.

"You know, we were hoping for a secret love story, not to be sent on a stupid errand for the keeper," Faolan teased.

"Am I supposed to make up things next time?" I fired back.

Instead of a reply, he gave me a worryingly encouraging grin.

Sadb got up from her seat. "We better get ready. Ceannasaí's right. The quicker we leave, the less chance our enemy will be able to set up something."

Faolan stood up as well, and they both headed for the door. Behind me, Riagán shifted with reluctance. I moved, letting him get up before he decided to steal a few more moments. He still leaned over and kissed me, making it longer than just a quick smooch, and there was everything in that kiss, from caring to desire, as if he wanted to give me a memory for the time he wasn't around. I kissed him back with the same intensity.

I could swear Lorcan looked up from his scroll that very moment, but he said nothing, and when Riagán moved away, Lorcan was the same way he was before. As Riagán left, an eerie silence hung in the day room. I glanced at the only mythborn around, but he seemed preoccupied with his task, and I wasn't sure whether he'd be up for some questions, especially ones that were only meant to sate my curiosity.

Cathal walked in, already wearing his full gear, and paused, looking around the almost empty room in slight surprise.

"They're getting ready," I said, feeling the burn of blush on my cheeks. There was little point in trying to conceal the truth.

It took him only a second to put two and two together, and he arched his eyebrow. "Weren't the humanborn the ones who invented the idea of privacy?" he asked dryly, though without anger.

"They also have a saying that all is fair in love and war," I challenged.

He smirked, but when he spoke, there was a warning in his tone. "And which one do you suggest applies in these circumstances?"

I knew when to keep my mouth shut, so I gave only a noncommittal shrug.

This time he offered me a genuine smile. "I suppose this serves me well, as I was the one to tell you the Scáthanna keep no secrets from each other." He sat down at the bench and helped himself to an apple. As he bit into it, he watched me intently. "You know you aren't going, then."

I nodded. It wasn't something I would argue about. "If you need Lorcan as well..."

Cathal shook his head. "If it's not a trap, it's going to be a straightforward hunt. Shrieks are common enough outside of the cities and back in our world, so most militant myth-born know how to hunt one safely. We're going because the Keeper of Flowers is trying to undermine the lady's position."

"But what if it *is* a trap? The MPF works with the Snake

and has the support of the mythborn outside of Dublin. What if they're all being manipulated?"

"Then I want you and Lorcan out of harm's way," Cathal said. He didn't dismiss my suspicions, which suggested he had his own. "You'll both stay here, in our quarters. The lady has agreed to post her trusted guards at the entrance, so they can assist you."

"But the lady..." I didn't finish when the obvious dawned on me. "That wasn't the end of your conversation."

"You've eavesdropped on me before, so I expected you might do it again and made my own provisions."

I couldn't help thinking he was amused that he'd managed to outwit me and perhaps even keep some things truly private.

"You shouldn't have told me. Now I know the trick."

He gave me a warm smile as he shook his head. "I meant what I said, Kaja. The Scáthanna have no secrets. It's not your fault that some of our team members are looking for things that aren't there."

I arched my eyebrow at that, because he *knew* that I'd actually heard how he spoke to Eithne in private. He might have spoken the truth about some passionate romance not being there, but it didn't mean there wasn't any love between them. I was sure Faolan would enjoy the tragic story of two would-be lovers separated by their duties, but I doubted Cathal would appreciate my speculations—because, of course, I had no proof. The way he looked at me made it clear I'd never get any, even if I made it my life's mission to listen in on his every conversation.

Shuffling outside of the room made his head turn. "Time to go. Stay safe, you both." He took one last bite of the apple and left it unfinished on a plate. "Do not leave the quarters unless you have no other choice."

Both Lorcan and I nodded. The Court was our haven, but it didn't mean it was safe. In the past, there had been explosives planted, and the Snake's spies posed as loyal members, so our enemy could have the means to reach us even here.

I listened to the rest of the team heading out. Cathal scolded them for abusing my listening skill, but just like with me, he didn't seem truly upset. Some ten minutes later, I lost them, suggesting they were making a good pace and were out of my skill's range quickly.

"Nobody was testing you on purpose today, but nevertheless, you did well," Lorcan said approvingly. "We appreciate that you're trying your best, especially given the circumstances." He put away the scroll. "I notice you glancing at me earlier. Was there something you wanted to ask?"

I hesitated, searching for the right words. "Sadb said you've been with the Scáthanna the longest, and I'd like to... hear some stories, if you're willing to share. Good, bad, serious, or lighthearted—anything, really. It's easier to learn and understand through stories, especially things that no one would even think to teach me."

"I'm not much of a storyteller," Lorcan replied, and I sensed some hesitation, "but I can tell you of some missions we did before we came to this world, and how Cathal approached the problems we faced." He moved to the table and poured himself some water. "Get comfortable. It'll take some time."

CHAPTER SEVENTEEN

Sweat was pouring off me as I repeatedly struck at an imaginary Sadb, then tried to dodge her equally imaginary strikes. Since the real Sadb wasn't here, I had a much better success rate, and my bruise count was close to zero. I was sure I got one or two when I tried to practice a smooth roll and getting on my feet quickly, but they were nothing in comparison to the collection I'd amass if Sadb was here.

Now that she wasn't, I found myself missing her scathing comments and scant praise. Fighting shadows felt like half-baked training, and I could hardly find satisfaction in defeating the imaginary Sadb.

What I did find instead was a lot of fear.

It'd been two days since Cathal and the others had left on their absurd assignment. He hadn't told us when they'd be back, and if they traveled far into the countryside, it could take weeks, but it didn't stop me from worrying. I was certain the keeper's request was a ploy to draw them away from the Court, and they were walking straight into an ambush. I pictured them dead, wounded, dying, tortured, surrounded... All the possible scenarios ran through my head as frequently as I took a breath.

Training helped some, because not only did I have to focus on my own moves, I also had to invent strikes and ripostes for my imaginary opponent.

After Lorcan spent the first day with me telling stories—or rather, giving accounts—of old missions, he subtly indicated that he'd rather be alone. It was hard to argue that we should sit together in the day room, staring at each other to make sure we were safe. The quarters were as secure as they could be, so we could just as well be doing something else.

He didn't avoid me, of course, and we passed each other in the showers or shared the odd meal, but he didn't seek my company, and I felt he'd prefer I leave him be, so I was left to my own devices—which meant training and working on my arsenal of charms and curses.

With my muscles weak from the workout I'd put myself through, I declared my defeat against imaginary Sadb, hung my head in shame as I tried to conjure appropriate comments from her, and headed downstairs. A long shower would help my body recover, and I'd deal with my worries later. Seeing as there was no one around, I considered conjuring an imaginary Riagán to accompany me in the showers, but somehow I was certain it would end up in disappointment. My imagination couldn't beat reality anyway, and I'd end up just worrying more.

I caught movement in the corner of my eye, so I turned with words of greeting to Lorcan. Instead, I saw a mythborn in a servant's outfit by one of the doors. The dull color of his outfit contrasted with his vibrant green hair and skin that shimmered like it had little scales.

It wasn't uncommon for the servants to enter the Scáthanna's quarters, bringing food, cleaning, collecting laundry, and restocking towels, but he was looking awfully guilty.

"Are you looking for someone?" I asked in a friendly way, hoping that I looked non-threatening.

As soon as I took a step in his direction, he darted away.

One of the perks of having worked in an international company before the war was the cultural and linguistic diversity of my coworkers, so as I chased the servant, I could swear in many more languages than I actually spoke. Too bad those curses weren't real curses—I could use a stun one at that very moment, but all I had were a few mock-ups from training.

"Stop him!" I yelled, hoping the guards outside our quarters would hear me.

The mythborn fished something out of his pocket and threw it at the doorway. Great, *he* had curses! There wasn't any explosion, so it had to be stun or sleep, and I braced myself in case he threw another one my way. Instead, he ran out of the door.

Chasing him was a bad idea.

He might have accomplices outside our quarters. This all could be a ruse to lure me out. He might even throw a nasty curse back into the corridor when he cleared it.

Yet I had no choice. After not getting anything from our raid on Donovan's place, we had no other clue or direction, and this mythborn could provide information we desperately needed.

So, I ran after him, ignoring my muscles' protest after the workout I'd just put myself through.

The courtyard was mostly empty, but there were guards

at the side gate, and some mythborn running errands, so I shouted, "Stop him!"

The guards stirred, and two out of the four headed in our direction. The mythborn I was chasing changed his route, heading for one of the Court's entrances. Despite my tiredness, I forced myself to pick up my pace even more. If he got inside, it would be easy for him to lose me in the many corridors. I didn't know the Court's layout well enough to anticipate the route he'd choose.

He made it all the way to the door, but by then, I was on his heels. A few more steps, and I'd be able to grab him.

The mythborn disappeared inside, and as a silhouette moved into the doorframe, I instinctively leaped away. It took only a second to recognize the person, but I'd already lost my momentum.

"Out of my way, keeper!" I barked. If I was lucky, I could still catch up to the culprit.

Of course, she didn't move from her spot, as if she had never intended to walk out that door.

"How dare you, commoner?"

Clearly, she hadn't bothered to remember my face from our last encounter, and my wearing plain workout clothes didn't help. I considered pushing my way past her, but these moments our exchange had taken meant my target was likely gone already.

"If you have a problem with me, bring it up with Ceannasaí Cathal," I replied. "I will surely inform him that your behavior aided the escape of a Snake spy." I had no proof, of course, but with that mythborn already gone, she had to take my word for it.

Her face changed, and for a blink, it showed fear. If I had to guess, she didn't have anything to do with the Snake or our enemy. She was just a prideful, shortsighted, power-drunk mythborn who cared little about any greater good as long as she got what she wanted.

Her expression shifted immediately, as if she'd gotten her control back, and her perfect, full lips twisted in a grimace. "You little, worthless myth-touched..." she hissed, her choice of words suggesting that she'd finally recognized me. "How dare you accuse your betters? You're here only because the lady took pity on you, and Cathal had no choice but to resort to recruiting the likes of you after the recent—"

"I'd be careful with your words, keeper." Lorcan approached from behind. Unlike me, he wore his uniform, and looked every bit as dangerous as a Scáthanna member should. "You've already put yourself at risk once because of the words you chose. The second time, you might not be so lucky."

Her beautiful face went a shade paler. "I think we're done here. Tell Cathal to train his experiments better. She hardly even looks the part."

Lorcan looked at her coldly. "The right look or not, she could take you down all the same. Think on it, keeper." He gestured at me to follow, and turned away.

I paid no attention to the keeper anymore, letting her stew in her own hate, disdain, or whatever other feelings she chose to poison herself with, and caught up to Lorcan.

"What happened?" he asked as we were approaching the entrance to our quarters. The guards from the gate were helping their stunned companions up.

"I saw a mythborn servant in our corridor poking his head into our quarters. When I questioned him, he ran," I said. "I almost had him, too, when the keeper got in my way."

Lorcan grimaced. "She dares to speak to us about

unearned privileges... The lady granted her more power than this mythborn deserves."

I was already piecing that together from the way the Scáthanna had treated her and Cathal's remarks during his conversation with Eithne, but I understood little of what the Keeper of Flowers' duties and position really were. It sure would be nice to learn more about the Court's customs, no matter how useless and stupid they were... One day, when I ran out of more important matters to see to.

"Do you think we should search the quarters for any curses he might have left?" I asked.

He shook his head. "Our enemy wants information. Killing us would get him nothing. It's likely that he heard the Scáthanna had set out, and sent someone to snoop around. But if you got a good look at him, give his description to the guards. Whether he was a real servant or not, he won't get to move freely around the Court anymore." He stood by the door to his room. "I'll be here if you need anything."

There was a pang of disappointment as he disappeared inside. After that encounter, as fruitless as all of our recent attempts to gain the upper hand against the mythborn who hunted us, I could use some company, but at the same time, my comfort wasn't more important than Lorcan's, and he wanted to be alone. I had to respect that and deal with my own feelings.

If the rest of the team didn't return the next day, I could send a message to Connor and see if he'd be willing to hang out. Making more curses together would be a good distraction.

But first, I needed a shower. After how the clash with the keeper went, I wanted to look presentable and wear my uniform before I talked to the guards. I had a feeling they'd listen more carefully if I did.

~

Two days after the unexpected intrusion, I felt with certainty that Lorcan wasn't in our quarters anymore. It wasn't even that I couldn't hear him. For my skill to pick him up, he'd have to talk to someone, and we were the only two people around, save some irregular servants, now diligently checked by the guards outside before they were permitted entry. Even without the skill, I never caught his footsteps or the door creaking, and there was never a sign of his having eaten any food in the day room. Of course, he could be avoiding me, but since he hadn't behaved like that in the previous few days, I was betting that he'd left. To where, and why, I had no idea. I couldn't even tell when exactly it had happened.

The longer his absence lasted, the harder it became to believe he was still somewhere around the Court, perhaps spending time with a friend. Even if Cathal made it clear we shouldn't leave the Scáthanna's quarters, he likely wouldn't mind that much if we still stayed on the Court's grounds. Lorcan had to have gone way further than that.

The lack of knowledge was the worst part. He hadn't left any message, at least not one meant for me.

Part of me wanted to head out and try to find him before the others returned. The other—more reasonable—part was adamant about staying put. Either Lorcan would return on his own, and all would be good, or he had been captured or killed, and by searching for him, I'd put myself in danger. One member gone was bad enough, and two spelled a disaster. Not to mention that I wasn't particularly keen on becoming a victim of some twisted torturer, and I also had no illusion that, in the unlikely event of my finding Lorcan, I'd be able to rescue him by myself. So I had no other alternative but to stay in the quarters.

Needless to say, being alone and having no clue what was happening to the rest of my team was agonizing in that mind-wrenching, gut-twisting, and unsettling way.

With nothing else to do, I practiced my listening skill, learning way too much about the Court's petty politics, mythborn crushes, and stupid schemes, getting adept on tuning out conversations and jumping between them, but I never learned anything of use. This seemed to be the theme of recent weeks, with every clue amounting to nothing, and it didn't help my mood.

I almost regretted that Cathal hadn't taken Eithne up on her offer of babysitting me. If I was to perform mental and verbal gymnastics dodging her inquiries about Trinity and Albert, at least I wouldn't have time to worry. I'd likely get frustrated, though. Playing mythborn games wasn't on my list of favorite pastimes.

Everything felt like a failure. *I* felt like a failure, and being idle and stuck only reassured me that I was right to think so. Anyone else in my place would have already come up with new plans, solutions, contacts to reach out to... and I was sitting alone in the Scáthanna's quarters, useless.

I hadn't felt like that since I witnessed my sister dying by a giant's hand. Or maybe since I witnessed one of my companions unexpectedly succumbing to the affliction, and we had to put her down like a rabid creature. Or since...

There were too many failures, too many moments in my life when I was helpless.

I forced my thoughts onto another path. Remembering all my past failures and figuring out once again whether I could have done something to prevent those events would cause me to become even more useless. Having a clear mind at least left some hope that I'd come up with a clever plan.

Maybe another locating charm... I hesitated. To barge into Lorcan's room and rummage through his things felt wrong, so I abandoned the idea. Yet if he didn't return by the time the others were back, I could suggest it to Cathal. Besides, for all I knew, Lorcan might have left a note to our ceannasaí in his office or somewhere else. I wouldn't be happy with such a display of mistrust over my ability to pass the message, but I could understand. After all, if he wanted to leave undisturbed, I couldn't have known about it.

I just had to be patient and wait for everyone to return.

Until then, all I could do was to find a solution to our biggest problem—the faceless, elusive enemy hunting us—and stuck alone in the quarters, I had plenty of time to do so. Too bad that my ideas weren't plenty.

I sat in the day room, looking through my old notes on curse and charm crafting. With the knowledge that Connor had shared with me, I could update some of them. Even though I didn't expect any trouble, I was wearing my uniform along with my weapon and some curses. I couldn't help thinking that the intruder wouldn't have gotten away if I'd worn it back then, even if doing so would have been impractical for training.

I half listened to what was going on in the Court, growing tired with the trivial and shallow conversation that made up the majority of what I eavesdropped on. Every now and then, I caught some tactical planning or political discussions, but they also felt of no consequence, since I had a hard time putting them into any broader context.

One, though, caught my attention, as I recognized a participating voice.

"Why aren't we allowed in?" Connor asked. "I've been welcomed in the Scáthanna's quarters before."

"We have orders to not let anyone in," a guard replied.

These weren't exactly the orders, as far as I knew. On the other hand, Lorcan might have told them so and forgotten to let me know.

I sprang to my feet and rushed out of the room. Connor definitely wasn't a threat, and I was desperate for some company. I made it to the entrance in record time, but once there, I slowed down enough to make my approach look casual.

"Are there any problems?" I asked the guards.

Connor stood nearby, nothing in his posture suggesting he was unhappy with the delay, and he brightened at the sight of me.

"Now that the member of the Scáthanna is here to vouch for me, will we be granted entry?" he asked.

The "we" part caught my attention. Behind Connor stood Clíodhna, looking less than her usual proud self. There was something apprehensive about her behavior, as if she didn't like being around but had no other choice. Still, from the little I'd gotten to know her, I would have expected her to express her displeasure for everyone to hear rather than behave in a way that could be considered meek.

"Let them in," I said, and walked back into the corridor, hoping that would stop any further discussions.

The guards didn't seem the types to argue, and soon the sound of Connor's uneven footsteps followed me in. Clíodhna walked in as well, more reluctant.

With the choice of the day room and my own room, I pointed at the former. "Please, come in. Make yourself comfortable."

Connor had already been here, but this must be the first

time for Clíodhna. She looked around with curiosity and slight surprise, suggesting she hadn't expected meager furnishing and the lack of any lavish decorations. I'd never thought of it, but the quarters stood out in comparison to the rest of the Court, which boasted subtle ornaments and trinkets everywhere—nothing gaudy, but enough to project messages of wealth and status. The Scáthanna's quarters had none of that.

While he sat down, she still lingered in the middle of the room, looking uncertain.

"What can I help you with?" I asked Connor. It seemed better to not add to Clíodhna's discomfort by addressing her.

Connor, though, looked straight at Clíodhna. She fidgeted. Swallowed. Looked at me and then away. Finally, she squared her shoulders ever so slightly and said, "I heard the Scáthanna are looking for a mythborn intruder... Someone with green hair and shimmery skin."

I gave her an encouraging nod.

"Well, it might be nothing, but I saw someone like that a few days ago. Talking to one of the servants in the kitchens. I think her name is Eabha..." She paused, looking at me with concern. "I'm quite sure they know I saw them."

She didn't have to say more. I could imagine fear nagging her enough for her to confide in Connor, who, in turn, convinced her to come here. He gave her a nod, and his neutral expression softened a bit, as if he were praising her for having done the right thing.

"You have the Scáthanna's gratitude for sharing this information," I said. "I'll let ceannasaí know, and he'll act accordingly."

As Clíodhna looked at me, I saw fear flash on her face. "Will I be in danger because of that?"

The truth was, I didn't know the answer to that question. Reasonably, I doubted that either Eabha or the intruder she'd spoken to remembered that Clíodhna had witnessed them talking, but I couldn't give reassurances. Who knew how perceptive mythborn were and how they connected facts?

"I don't think you are in danger because you saw them," I replied. It'd been two days, so if they cared about what Clíodhna saw, they would have acted already. "And if you're willing to participate in a little deception, no one will ever know you were the one to bring us this information."

She looked at me with suspicion. "What do you have in mind?"

I couldn't help smiling, because I was certain she wouldn't oppose my idea. "If you storm out of here being loud about how I insulted you or how you won't be the one to apologize, it would seem to any witnesses that we had some sort of an altercation, and it was likely a private matter that brought you here. People will gossip, but then, they always do." I shrugged. "And I don't care what kind of story you tell about what happened here."

"You would give me such power over you?" She arched her eyebrow with disbelief. I could almost see the wild stories about me she was considering telling.

"I would if it ensures you're out of harm's way." I doubted anything she did could harm me in any real way, and it would be interesting to see how far she'd dare go with my permission given.

Clíodhna nodded, and I didn't expect more than that. After all, this was a transaction, and my offer was a payment for her willingness to share what she knew. She looked at Connor. "Let's go."

Connor moved, but instead of getting off the bench, he

stumbled, and slight pain twisted his face. Clíodhna paled and looked away. Then, without a word, she left the room.

I shook my head at her as I approached Connor to help him. "Worse day today, I take it?"

"Can't only have good days, right?" His smile was forced, and the corner of his lip trembled as if he was trying to conceal a grimace. "Otherwise I wouldn't appreciate them anymore." He arched his eyebrows as I pulled him up. "You've become stronger."

"At the cost of many bruises, I assure you."

He chuckled.

"You know," I said, letting him go when he caught his balance, "you could have come alone."

Once he'd learned about Eabha from Clíodhna, there was no need to drag her all the way here. Not to mention that if he was alone, we could have a much longer conversation, and a more pleasant one too.

"I could have." His reply was that of acknowledgment, not agreement. He looked at the open door. "But Clíodhna has some growing up to do."

Hearing the caring so clear in his voice, I said nothing. I might consider his cousin immature and spoiled, and Connor wasn't oblivious to those traits either, but there had to be something more to her that made him consider her worth the effort. I had a hard time believing it was only sentiment or love. Connor was too mature to allow himself to be blinded like that.

"See you around, Kaja." He left, his limp marking the uneven rhythm of his steps.

As they were leaving the quarters, I eavesdropped on them to know what kind of story I'd have to confirm later.

Clíodhna did make quite a scene, but to my surprise, it wasn't any tall tale. She was just complaining that no matter how beneficial Connor deemed knowing a Scáthanna member, associating with a myth-touched was beneath their status. Even though she spoke of how unrefined the myth-touched were and how bluntly humanborn they could be in their ways, it didn't feel like she was trying too hard to exert the "power" over me that I'd given her.

Perhaps there was more to that mythborn female that, until now, I'd thought to be a typical Court noble, and Connor was right—she just had some growing up to do.

CHAPTER EIGHTEEN

As much as I wanted to find Eabha the minute Connor and Clíodhna left, I didn't do it. With Lorcan gone, I was on my own, and everything that required leaving our quarters seemed like an unnecessary risk. Part of me argued that nothing would happen to me within the Court, and even if someone tried anything, I had enough training to defend myself, but I couldn't shake off my instinctive fears. If I was wrong and something *did* happen, the rest of the team would arrive back at the Court with both Lorcan and me gone and no knowledge of what happened to us.

And, in the end, time wasn't of the essence anymore. Either Eabha had already fled the Court, if she was an accomplice to the intruder, or she was still working in the kitchens, unaware and unsuspecting. This could wait, and I could wait too, no matter how anxious I was to do something... *anything*.

So, with nothing else to do, and with the notes of charms and curses looking boring after the two days I'd spent working on them, I engaged my skill. I doubted the conversations around the Court would provide me with any clues, but at least I could amuse myself with the thought of getting to know all the latest gossip. If nothing else, maybe I could win some points with Faolan if I offered to share it.

"Now, with Kaja around, you'll have to watch out for what you *thought* she didn't hear you saying."

I almost jumped at the sound of Sadb's voice, but my heart sank a little when I realized I'd likely picked up a distant conversation. Yet it had to mean they were coming back!

Then Faolan's laughter sounded in the corridor, and I actually jumped up, rushing out of my room. I didn't care whether I looked like an overeager puppy. I just wanted to make sure they were all fine.

Cathal was first, of course. His uniform bore marks of dirt and blood and was torn in places, but he walked on his own, and I noticed no sign of serious wounds. Behind him, Faolan and Riagán, equally battered but alive.

Sadb was last, protecting their rear, and even she looked less perfect than her usual unbreakable warrioress image. Yet she still nudged Faolan with an amused "Told you."

They all shuffled, ready to go about their business, likely showers, food, and bed, not necessarily in that order, but Cathal was still looking at me, and he lifted his hand. Everyone stopped what they were doing.

"Lorcan?" Cathal asked quietly. He must have read trouble from my expression.

I shook my head. "I don't know. He didn't tell me anything. I'm guessing he left some time after the incident with a servant."

Without any prompting, I relayed the short and eerie encounter, including the Keeper of Flowers' appearance. I didn't believe she had anything to do with what happened, but I didn't know her as well as the others did, so she could have fooled me.

"The guards, of course, found no servant or other mythborn fitting my description, but I've received information that a mythborn named Eabha working in the kitchens might have spoken to her. I have not... approached her yet," I finished awkwardly. Would Cathal had expected me to have acted?

He looked to the side, at Sadb and Riagán. "Once you clean up and change, bring her over if she's still around. Tell whoever's her superior that she might have knowledge beneficial to Court matters. No need to alarm the people she will have to work with later."

They nodded with solemn expressions and headed for the showers. On his way, Riagán shot me a glance of apology. I didn't think it was necessary—we were both on the team, and Scáthanna business was more important than any personal affections—but I appreciated the thought.

Cathal turned back to me. "And what of Lorcan?"

"Some time later, I noticed Lorcan wasn't here, and I couldn't... *locate* him anywhere around the Court," I replied, careful not to mention my skill directly. With the days of solitude having fueled my paranoia, it didn't feel safe to mention it even here. "I thought it'd be better if I didn't set out on my own to look for him."

He waved at Faolan. "Check with the guards. See if they know anything about his departure."

Faolan left without delay.

I hesitated. "Ceannasaí... He might have left on his own, maybe to see a friend or chase down a clue. He might have not told me because our orders were clear. But he's been gone long enough to suggest that he's in trouble. I know it didn't work the last time, but maybe we should try making a tracking charm again. The sooner, the better."

As the last charm stopped working when Cait died, we had to act quickly. We'd already lost who knew how much time, because I didn't know when Lorcan left or when he was captured—if at all.

Cathal gestured for me to follow, and we entered Lorcan's room. It looked... pristine. Not spartan, not meager, not minimalistic—pristine. As if Lorcan had never lived there.

"All of his personal belongings are gone," Cathal said in surprise.

Seeing as Lorcan had partaken in the search for Cait and knew of the locating charms, the message was clear. He didn't want to be found. I looked at Cathal, but he shook his head.

"I have no explanation for this," he said. "Lorcan wouldn't abandon the Scáthanna."

I could hear confusion in his voice. Lorcan's behavior made as little sense to him as it did to me.

"We'll let everyone know once they're back."

"How did the hunt go?" I asked.

He gave me a tired glance. "We killed all three shrieks. The keeper will have flowers for her important ceremonies." He paused as if considering something. "Perhaps you should go and observe one day. From what I know of you, you don't to seem to be overly spiritual, but you would learn something of our customs, even if I personally find them hollow."

I arched an eyebrow. "It's more likely that I'll annoy the keeper with my presence," I said with a hint of sarcasm. "Especially if I admit that I attended following your suggestion."

Undoubtedly, the keeper would suspect Cathal had sent me for the sole purpose of annoying her, and she would be offended by my presence alone, but I could think of many other ways to make her experience even worse.

That earned me a smile, and he waved a finger at me. "Don't get ahead of yourself, Kaja. We'll make another enemy when we're done with this one."

I cherished the ring of amusement in his words. I knew that soon enough his many concerns would return, but for this heartbeat, I'd made his mood lighter. That was what team members, *family* members, were supposed to do for each other.

He left Lorcan's room, and I followed.

As we walked down the corridor, Faolan returned. He shook his head as soon as he saw us. "The guards don't know anything. Members of the Scáthanna don't get questioned upon their departure, so no one even paid attention to Lorcan leaving."

My first reaction was that we had to question everyone, because somebody would have noticed something. My second reaction was surrender. A witness could tell us when Lorcan left exactly, and perhaps whether he was alone, but nothing beyond that. We'd waste time and learn nothing, likely annoying people around the Court in the process.

Cathal nodded. "That's all. Get cleaned up and changed. I'll call for you once Sadb and Riagán are back." He glanced at me while Faolan was already taking off. "Being both alone and unable to do anything must have been a torment. I appreciate that you endured. Otherwise, we could have come home to more questions than answers."

The tone of his voice reassured me that those weren't empty words. Cathal recognized that I'd learned my lessons and was trying to be a part of the team. I didn't reply, but I doubted he expected any response to his praise.

"Wait for the others in the day room," he said. "I'll be there shortly. If Sadb and Riagán bring Eabha before I'm back, ask them all to wait."

"Yes, ceannasaí."

The corner of his lip twitched and a flash of amusement passed over his face, but he said nothing as he headed for the showers, and I had a strong feeling that he remembered the humanborn Kaja who didn't accept his orders so readily... but our relationship had changed since then, and I'd changed as well.

And even if I wouldn't admit it out loud, saving the leftovers of my pride, he could claim it as his victory. Even Albert hadn't managed to muster such a level of deference observance in me, so Cathal deserved all the credit for finding a way to harness my insubordinate nature.

To mythborn, Eabha probably looked plain. Her skin resembled a human's, its only somewhat unnatural feature being the hue of a strong tan that was nearly unachievable in Eireland even before the Magiclysm, unless someone went on vacation abroad. Her hair, straight and cut at chin level, had that ash-blond color that never drew attention. Yet she was a mythborn, so her eyes of vibrant cobalt were beautiful.

She stood in the day room, fidgeting, and she looked from me to Faolan and back, making an effort to avoid meeting Cathal's eyes. With Sadb and Riagán behind her, as they'd let her enter first, she had to feel trapped.

I sent her a warm, comforting smile.

"Please, take a seat," Cathal said. "Or perhaps you'd prefer to talk in my office."

"No, 'tis fine, ceannasaí," she replied so quickly, it had all the hallmarks of desperation. "I was told youse have questions?" She didn't move from her spot, making it clear she wasn't about to sit down, despite the invitation.

I didn't understand why she, without a doubt uneasy in the presence of all of us, didn't take Cathal's offer to have a private conversation. I could see how he intimidated her more than anyone else, but since we were all on his team, she wasn't really safer here than she was in his office if he wanted to do something underhanded.

"Yes, about a mythborn you might know. A male with green hair and shimmering skin."

While Riagán made his way around, to sit down by the wall opposite me and Faolan, Sadb stayed where she was, leaning against the doorframe. Her pose seemed casual, but I had no doubt that she'd chosen the spot to block the only way out of the room.

Eabha looked at Cathal, confused. "You mean Calbhach? I know him because he's courting my spouse's cousin. He's a messenger, so he stops by to chat whenever he's at the Court."

"A messenger?" Cathal asked.

"With Emerald Messages." She looked at him with suspicion. "What is this about? Is he in trouble?"

Cathal shook his head. "We have questions about a message delivered to the Court." He was quick to use the information she already gave him to ease her distrust.

Eabha shrugged. "Someone at Emerald can answer that, but when Calbhach comes next time, I'll tell him to stop by, ceannasaí." She furrowed her brow. "He hasn't been around for the last few days, so he's bound to come soon."

I kept my comment to myself, but I could see Cathal and the others thought what I did—that mythborn hadn't shown up at the Court again because he was hiding. He knew I'd gotten a good look at him, so he wouldn't risk coming back.

"I see, thank you."

"Is that all, ceannasaí? I'd like to get back to work before my supervisor misses me."

I couldn't shake the feeling that there was something odd about her. On one hand, her posture and voice suggested a simple mythborn who didn't want any trouble, but on the other, it felt like she slipped the act every now and then, with her speech patterns and vocabulary reverting to what they naturally were. I was an expert neither on linguistics nor on mythborn culture, but I trusted my instinct.

Cathal was about to wave her off, so I butted in. "Just one more question."

If my ceannasaí didn't like it, he didn't show it. Instead, he nodded to Eabha, pointing at me.

"Why didn't you come forward sooner?" I looked her in the eye. "The guards were asking around."

For a split second, she shifted as if readying to flee, then she shrugged again. "Guards talked about an attack. That's not something Calbhach would ever do. He's such a sweet boy, after all. I thought for a moment that maybe I should say something, but many mythborn fit the description. I didn't want to get him in trouble for nothing." She turned back to Cathal. "It was only about a message, yes?"

The concern in her voice sounded genuine, and I couldn't tell whether I was picking up on some subtle cue or simply developing paranoia because of our invisible enemy.

"Yes, all is well. You needn't worry. Our new member wasn't around during the incident, so she didn't know the two things weren't related," Cathal replied smoothly. If I didn't already know he was lying, I'd never be able to tell. "It's all we need to know. I'll have Sadb escort you back, so that she can reassure your supervisor that everything is well. I'd hate for you to suffer from malicious tongues just because you were helpful to us."

"'Twas my pleasure, ceannasaí." She'd already slipped back into the simple servant persona, with a servile tone and rushed bows.

She left, and Sadb followed.

Cathal looked at Faolan. "Go, alert Aengus. Make sure he has her followed, no matter when she leaves."

I didn't like the idea of trusting someone else with Eabha, but we didn't have the resources to handle it ourselves, especially not with the danger still looming over us and Lorcan absent. Besides, Cathal seemed to know Aengus well, and they had history. To him, it must be as natural as me asking Albert or some other Trinitian for help.

"I'll take Sadb and Faolan to check Emerald Messages. It's unlikely they'll know anything about what Calbhach was doing here, but we have no other clues to chase down, unless Eabha's behavior reveals something. You two stay here until we return."

As soon as we both acknowledged that, he left the room.

Riagán looked at me. "So, what about Lorcan? Ceannasaí didn't mention him at all."

With a heavy heart, I told him about the discovery Cathal and I had made in Lorcan's room.

He closed his fists. The silver of his eyes dimmed and darkened, and his face hardened. "This is not like him. We could always rely on him."

It sounded like he wanted to convince himself and

maybe even force the reality to shift to match what he considered true. Then his expression softened.

"I'm sorry that you were left alone." A flash of anger passed over his face, as if saying that had made him realize once more that Lorcan had surprised and perhaps even disappointed him by abandoning me.

"I'm sure he had a good reason to leave." I meant what I said. I couldn't picture Lorcan doing something like that out of cowardice or a lack of trust.

I wanted to reassure Riagán that all would become clear once Lorcan returned, but the pristine room he'd left behind made it obvious there would be no coming back.

He walked over and enclosed me in his arms. "I'm so sorry, Kaja. This is not who we are. This is not how you were supposed to join us."

"Maybe it's better that way," I replied, forcing in a light-hearted note. "If you were all perfect, I'd have a much harder time fitting in. But all those mistakes just make you more..." I bit my tongue before saying that mistakes made them more *human*. I doubted that a mythborn would under-stand the pre-Magiclysm figure of speech. "More real, approachable," I finished awkwardly.

The tension in his muscles eased. "That can be danger-ous..." There was a trace of teasing in his voice. "If we don't watch you closely, you could go and tell the Trinitians that the Scáthanna are nothing special."

I snorted. "Seeing as I wear your uniform now, it would be like a shriek trying to vouch for other shrieks."

"A well-chosen metaphor," he said amused. "I don't doubt that to Trinity we're likely as reasonable as shrieks."

"And definitely as deadly," I added.

I was lucky to have only encountered a few shrieks, but the memory of a hunt I did with the Scáthanna back when I was a humanborn still gave me chills, because I'd come dangerously close to being frozen solid by a shriek's breath. At the same time, though I wasn't on the team yet, both Riagán and Sadb had come to my aid without hesitation, and neither thought less of me for needing their help. Quite the contrary—everyone back then seemed impressed that I'd actually survived long enough to receive said aid.

"Speaking of which..." I gave Riagán a nudge to sit down beside me. "I'd love to hear something more about your hunt. Cathal only gave me the dead shriek count. Have some food, drink, and share stories of bravery and daring deeds. The more colorful, the better!"

That earned me a broad smile. For at least a while, Riagán would be back to his old cocky and confident self, and neither of us would think about Lorcan or the mysterious enemy who was out to get us.

I believed he needed it as much as I did.

CHAPTER NINETEEN

One thing I had learned about the Scáthanna was that they kept together, especially in dire moments. They didn't commiserate, though, instead acting as if life went on as usual.

If I had my way, I would worry, but others seemed to have taken Lorcan's disappearance in stride—just another setback in a sequence of many. And apparently, they expected the same of me. Perhaps it was because it felt different this time. Even though nobody expected to see Lorcan again, it wasn't because he was taken. He'd left on his own and in a manner that suggested cutting ties with the Scáthanna. It still hurt, especially the trust he'd broken, but it removed the worry that would have come if he was still a team member. He'd chosen to not be one of us.

Yet the draw to not be alone in such a time was strong, pulling us all together like magic. I was starting to suspect there was something more to the team, like a secret ritual creating a connection between us so that we could always find each other and know if one of us was in danger... But that was the wishful thinking of a human mind fed by books and movies. All there was to the Scáthanna's bond was the same companionship I'd experienced with my humanborn team back in the war. Strong emotions and grueling experiences brought people together and made them seek solace, knowing that others understood it.

That was why I was sitting by the training room's wall, sweating and sore from my morning training with Sadb, because nothing could be a good enough reason to cancel a beating session. At least she didn't go on me any harder than usual. Still, I was overjoyed when she let me off the hook and Faolan volunteered in my place.

They went all in, dealing strikes without mercy. Their training weapons must have been amulet enhanced, because otherwise they'd have broken them in the first five minutes of sparring. The broad-shouldered mythborn had a clear strength advantage over Sadb, but with her fierce attacks all over him, he didn't look like he was in for an easy win... or any kind of win, for that matter. Sadb looked like she could take on an army.

Every now and then, I tossed one of my pretend curses in their general direction, simulating distractions and sneak attacks. They paid hardly any attention to my attempts, but they insisted I kept going.

"Alternatively, you could join us." Faolan grinned while blocking Sadb's strike. "I could use some help."

I gave him my best skeptical glare. "No thanks. I've had enough beating from Sadb already. And she isn't going easy on you. With that treatment, I'd end up with more than just bruises."

Faolan threw out something in the mythborn language, and Sadb laughed. I wouldn't be surprised if he was calling me a pussy or a chicken, or whatever the mythborn equivalent of those insults was. At some point, I'd have to ask

Riagán for a crash course on mythborn invectives, so I'd know whether and when a response was necessary.

Riagán, of course, walked in right then. He must have some magical instinct to always time his entrances just right. Even when I was facing an Afflicted on my own, he'd appeared at the last minute and saved me from immediate death. Though back then he did find me thanks to a locating charm, so maybe it was pure luck—mine more than his—that he had made it on time.

He circled the fighters at a distance that indicated he wasn't about to get in between them, but as soon as he was behind Sadb's back, he attacked without warning.

I snorted when he failed to surprise her.

With her eyes still on Faolan, never giving him an opening, Sadb kicked backward, hitting Riagán square in the chest. He flew backward and stopped short of the wall with a huff that reassured me her strike was every bit painful it looked.

"Too slow!" Sadb called out without looking over her shoulder, while she delivered more strikes to her actual opponent.

Riagán grinned at her back, unmoved by his own failure. "But it keeps you on your toes."

He made his way to me, this time staying away from the fighting duo. Smart. If he failed to get a drop on her once, when she wasn't expecting it, there was no point in trying again unless he wanted to join the sparring match and get a proper beating from her. And as much as I knew he wasn't a bad fighter—none of them were—I also knew he stood no chance against Sadb.

"Still nothing?" I asked as soon as he sat beside me.

Riagán shook his head.

The previous day, Cathal and the others had returned

with nothing. Emerald Messages' owner had confirmed that a mythborn named Calbhach worked for them, but he hadn't shown up for work in a few days, and his family didn't know where he was. Since Emerald Messages had no record of him doing deliveries to the Court before his disappearance, it felt like another dead end, despite their promise to let the Scáthanna know if Calbhach returned to work. I doubted he would, and the rest of the team did as well. He was likely hiding, probably out of Dublin already.

Riagán sat beside me, his expression pained. An afternoon of light storytelling and laughter while we enjoyed each other's company wasn't enough to alleviate all of what he—and others—was going through. Lorcan's betrayal, because I was sure they all saw it that way, hurt him in a different, more damaging way than the recent deaths.

I gently touched his shoulder, to remind him that I was there, but offered no words otherwise. There were none that would ring true and encompass all the emotions that rattled the team. He sent me a weak smile, his eyes still marred by pain, and then looked back at the training duo, his expression softening and shifting into slight amusement. He wasn't hiding his feelings, from what I could tell, only finding solace in the normalcy of his teammates' presence.

Faolan came to a sliding stop right beside us, then lowered his weapon before Sadb could launch another assault. Large patches of sweat marked the tunic he was wearing, and droplets of perspiration trickled down his face.

"Unbeatable, as always." The way he looked at Sadb made it clear he meant it as the highest praise.

Sadb smirked at him as she approached, massaging her arm. He got a few hits on her, and they looked anything but gentle.

"At least you're somewhat of a challenge, not like a

certain myth-touched." She glanced at me without malice. "Fancy some more training? Faolan wore me down, so it's going to be easier than in the morning."

I openly snorted. Sure, Sadb looked like someone who'd been training for a while, and I could actually see a tiny patch of sweat on her tunic, but she was nowhere near winded.

"I don't think you really believe that I'd do any better than I did in the morning," I replied.

"Don't even ask," Riagán said quickly as Sadb's gaze found a new target.

"If you don't train, you won't get better," she threw at no one in particular. "All three of you against me?" She lifted her training weapon in anticipation. "You land ten hits total, and I'll call it your win."

I looked at the others. They must have noticed as well that Sadb's offer was lined with desperation. She needed more distraction, and for her, training was the best solution.

"That will have to wait," Cathal said as he entered, his expression solemn. "Lorcan's been found."

In a blink, we were all on our feet and around him, even though his posture and voice had already told us enough.

"His body is being brought to the Court now," he said. "It seems that he took his own life. No signs of fighting on the scene, no signs of torture."

His words seemed to linger in the complete silence that followed, and as I fought my own disbelief, the others' faces showed similar emotions. I hadn't known Lorcan all that well, but such behavior seemed out of character for him, and clearly they couldn't make any sense of it either.

"I doubt we'd learn anything where he died... if it was even the place of his death," Cathal continued. "I know you're all tired with the lack of progress and what seems like a string of failures. So instead of chasing elusive leads, we should do what we do best—hunt. We're going to set up a trap."

The Scáthanna livened up. With that one word, "hunt," Cathal had reignited everyone's hope and determination. I could feel it too: his plan, though probably risking all of our lives, gave us the initiative. We'd finally be doing something instead of feeling helpless and clueless. For once, we would be one step ahead in the game.

"A trap needs bait." Faolan eyed me, since it was obvious who would play the part. "That's a huge risk, ceannasaí."

Sadb and Riagán nodded, confirming he'd voiced their thoughts as well.

"That's why we need to play it smart, so Kaja's never in real danger," Cathal replied. "I spoke to Aengus, and he's willing to provide us a plausible excuse. He'll hold a gratitude celebration for Kaja saving his life. Given his status at the Court, I'd be in no position to refuse Kaja's attendance, and since she performed the deed alone, the rest of you wouldn't be invited. As Aengus's friend and also the one invited, I'll accompany her to Faoinn Crann, and the rest of you will lie in wait."

I knew the place he mentioned, though I'd only been there once. Back then, we were setting up a trap as well, and Laoise was our bait. Things went wrong, as they often do, and she would have died if Sadb hadn't intervened. Knowing the relationship between the two of them, the memory of Sadb's fury as she rushed to Laoise's aid made much more sense now, but I hoped she'd come to my aid in a similar manner. If not because she cared for me enough, then because of her desire of revenge.

I gave Cathal a nod. All things considered, it was a good plan, and I was the best bait: the weakest and most vulnerable of the team, and our enemy always went for the easiest targets... I couldn't help wondering what he'd do when there were only Cathal, Faolan, and Sadb left.

"They might not try anything with you around, ceannasaí," Riagán said.

"I could pretend to sneak away," I offered. "If our enemy has done his homework, he won't be surprised to see me acting this way."

"That could work," Cathal said, "but I'd rather not lose sight of you. You'd be on your own before we get to you, and if something goes wrong, we might not reach you in time."

I wasn't about to argue when we were discussing my life. He knew better what the safest way to play it out was. Yet, in the end, I needed to be alone for long enough to tempt our enemy.

"Under the guise of arranging the celebration with Aengus, I'll check the route and plan everything. Sadb, Faolan, you'll be with me. Riagán and Kaja will stay here." Cathal looked around. "I'll give you an hour for showering and food before we set out."

Sadb and Faolan left immediately, and Riagán took a step toward the door, but looked over his shoulder, clearly waiting for me. I waved at him. "I'll be down in a minute."

Cathal watched me with narrowed eyes. "There's something bothering you about the trap we're about to set. And it's not your role in it."

I nodded. Being bait didn't bother me, especially as it made sense in the light of what we knew about our enemy. It was what we didn't know that made me worried. "What if... What if our enemy doesn't care about me?" I asked. "What if I don't know or have what he wants from the Scáthanna?"

"You're concerned that while we set the trap, he'll go after Riagán instead."

I swallowed and nodded. In assignments, Riagán usually stayed behind, his bow skills being of little use in close quarters. That would make him a perfect target, and a much more valuable one than some myth-touched who hadn't been on the team long enough to learn any secrets.

"Faolan will be by his side the whole time," Cathal said. "The two of them can hold their own. Sadb's orders will be to get to you as soon as possible, and assuming you're separated, I'll aid the one who needs help more."

"Thank you, ceannasaí," I said.

I knew he couldn't give me any real reassurances, and things could always go wrong, but there was comfort in being able to trust someone with my life, even if he was bound to put it at risk more often than not.

Dear Albert, if you're reading this, it means that I'm dead.

I paused, finding grim amusement in imagining Albert's reaction to a letter beginning like that. It wouldn't be good, that was certain, but Albert usually reacted badly no matter what I did. At least in this particular case, it wouldn't be my problem anymore.

I sighed. I'd rather not write it at all, but I owed him an explanation and could hope that getting it from me, even a dead me, rather than from Eithne or Cathal, would stop him from doing something unreasonable, like breaking peace. My death wasn't worth it.

With that thought, I put pen back to paper, detailing what had happened since the ritual that made me a myth-touched. Of course, I put a lot of effort in describing the events in a diplomatic way rather than writing plainly that Eithne was a lying bitch. I also made sure it was clear that Cathal didn't blackmail me to make me join the Scáthanna... or force me to stay when things went bad. It was better if Albert blamed my usual stubbornness for what happened than anyone still alive, especially any mythborn.

Then there was the difficult part. Somehow, I had to explain our trap to him without revealing that I was to play the role of bait, and at the same time make the risk big enough to explain why I'd written the letter beforehand.

A hand touching my shoulder almost made me jump up and toss a curse before Riagán said, "I'm sorry. I knocked several times, but you weren't answering, and I got worried."

"I was writing and got lost in thought." I moved to the side, revealing the letter.

He glanced at the paper, and then turned his eyes away from it. "I can come back later."

"Albert can wait," I said firmly. In fact, he wouldn't get this letter until I was dead, so I hoped he'd get a real exercise in patience. Or that instead of getting it, he'd finally get to meet the new me once the Scáthanna were safe. "You wanted to talk... about tomorrow?"

My stomach twisted at the thought of the risks we were all about to take.

He hesitated, so I got up from the chair and walked over to the bed, pulling him to sit down with me. I let the silence between us linger.

"I just wanted you to know that we all are going to make sure you stay safe," he said finally. "Faolan, Sadb... It might feel like neither have truly warmed up to you, but they won't hesitate. You can trust them. Nobody on this team thinks you're expendable just because you're a myth-touched or you haven't been with us long."

I nodded but said nothing. As comforting and reassuring as those words were, I sensed this wasn't the real reason he'd come. His expression was one of pure torment. I leaned against his shoulder, expecting him to embrace me so that we could find comfort in it, but he didn't move.

"I have no right to ask this of you... especially not for selfish reasons," he said, his voice breaking, "but should it come to the worst... I beg you, give us as much time as you can to find you. You know we won't stop looking." His hands trembled, and he closed them into fists, crumpling the fabric of his gray pants. "I'm sorry. I shouldn't have. It should be your choice."

With this, the source of his torment became clear. He didn't want me to die, but he was torn about asking me to endure possibly endless days of torture... for him. He must consider it selfish.

I touched his chin and, with a gentle tug, made him look at me. "It's okay. I understand. You want me to live because you care for me." No matter how broken I'd be when they rescued me, I'd be alive, and he believed he could fix everything else.

He was about to argue; I could see it in his eyes. I could even guess the words he would use: that it was selfish to put such pressure on me, perhaps make me feel guilty about using the death curse, and taking away my choice. These were all valid arguments, and I had no reassurances.

So I kissed him instead.

"Last time, it was you who helped me to survive," I whispered. "You convinced everyone, Cathal and others, to try to save my life. You even convinced me that I shouldn't give up and try the ritual. Without you, I wouldn't be here. I think you deserve a promise that I'll hold on to life as desperately and for as long as I can." I smiled gently. "But only if you promise me the same."

That finally chased away his uneasiness, and he pulled me closer. "That's fair," he whispered. "I do promise you the same."

I chuckled, because a thought struck me. "You know, in situations like that, humans usually reconfirm their feelings for each other, not promise that they will endure gruesome torture for each other." Though, in a way, both meant exactly the same.

"I suppose we could try the humanborn way next week," he replied, amused.

It felt good to have him back to his usual self. Back when I was literally dying of the affliction and figuratively dying to know what secrets he'd been keeping from me, he'd made me a similar promise: that he'd tell me the following week. It meant that I had to survive the ritual, to keep on living, to know.

I leaned against him, putting my arms around his chest and holding tight. The letter to Albert could wait, especially since it wouldn't change anything at the time it was meant to be sent. But holding Riagán, feeling his inner magic and smelling the scents of pine and campfire smoke... That gave me strength.

I was alive. I had a future, a future with him. And I intended to keep it that way.

"Next week it is," I said.

CHAPTER TWENTY

Faoinn Crann was much like I remembered.

Tall, magically grown trees provided a canopy ceiling over the square, and the charms hanging among their branches emanated warmth and light, changing an early spring evening into a summery one—if Eireland had such a thing as real summer to begin with. With the temperatures barely ever exceeding so-called room temperature and rains as common as any other time of the year, it was easy to forget this country actually had four seasons instead of what felt like perpetual autumn... Here, with their skillful use of nature and magic, mythborn artisans had managed to evoke the feeling of an everlasting summer evening.

Mythborn-only guests sat at countless tables, enjoying drinks and food served from the kitchens set up in the neighboring buildings, and engaged in lively conversation. Every now and then, a burst of laughter rose toward the gnarly branches, proving that even the mythborn were sometimes carefree and honest. On the other hand, my benevolent perception of the place might have sprouted from the fact that, contrary to my previous visit to Faoinn Crann, nobody was looking at me with poorly concealed disgust. It was a benefit of being a myth-touched, because most of the self-absorbed mythborn nobles likely had no idea beings like me even existed and wouldn't be able to tell the difference between me and a mythborn.

Cathal walked beside me, and our uniforms drew everyone's attention. I caught glances of respect and ones of curiosity, as if they were trying to figure out whether we were on some official business or had simply failed to wear anything casual. Several mythborn ladies eyed my ceannasaí as if gauging his tastes and their chances. They looked away as soon as they spotted his stonelike expression, which made it clear he wouldn't be interested in any beauty who crossed his path. Our weapons might have been a tell as well, even though we hadn't brought much other gear with us, since we were supposed to be joining a celebration, not going to war. If the trap was to work, we needed to keep up the appearance of that minimal amount of equipment to go with the Scáthanna's formal dress, which was pretty much our uniforms, just with less... stuff. Cathal sure liked simplicity.

At least most of my curses were meant to be concealed, so I could take them with me, because if I had to rely solely on my blade, I might just as well surrender to our enemy, sparing myself the humiliation of trying to fight my way out of any ambush.

Aengus waved to us, smiling. He was sitting at a big table with several other mythborn. All of them wore exuberant clothes, a mix of the otherworld fashion and Earth influences, with complex Celtic weaves embroidered on their shoulders and hems.

Cathal sighed then forced a polite smile. It seemed that

he was looking forward to socializing as much as I was, but we both had our minds on the trap. Passing time with myth-born noblemen was just a means to an end. Yet I could easily picture how, in some other circumstances, Cathal would blend right in with the other nobles, discussing whatever topics they found worth their time. Even since Connor had mentioned my ceannasaí's birthright during my first official evening at the Court, I'd been picking up subtle cues confirming it, though I had yet to witness Cathal looking down at anyone in that snobbish nobleman way, be it at the members of his team or the Court's servants. It almost seemed that vain pride and condescension were beyond someone of his status.

As we approached, it didn't escape me that everyone at the table spoke in the mythborn language. None bothered to switch, but then, why would they if they saw what looked like two other mythborn approaching? I gave up on trying to make sense of the conversation we walked onto.

"Cathal, Kaja," Aengus said in English. "I appreciate you made time for me." He stood up, lifting his cup and turning toward his other guests. "My friends, the only reason I'm here today with you, drinking and enjoying life, is this brave myth-touched, one of Cathal's finest warriors." He made a short pause while others eyed me with not-so-well-concealed doubts. "I'm sure you're wondering what could be so special about her, like I did not so long ago. I thought little of her, yet her very actions proved me wrong. Not only did she defend me in the heat of battle, risking her own life while trying to preserve mine, but she also ensured I didn't die from a flesh-eating curse."

Cathal arched his eyebrow in an unvoiced question, and I gave him a quick nod. With all that had happened back then, Cait's kidnapping and everyone's suspicions toward me, I didn't have time to tell him the details of how, exactly, I saved Aengus's life.

I bowed. "I was merely following orders." Even if Cathal hadn't instructed me earlier to downplay my deeds, I'd have done so anyway. Being in the limelight under the other mythborn's scrutiny didn't appeal to me. The sooner we were done with the official part, the sooner they all returned to their private conversations, and the happier I'd be.

It would be perfect if I could sneak away as soon as Aengus finished the gratitude show, even though it meant I was to risk my life being bait. I supposed it spoke volumes of what I thought about social gatherings with mythborn nobles, but the rules of setting a trap were much simpler: lure the enemy out, don't get killed or kidnapped, and catch the son of a bitch who was after us. No politics, no false smiles, and no navigating a strange culture in the company of people who likely thought less of me than a bridge dweller.

"You did well where my adjutants failed. Let my gratitude be known." Aengus lifted a cup, drank from it, and then offered it to me.

As I accepted and took a sip as well, I caught Cathal's smirk. If not for the instructions he'd given me on our way to Faoinn Crann, I wouldn't have the slightest clue what to do.

"Your veenya is all the gratitude I need," I offered the standard reply, making it clear I didn't consider him indebted. Supposedly, it was poor form to hold a life debt over a noble mythborn's head, and I couldn't help wondering whether that rule didn't apply to other mythborn and humanborn, or whether Riagán had conveniently ignored it when it came to *my* debts. On the other hand, as my conscience reminded me, he was never quick to bring them up or demand any payments. I was the one to insist, and it could be considered a courtesy that he followed my lead rather than taking offense.

"Let's drink, then!" Aengus picked another cup, and this concluded the official part.

The mythborn returned to their conversations. None of them bothered switching to English, but I didn't mind. I hoped I could sit in a corner without drawing too much attention, but Aengus waved us over.

"Do you speak mythborn or Irish, Kaja?" he asked as we sat down beside him. "English feels so... foreign."

"I'm afraid not. But if you wish to speak Irish with my ceannasaí, I'll gladly listen. I know a few words and expressions, and I'm hoping to learn more one day, so it'd be a pleasant opportunity to get used to it," I politely lied.

Irish, no matter how alluring, wasn't on my priority list, but if Aengus obliged, it would give me an excuse to be silent and listen to other, more important things. If I could catch our enemy's voice before the trap was sprung, perhaps I could gain us an advantage. I knew he was somewhere out there. The celebration wasn't a secret, and we were certain he had well-placed spies at the Court that would give him all the necessary details. To hear his voice again, to know he was close and within our reach... I wanted it.

"This celebration is in your name, Kaja. It would be rude if I left you out of this," Aengus said louder than necessary, attracting glances of his other guests as if reminding them to behave properly. "And the scar I have will ensure I'll never forget what you did for me." He toasted me once more.

"Scar? Has your wound healed already?" Cathal drew attention away from me and engaged Aengus in a conversation, saving me from more formal evasions and courteous rejections.

Reluctantly, other mythborn switched to English, though from the bits of their exchanges I caught, I wasn't missing out on much to begin with. Some Court politics, discussions about the future of the countryside, which was mostly mythborn-controlled, and arrangements for the next social event.

I was ready to use my new skill when one of the mythborn got up from his seat and carried his chair over to my side of the table. His eyes, locked on me, made it clear he wasn't going to join Cathal and Aengus.

"The first myth-touched to join the Scáthanna. That's quite an honor." He set his chair beside me.

His skin was a mix of grays and greens, though his hair was black, not fair like Aengus's. With the way he spoke and carried himself, I had no doubt him and Aengus were family, so with his young face, he must be Diarmuid. Unless, of course, the mythborn noble had more than one son.

"My father says you saved his life, so I should express my gratitude as well." He toasted me, and I reciprocated. He didn't offer me his cup, so it had to be an informal phrase and not something I was obliged to respond to. "You must have some remarkable skill for the ceannasaí to have chosen you."

I smiled at the rather straightforward remark accompanied by an unapologetic stare. Diarmuid didn't even try to conceal that he was questioning my right to be one of the Scáthanna.

"I shouldn't speak for my ceannasaí or assume his motives," I replied. He needed more than that to make me feel uncomfortable.

"Of course you shouldn't." Diarmuid smiled as if he'd expected such a response. In his eyes, this must have been an evasion. "But it's my right to have doubts."

I moved my chair back just enough for Cathal to be visible and pointed at him. "He's sitting right here, if you'd like to bring it up with him," I said.

It was easy to complain behind someone's back, but I doubted Diarmuid had the balls to tell Cathal to his face that he'd made a bad decision letting some lowly myth-touched join the Scáthanna.

To my surprise, Diarmuid laughed. "You might be born of a human, but you sure carry yourself like someone who's been around mythborn long enough." His cup clinked against mine. "This is how your people do it, isn't it?"

He was doing his best to come across as approachable, but I didn't have to read his mind to know he still considered me beneath him, or *any* mythborn, and his behavior was only covering for his lack of courage to actually ask Cathal how someone like me became a member of the mythborn elite unit.

At least he'd decided to keep civil, likely out of respect for his father, but his presence still annoyed me, as it disrupted my plans of searching for our enemy.

"You seem distracted." Diarmuid studied me. "Or maybe intimidated by the company?" There was another challenge in his voice, but he lacked Riagán's charming confidence to pull it off, so he sounded like a bratty child, which anyone would prefer to ignore if given such an option.

I took another sip of veenya. According to Cathal, I needed to drink it all, but he'd also advised me to take it slow, and rightly so. Being drunk on my way back wouldn't do me any good. Diarmuid was still staring at me, clearly expecting an answer, and made me desperate to be done with both gratitude parties and conversations with no-so-grateful sons.

"There's a lot to take in here." I forced a smile. Cathal's

plan didn't include me offending everyone around and being thrown out of the party, and I could bet he wouldn't appreciate if I added such a twist to it. "I only visited Faoinn Crann once before, and since I was accompanying the Scáthanna, who had business here, I didn't get the opportunity to truly enjoy it." I hoped that would suffice for an excuse.

"It's one of the finest places in the area, though you should visit the social nodes around... What do the human-born call it...? Henry Street, I believe." He stretched on his chair. "As a myth-touched, you won't need a special invitation anymore."

Another jab, and I wished I could roll my eyes or sigh theatrically in response. If he wanted to hurt my pride, he was doing a horrible job.

"Thank you for the recommendation," I replied. "I'll be sure to visit the area as soon as my duties allow me."

Yeah, I had better things to do than socialize with self-important mythborn, and having taken more than a glimpse at Henry Street while we crossed it on our way to Max, I doubted there would be anyone around worthy of the trip he was suggesting.

I almost chuckled when he cringed at my remark. I hadn't meant it as payback, but it seemed that the mere mention of my work with the Scáthanna was enough to push his button. I could see why Cathal preferred me on his team, no matter how skilled Diarmuid might be. Sure, I brought a lot of my own issues into the fold, but at least I could get over my personal dislikes and work with them instead of hunting for opportunities to jab at them.

"I see you two found some common topics." Aengus leaned toward us with the smile of a successful matchmaker. "I'm hoping that one day you'll have even more in common as teammates." He winked at Cathal, as if they shared a secret. Too bad I couldn't tell him I was aware of the conversation they'd had before the ambush in the Botanical Gardens, and that I knew Diarmuid wasn't even under consideration.

"I don't intend to give Kaja away." Cathal had a slightly amused expression on his face. He glanced at me in that telling way that reassured me he remembered I had eavesdropped back then. "Ever since she started working with us, her skills and insights have proven quite valuable, and I hope that in time she'll become as irreplaceable as any other member of the Scáthanna."

It was nice to hear such praise from him, especially in public, though I sensed his words were meant more for our audience than me. I already knew I was of worth to him and the team, so it sounded like he was sending a message to other mythborn to stop questioning his decisions.

"I thought she joined only recently." Diarmuid gave him a challenging stare.

I hadn't expected for the mythborn kid to have it in him to question Cathal's truthfulness so openly. Aengus's son either had bigger balls than I'd granted him or no clue what he was doing. I wouldn't be surprised if his noble blood made him believe everything was allowed, and if that was the case, I would enjoy the show of Cathal putting him back in his place. My ceannasaí might respect Aengus and value their friendship, but I doubted those feelings extended to the mythborn's irksome offspring.

"Kaja worked with us before she became a myth-touched." Cathal's reply was calm, but his expression hardened. I read a clear warning in his voice, and were I in Diarmuid's place, I'd drop the subject and top it up with an apology as soon as I had the chance. "She helped us find agents of the Snake, faced a shriek with us, and killed a Léanmhar—twice."

That was quite an impressive list of feats I'd accomplished... if one didn't know the details. I might have actually helped with tracing down the Snake's agents, but I found the last one investigating something else and ended up being in the wrong place at the wrong time. I also wouldn't have survived that shriek if Sadb didn't come to my aid, and as for the Afflicted... I almost cringed at the memories. With the first one, I used the curse I'd designed specifically to kill those things, so I could hardly call it an achievement. And I'd rather forget all about my second encounter... If the Scáthanna hadn't arrived back then, I'd be dead—or worse. Even though the vision of a magically mutated Kaja lookalike wandering Dublin and killing indiscriminately hadn't come to pass, the thought still soured my mood, and I fought to keep my expression neutral to match the supposedly pleasant circumstances. Oh, how I wished for this shindig to end already!

Yet it was satisfying to see Diarmuid's dumbfounded stare. He hadn't expected me to have done anything except for saving his father's life, which he likely believed to have been an accident or a stroke of luck anyway.

"Impressive." Aengus got his composure back first, and looked at Cathal. "I can only hope you'll give Diarmuid a chance to prove himself as well."

"I'm sure your son has many fine skills that will shine when given opportunity," I replied before Cathal had a chance. "Now, if you excuse my unrefined behavior, there's something I have to discuss with my ceannasaí in private," I added as I put my cup away. It was half-empty already, and I was growing tired of the social gymnastics we were performing to satisfy etiquette.

What was even more frustrating was that even if Aengus was inclined to acknowledge my value, he still couldn't resist trying to convince Cathal to invite Diarmuid into the Scáthanna, and my presence was grist for that mill. Both the frequency of Aengus's not-so-subtle remarks and the excuses to make them were approaching absurd levels at collision speed, so if a team of cheerleaders suddenly rushed in, performing breathtaking acrobatics and chanting, "Let Diarmuid join, go, go, go, Cathal, let him join!" I'd be only mildly baffled at the sight.

"Kaja has training with Sadb tomorrow morning," Cathal explained when Aengus looked at us confused. "I'm sure she's torn between appreciating your hospitality and being on time and adequately rested."

I did my best to hide my surprise. There was no training, and this wasn't part of the plan. Whatever Cathal intended, I didn't like that he'd given me no warning. I trusted him, of course, but it would have been nice if he'd told me beforehand. In the end, though, it mattered little what kind of excuse we fabricated, as long as I was on my way.

"I didn't realize my personal pleasures were interfering with your duties," Aengus replied, and I couldn't decide whether his words were genuine or if he was that good of an actor. Likely the latter, since he was in on the trap. "Such dedication is nothing but commendable, so if you wish to leave early, Kaja, I won't hold it against you. More so, I'll have Diarmuid accompany you back to the Court. It's the least I can do."

Before I could come up with a polite way to decline his offer, Cathal smiled and nodded. "Excellent idea. On her way back, if Diarmuid's interested, Kaja can tell him more of what the Scáthanna expect of their members."

His response made me want that private conversation

after all. As much as the excuse didn't really matter, I disliked that Diarmuid was now mixed into the plan. Cathal knew I would be walking into a trap, yet he was sending Aengus's son along. Being bait and babysitting an insufferable mythborn felt like mutually exclusive goals.

"Ceannasaí…" I hoped he could read on my face what I couldn't say.

"You should drink your veenya, Kaja," Cathal replied, as if he shared none of my concerns. "While it's fine to leave early, it would be impolite to leave the gratitude cup unfinished."

He passed me the cup. He must have switched it, because there was much less veenya in it now. I nodded. I still didn't understand why he was letting Diarmuid tag along with me, but at least Cathal had ensured I wouldn't be drunk.

"To your health!" I toasted Aengus and drank the last of veenya. Then, just like Cathal had told me earlier, I placed the cup upside down on the table, and as a reward I received approving glances from the mythborn around. The cup was empty, which meant there was no more debt to be paid.

"Are you ready?" Diarmuid got up from his seat, and only then did I spot a rapier-like blade by his side. At least he wouldn't be a total burden.

"Yes, but there really is no need for you to rob yourself of this celebration's pleasures," I replied.

He was smiling, but he looked at me with a sudden seriousness. "I'd hate to see my father's guest of honor walk on her own, vulnerable to thoughts that *ambush* one when they're alone. I'm sure I'll be able to provide enough distractions to keep your mood up." His hand leisurely skimmed past the grip of his weapon.

The emphasis on the "ambush" and the gesture made it

clear that he at least had an idea of what he was getting into. Perhaps Cathal, unable to go with me or send any other team member along, was choosing the second-best option—a mythborn considered well trained but who also looked quite inconspicuous in his noble outfit. Or it might have been Aengus's insistence, and Cathal had no choice but to play along if he wanted his friend to help set up the trap.

Either way, robbed of all arguments, I gave Diarmuid a nod. "I welcome and appreciate your company, then." I turned to my host. "Aengus, thank you for inviting me. It's been a pleasure and an honor." Then I glanced at Cathal. "Ceannasaí, I'll see you back at the Court."

Before leaving, we exchanged a round of pleasantries with all the mythborn. They seemed almost genuine when they expressed wishes to see me again soon, and I responded in an appropriate manner, but when Diarmuid and I finally left Faoinn Crann behind, it was a relief. Only the inquisitive glare of the mythborn accompanying me kept me on guard, and I concealed my feelings. Even if I personally cared little of what he thought of me, my behavior would either validate or undermine Cathal's decisions, and my ceannasaí didn't need to be questioned by the likes of Aengus and his son.

Diarmuid walked beside me with confidence and in a good mood, while I couldn't chase away concerns of how he'd react when we fell into an ambush, even if he was prepared that there could be one. If he had never fought in the war and only practiced in training situations, he could freeze or stumble no matter how good his training was, and that thought kept me on edge more than knowing that I was a piece of cheese in a mousetrap.

As much as I wanted to catch the mythborn responsible

for my teammates' deaths, part of me was praying nothing would happen on our way back to the Court.

After all, I didn't want to have saved Aengus's life only to get his son killed.

~

DIARMUID'S LACK of concern kept grating on my nerves as we walked the empty streets of Dublin's north side, and it once more made me ponder Cathal's insistence on sending an inexperienced mythborn along. I might not be a warrior myself, but the war had trained me in survival, and I was prepared for being outnumbered and overwhelmed.

I also had more common sense than honor, so if things went awry and I saw an opening, I wouldn't hesitate to flee. Diarmuid, on the other hand, had the posture and gait of someone convinced he couldn't be taken down, and that was begging for trouble.

But the route we took was eerily empty. Even with the postwar drastic drop in Dublin's population, I expected to see more passersby. Perhaps most locals preferred early nights, or they'd gotten wind something was brewing in the neighborhood and wisely chosen to not get involved. Every now and then, a shadowy figure moved in the dark of the ruined buildings, and I couldn't help wondering whether the local mythborn, who from my experience could be feisty and troublesome, were keeping away at the sight of my gray uniform.

"You seem on edge. Are you worried that I'll prove I'm better than you and take your place in the Scáthanna?" Diarmuid asked all of a sudden, destroying the silence I was quite enjoying.

"I wasn't aware you were a scout," I replied.

"Why would I be?" His eyebrow arched in genuine surprise. "Lowborn can handle such unimportant tasks."

"And thus you answered your own question about my concerns." I sent him a smile. "Though I wouldn't repeat your opinion about scouts when Sadb is around. She might react strongly to it."

That gave him pause. I could almost see the gears turning in his head. "You're right. Every role is important on the team. My apologies." He didn't mention Sadb, but his reaction suggested her relationship with Laoise wasn't a secret. "Is that why your ceannasaí didn't want to send you alone? Because you're... a scout?"

"I can hold my own," I said, throwing Sadb's assessment at him. It was polite of him to refrain from openly suggesting I wasn't a warrior.

"You fought in the war, didn't you?" His voice rang with sudden interest. "Is this why Cathal let you join? You were helping us back then?"

I laughed. Diarmuid's circles must be narrow, limited only to the Court's nobles, if he truly had no idea who I was.

I might not be famous Dublin-wide, but the name Kaja Modrzewska had always been associated with the all-humanborn Trinity, and I'd never hidden my ties to them, in the past balancing on the fine line of staying neutral while still favoring them when it came to the flow of information. Then, of course, Eithne had come into the picture, swaying me to work with the Scáthanna, and I'd found myself balancing on another line, the one between the trust Albert had in me and keeping all the secrets Eithne and Cathal deemed necessary to keep.

"If ceannasaí and I had ever met back then, we wouldn't be talking now." I savored Diarmuid's confusion but saw no point in concealing the truth. "During the war, I was helping

Trinitians, and ever after the treaty was signed, my ties to them remained strong."

I didn't remark that they were *still* strong. I wasn't worried that he'd take it as a confession of my being a Trinitian spy. I just couldn't be sure whether, after all that had happened, I had any ties left. Especially after months of radio silence that might have pushed Albert over the edge and made him question our bond or mutual trust, because the infrequent, short, and somewhat impersonal letters could have just as well been written by someone else.

Diarmuid regained his composure quicker than I'd thought he would. "That's unexpected, but I still can't see the reasons to make you part of the team."

I shook my head. "You're grasping at straws." I didn't want to hear next that I'd only gotten in because Riagán vouched for me. Even if it wasn't going to happen this time, because I doubted Diarmuid knew about it, such an argument was sure to come later, when my relationship with said archer became obvious to everyone, and I wasn't going to hide it just to avoid gossip. "Cathal needed a scout, and I've worked with the Scáthanna before, chasing the Snake's agents. That's it."

He didn't look convinced, but he dropped the topic, and that was all I'd wanted.

Since we were halfway to the Court already, I engaged my listening skill. Lorcan had warned me about using it when I needed all my strength and focus, but this time, it was worth the risk. I had to know when the trap was about to spring and what our adversary was planning.

There weren't many conversations around to pick from, and soon enough, I caught the voice I was hoping to hear.

"Such a lousy attempt," said the mythborn. "I expected more from the *famous* Scáthanna."

"Master?" Another voice joined him. His accent sounded French, so he was likely a humanborn.

"After three of them already died, they're sending their weakest member accompanied only by some noble-blooded child. Cathal is wiser than that, so it means they're trying to set up a trap," the mythborn replied with the slight ire of someone explaining the obvious.

"Shall we withdraw, then, master?"

"No, I still want her. Alive, no matter the cost. I'll be waiting for you at the Smithfield stop, as we planned."

For a heartbeat, I wished I could follow that voice and find our enemy, but Cathal's orders were clear: I was only supposed to spring the trap, so we could capture as many of his lackeys as we could. One of them would value his or her life more than staying loyal, and we'd have a solid lead. To risk my life chasing after the enemy himself would be foolish.

"Get ready," I muttered as I reached for my blade and one of my curses. "They're coming."

"How can you—"

The ambushers stormed out of an adjacent alley, and more poured out behind us, cutting off the way back to Faoinn Crann. I didn't have time to count them all, but they were at least twenty strong. I swallowed. Many more than I had expected.

Diarmuid took a fencing stance, his rapier held to form, but his previous confident expression had vanished. It must have dawned on him that our opponents wouldn't line up to have an honorable duel with him one by one. The time had come when the poor noble boy would show whether he was worth anything at all.

I threw a fiery curse, one of my stronger ones, and a wall of flames separated us from the attackers in the back.

But the others were approaching, already too close to risk more flames, so instead, I activated my magic flare. The rest of the Scáthanna was supposed to be nearby, so I only had to survive for a couple of minutes on my own... A time Sadb had estimated I'd be able to last. I preferred not to ponder what kind of enemy numbers she'd used for that calculation, and whether she'd been honest or had tried to give me a confidence boost while hoping for the best.

One of the humanborn lunged, a lousy and unskilled attack, so I sidestepped and snapped my sword against his neck—a move Sadb had made me practice in endless loops, a simple but effective arterial strike.

Maybe staying alive wouldn't turn out so difficult after all... I cursed under my breath when I remembered that I also had to keep Diarmuid breathing. Judging by his fencing stance, he wasn't going to do a good job himself. Yet, to my surprise, he dodged with quite the precision and drew his sword across his adversary's blade arm, rendering it useless, then spun and grabbed his other opponent, a thin woman, and slung her back toward the other ambushers.

"They aren't honorable in their ways," Diarmuid said casually while ducking to avoid a brick thrown at him.

"Neither am I."

I tossed another curse. This would be a valuable lesson for Diarmuid, teaching him the difference between fencing bouts and real fights. One could hope it wouldn't be his last.

I needed to thin their numbers quickly, and a stun curse was just the thing. It would only buy us a few seconds, but it would be worth it, especially if Diarmuid used the advantage as well.

The flash of light, loud pop, and blast of magic had all the expected effects, and I didn't want to waste a single moment. I launched into the group to deliver one slash each, to the neck, to as many as I could.

Arterial strikes didn't render their recipients immediately dead or unable to fight, but they quickly made people figure out that they were doomed, causing them to either fly into a rage, trying to take their adversaries with them, or frantically try to remedy the wound, effectively removing them from the engagement. If I moved between them fast enough, I'd never have to learn which option they chose in their final moments.

Much to my relief, Diarmuid followed suit, practically doubling the effectiveness of the tactic—though, busy with my own opponents, I could only guess what sort of strategy he used.

Of course, the trick was also recognizing when the curse's effects were wearing off—usually three to four seconds—and regaining some distance before finding yourself stuck surrounded by your enemies. Diarmuid must have figured it out as well, or perhaps he had some training that taught him to read the situation, because we both pulled back at the same time.

Then two curses exploded right beside us. The first was a stun, and a well-made one at that. I kept my own footing enough, hardened by years of war and those training sessions with Sadb, when she'd insisted on practicing with live curses, and my own trinkets often threw me around more than distracted her. If I got out of this fray alive, I was definitely giving her the credit for getting me ready.

Diarmuid, on the other hand, lacked my painful but valuable experiences, and he collapsed to the ground amongst the growing effects of the second curse—in simple terms, the equivalent to a smoke bomb—and I suddenly had a choice to make: stay with Diarmuid, so both of us would be easy targets, or keep moving in the hopes I'd draw our opponents away from him. With Diarmuid dazed on the ground and dark plumes of smoke everywhere, he could easily be missed or taken for dead, so with a hint of guilt, I chose the latter.

The benefit of smoke bombs was their ability to cast opponents into confusion, impair vision and recognition, and sometimes bring on quite the fit of coughing, but the downsides included impairing the attacker's own vision and recognition, amongst other things. And that meant I gained a lead on my pursuers, the remainder of the group. It also meant they had abandoned Diarmuid for the chase. If that mythborn had any self-preservation instinct, he'd stay on the ground and in the cover of the smoke for as long he could.

The second group was already past the flame wall, and they were the ones who had tossed the two curses with disregard for their own companions' safety. I repaid them in kind, throwing three trinkets in their general direction. There wasn't time for being choosy, nor aiming, but I couldn't complain about my luck when the front runners stumbled between two stun curses exploding at the same time as a fire curse engulfed the lot of them, bringing the short chase to a decisive end.

Diarmuid crawled out of the smoke, coughing but determined to rejoin the fight. He still held his weapon, and as he got back onto his feet, even in his miserable state, he looked like he was willing to take on anyone and everyone.

I looked around. Where was the rest of my team? They were meant to follow me at a close distance, so it shouldn't have taken them long to catch up. Unless...

My heart skipped a beat, but I didn't allow myself to ponder the possibility that they also had fallen into a trap.

Another group was apparently waiting in the same alley as the group that originally greeted us. Only five strong, but the three humanborn and two mythborn, both massive bridge dwellers, all looked like seasoned warriors. As if the previous ambushers' goal was to wear us down, leaving us open and bleeding for the sweep team.

I needed to get back to Diarmuid. Alone, neither of us stood a chance.

The new group was still approaching slowly, likely sizing us up, while the remainder of the previous group were putting together what had happened and where their targets were.

The seasoned warriors were further off, so I cut off the other group's advance with an ice curse. Their screams echoed in the street as magic exploded, forming long icicles. A nasty kind of death, but I couldn't pity them when the image of Cait's mutilated corpse was forever etched in my memory. I hoped that some survived, though, because this whole trap was about getting information, not my rite of passage as a Scáthanna member, nor my seeing to my own desire for revenge.

"So these are our real enemies," Diarmuid said as I got closer. He was eyeing the newcomers with a wariness that suggested he at least had some sense of threat.

We both turned to them. They were slowly spreading out, and the way they moved told of experience, real experience. I knew they had orders to take me alive, but the same likely didn't apply to Diarmuid. Besides, in the heat of a fight, instincts could kick in and ignore any orders that went against the will of survival. One of them could kill me before even realizing they'd dealt a killing blow.

My own instincts were desperately looking for a way out. I had more curses, but the group's wary expressions told me

I'd have to be lucky to even throw them in disarray. With nothing else coming to mind, I took a slow breath and ensured a correct grip on my weapon. Once the fight started, I'd have to find the opportunity to alter our odds.

Then one of them dropped.

I didn't have to see the gray band on the arrow sticking from the back of his head to know who'd shot it. Sure, there were many skilled archers in Dublin, but only one could place a perfect shot on target in the dark, with smoke concealing both the humanoid silhouettes and their movements... To be fair, there were a few more who could do that, including my old Trinitian companion Orla, and my judgment was being clouded by the emotions I had for said archer—and because he'd once more arrived at the last minute to help me out of a bind.

Before the other four reacted, Sadb was among them, and both Diarmuid and I got to stand motionless, admiring the beauty of her handiwork. She was like a tornado of blades with the blond swirl of her ponytail among the flurry of steel. And, of course, there was blood spraying, screams rising, and disembodied limbs flying.

Yes, Sadb definitely knew how to make killing impressive.

"Weren't we supposed to take some alive?" Diarmuid whispered, smart enough to not voice his objections any louder.

I did note that he didn't look disgusted. He was watching the gory scene with the composure of someone who'd seen similar things many times. No matter how spoiled of a nobleman he might be, it seemed that Aengus had ensured his son had some proper training and maybe even real battle experience.

I motioned to the side, where Faolan was knocking out

the survivors who still clung to their lives. "We'll have some."

Nearby, Riagán landed as smoothly as if he'd jumped off a curb, not dropped from the top of a four-story building. I tried not to look envious. Back when Cait brought me my gear, she'd included a jump charm, but I'd neither had a chance to try it nor was ready to leap off high places trusting it would protect me. Sure, magic could do a lot of things, but such blatantly physics-defying feats still left me dubious. No matter what the Magiclysm had done to this island, gravity was still a fact... a deadly fact if one ignored it.

Yet the Scáthanna seemed to make good use of them, and someday, I'd have to ask one of them teach me.

"I'm sorry," Riagán said as soon as he got to me. "We had unexpected company that kept us." He was already scanning me, looking for wounds, and only when he was satisfied with his inspection did he spare a nod to Diarmuid.

So our enemy had planned for the ambush we set. I had a feeling someone had informed him of it, and once more it reminded me that, until we caught him, no place was a safe haven anymore.

"You made it in time," I replied.

What I didn't add out loud, since we had an audience, was that he'd made it out of his own ambush alive.

Cathal and Aengus were coming from the direction of Faoinn Crann, and they led the group of mythborn I'd met at the gratitude party. As the males and females spread out in quite a military manner, it became clear Aengus hadn't invited useless noblemen to the celebration, but hand-picked warriors.

They all bore the marks of a skirmish, suggesting that our enemy had had yet another group ready to cut off anyone coming to my aid.

As Cathal and Aengus approached, I headed straight for them. "Ceannasaí, he said he'd be waiting at the Smithfield stop."

I didn't care that Aengus would likely question later how I knew. We had no time to waste. If any of the ambushers managed to sneak away, or they had lookouts who hadn't engaged in battle, our enemy could receive warning before we got to him.

Cathal didn't hesitate. "Aengus—"

"I'll have everything under control here," Aengus replied, "and the squad from the Court should arrive shortly. But if you don't mind allowing Kaja to stay with us, we'd appreciate help from a Scáthanna member," he added, a little louder.

"Very well. Kaja, stay with Aengus, and if the Court's guards prove difficult in any way, remind them who's running this operation." He also didn't speak quietly, and his tone made it clear that I shouldn't be shy about it either. Myth-touched or not, the grunts were to listen to the elite group's member.

He didn't wait for my "Yes, ceannasaí," and at his sign, the rest of the Scáthanna headed out.

I stood, alone, letting Aengus handle his men, as his request didn't have anything to do with having Cathal's representative around, even if they'd both made it look like I was needed.

"He just left you here." Diarmuid stopped by my side, his voice quiet, as if he didn't want to draw anyone's attention. "You're one of them, but Ceannasaí Cathal left you here." The way he said it made me guess he couldn't understand either Cathal's motives or my stoic reaction.

I looked at him. He wasn't half as bad in a fight as I'd thought he'd be, but in other aspects, he still acted like a kid. Yet not only had he held his own and helped me in the ambush, he'd also tried to be discreet discussing this topic, as if he wanted to make sure no one else noticed what he pointed out.

"It was a reasonable thing to do," I replied. "I'm still the enemy's target. If they walk into another ambush, they don't have to worry about me."

Diarmuid shifted uneasily. "But he shouldn't treat you like..." He looked me in the eye with a bluntness unusual for the mythborn. "Like you're worse than mythborn. No matter what I or others think about it, you are a member of the Scáthanna now."

"And like others, I do what the job requires of me, even if it means staying behind."

He didn't look convinced. "But—"

"If Cathal thought less of me, he'd never let me walk alone into a trap," I said. "I'd stay safe at the Court, and someone else would be the bait." And to be even more precise, if he didn't think I was capable, I'd have never made it onto his team.

Contrary to my expectations, Diarmuid fell silent, so we stood watching others do their work. The Court's guards arrived and helped with the prisoners. Their medics took care of the survivors while other mythborn pulled bodies away to the side. It would be nice to search them for clues, but I doubted I'd find anything important. With so many people involved, our enemy had to rely on henchmen and maybe even local criminals, so while they could still know some details about him and his operations, they were unlikely to carry any important documents.

Finally, Aengus approached us. He gave a short nod to his son, as if approving that Diarmuid had stayed by my side all that time. Perhaps it was a test for him, too, one to see if he was ready to join the grownups rather than stay a boy.

"Kaja, we're done here," Aengus said in a formal manner. "We're ready to head back, but if you'd rather wait for the rest of the Scáthanna to return..."

I shook my head. "Give your men the order." I doubted Cathal would expect us to wait, and the sooner we got the prisoners to the Court, or wherever the mythborn held them, the safer. It'd be a waste to go through the whole trap and lose the captives if something unexpected happened. Of course, I hoped they'd catch the mastermind at Smithfield, but until I saw that mythborn in binds, I had to assume he'd slip away.

We headed out without delay, and Diarmuid walked beside me all the way back to the Court, though we spoke little.

The night was dark, with clouds covering the moon and stars, and I kept listening for any hints of another ambush. It made no sense, of course, after he'd put so much effort into the first one, but I refused to be caught off guard just because I didn't think a second trap was likely.

When we came through the Court's gates, the group split, some escorting the prisoners, some heading for the barracks, and Aengus left with just a few words of courtesy, rushing off to the main entrance. No wonder—with me back at the Court and safe, there was no reason to keep up the charade of my presence being required for anything.

I glanced at Diarmuid, expecting him to follow, but instead he lingered, his eyes focused, as if he was evaluating me.

"You aren't what I expected," he offered in an amicable manner, as if he was admitting to having made a mistake. "Maybe the lady is right about myth-touched being worth our time." He beamed widely all of a sudden. "But I'd still beat you in a fair duel."

I snickered. "I don't do fair duels. But if you're looking for a challenge... Your father is friends with my ceannasaí. He could arrange a sparring match for you with Sadb or Faolan. You'd learn a lot, and maybe that could help you in future as well. Judging from my own experience, the Scáthanna like to get to know their potential members beforehand."

His face brightened at that. I had no way of knowing whether Cathal would ever consider Diarmuid as a recruit, but a little hope wouldn't hurt. If he was insistent enough, he would at least get to train with Sadb, and maybe a few painful lessons with her would make him change his mind about joining. Or he'd adapt quickly enough to actually become of value to the Scáthanna. Though, with Lorcan and Cait gone, I'd wager Cathal would be looking for a field medic or a curse expert rather than another warrior.

Diarmuid bowed. "I appreciate your advice. Be well, Kaja."

As soon as I reciprocated, he left, and with nothing else to do, I headed to the Scáthanna's quarters. The thought of how dark and empty they would be reminded me that everyone else was still out there, hunting. It made me hate the prospect of sitting alone again all the more. No matter how reasonable it was to leave me behind, it also made me feel like I wasn't pulling my weight.

A lone figure peeled away from the wall opposite the entrance, and my first instinct was to prepare for a fight, with both my mind and body still on edge after the ambush, but I recognized that uneven gait and relaxed.

"The word around here is that the Scáthanna had something big going on tonight," Connor said when he got closer, "so I thought I'd check if you were fine." He didn't miss that I was the only team member around, so his face expressed unvoiced concern.

"They're still out there, chasing a lead," I replied. "It's going to be a while before I return."

"Care for some company until then?"

"I'd appreciate it greatly." I wasn't shy with my gratitude. Connor deserved to know he was saving me from myself. "Come, I'm sure there's some food ready."

We entered the quarters together.

CHAPTER TWENTY-ONE

The Scáthanna returned in the middle of the night. They walked into the quarters and into the day room as soon as they saw that I was still awake. As expected, their clothes bore the marks of a fight, and I hoped that none of them were seriously injured... At least they were all walking on their own.

Connor, who had been dutifully keeping me company, allowing the conversation to meander through charm crafting, Court politics and gossip, and even humanborn history and pop culture, immediately stood up. "I'll see you later. Thank you for your time," he said in a more formal manner than he was using moments ago.

He was about to head for the door when Cathal's gesture stopped him. "There's no need for you to leave. Unless you have an urgent task waiting for you, you're welcome to stay."

"Maybe he's just had enough of Kaja's company," Faolan murmured.

Connor glanced at him, clearly unsure whether it was truly a joke, despite Faolan's amused tone.

I nudged him. "You heard our ceannasaí," I said lightly.

"So, unless you have any good excuses..." I motioned back at the bench.

He sat down, and I sent him a quick smile. If he spent more time with us, other mythborn, if only servants, would see him in the company of the Scáthanna, and gossip would follow, and maybe his life would get a bit easier and the Court mythborn would finally look past his injury.

"You didn't get him, did you?" I asked.

Cathal shook his head. "There was another ambush waiting for us. It was as if he knew we'd go to Smithfield. We killed many of them and took a few prisoner, but I doubt he'd ever been among them."

"He must have assumed we could question the captives immediately and get that information," I said, but I was thinking of something else. Was it possible that the enemy knew about my skill? The Scáthanna had kept it secret, but if he had someone good enough to eavesdrop on us, a single conversation would be enough...

I looked at Cathal, not willing to voice this idea out loud. I trusted Connor, but it didn't mean someone else didn't have the means to listen in. Perhaps I wasn't the only myth-touched gifted with such a skill.

"It's possible." Cathal gave me a slight nod, and his focused eyes suggested he was also responding to what I didn't say.

Meanwhile, Faolan plopped heavily on the bench, and only then did I notice a large red patch on his shoulder. "Got any of your healing charms at hand?" he asked. "We've already used all of ours."

I fished them out without delay. "What happened?"

"He failed to move away from a blade's path," Sadb said with a hint of a reprimand.

She, though covered in blood, looked unscathed, of

course. I was starting to believe it would take a small army to take her down.

"I was shielding a team member."

The way he glanced at Riagán and turned his gaze away immediately when he noticed me watching told me enough. If not for Faolan, Riagán would be dead or seriously injured.

"I don't think this humanborn was trying to kill me," Riagán objected, and with the way he said it, I had no doubt it wasn't just for my benefit, but that he truly thought so. But if he was right, it meant he was our enemy's target as well, and also was to be taken alive.

I pushed any other thoughts away, unwilling to consider what it meant. I didn't need to feed my fears any more.

"The idea is to avert the blade, not stop it with your own body," Sadb remarked, cutting through his uniform.

Magically enhanced for protection, it resisted her efforts, and as she pulled on it with visible frustration, I knew it wasn't about the fabric. She was blaming herself for one of her teammates getting injured. I had no doubt that this feeling was built on the foundation of the blame for Laoise's death she likely shouldered too, even if she couldn't have done anything to prevent it. I knew. I carried similar self-blame, after all.

"I'll report to the lady," Cathal said, "and see if Aengus's people got anything from our captives. Someone is bound to talk."

"If they don't, we should get a turn at making them speak," Faolan called after him, but I doubted Cathal had heard him. He waved at me. "About that healing charm?"

I rushed over. The wound was already partially healed, but if it had taken all their charms to get it there, I doubted one more would finish the job.

Connor called my name, and when I turned, he tossed

me a charm he'd recovered from the harness on his leg. "This should help. Just hold it in the same hand."

I activated the charm, and the strength of magic almost stunned me. Careful not to waste it on idleness, I put it closer to Faolan's wound.

He huffed in shock. "It's strong."

"I've been working on enhancing charms that don't do anything but augment other magic. They can help amulets or charms last longer or gain additional power for a short time," Connor said. "It's a work in progress, as ideally, they wouldn't deplete at all, but I can't get it right yet."

"Magic batteries," I said under my breath, but nobody paid attention to my joke, and maybe it was for the better. I doubted they'd get it anyway. I supposed, if I was to truly become a part of this team, I had to teach them more of human culture, so at least they would get some references.

"But why not just make a stronger healing charm instead?" Riagán asked.

"Because then you can't choose to use just a little," Sadb replied in the tone of someone explaining an obvious thing. "One would think that spending so much time with Kaja would have given you at least basic knowledge of amulets and charms. You should try talking to her sometimes instead of... pursuing other pastimes. She could teach you a thing or two."

"Maybe we should sent him to apprentice with Connor," Faolan added.

I was happy that my back was to Connor, because I didn't want him to see my confusion. Riagán knew enough of charms to figure out a locating charm could be made out of the silver brooch I'd given him in gratitude for saving my life, so he wasn't as clueless as he appeared to be, and Sadb and Faolan likely knew.

Faolan winked at me, clearly amused, and I understood. They were trying to make Connor feel comfortable among them.

"I think I'll pass," Connor said. "But I'll take Kaja back, if you're offering. At least she already knows the basics."

"That's more than can be said about her blade skills," Sadb said in quite a theatrical whisper.

I chuckled. "I'd rather torture you than Connor. He's nice to me at times."

She sent me a grin that promised she was happy to reciprocate the torture.

The healing charm, despite being augmented with Connor's invention, spat out its last bursts of magic. Faolan's wound looked much better now, like a surface scratch— long, but barely bleeding.

"Thank you." I handed the enhancer back to Connor.

He accepted it and stood up. "I'd better go now. Without it, my harness might not be as effective, and I'd rather avoid the humiliation of being carried back to my quarters." He looked around. "Thank you for your hospitality."

"It's the least we could do," Faolan said. "You cared to see that one of our own had company and help if danger came, and that's more than the Court's supposedly finest bothered with."

I didn't argue that I should have said something to Aengus or Diarmuid, because ultimately, Faolan was right. Both of them knew about the trap and that I was our enemy's target, but as soon as I was back in the relative safety of the Court's walls, neither had spared me a second thought.

"It was a pleasure." Connor gave me a nod. "Be well, all of you."

He left as soon as we said our goodbyes, and the atmosphere lost some of its lightness.

"He wasn't even there, was he?" I asked, dismayed.

Faolan shrugged. "Not that we could tell. It wasn't a well-executed ambush like the one prepared for you, and nobody seemed to be leading them."

"So, it was all for nothing again." It was hard to keep dismay from my voice.

"Not for nothing." Cathal walked in, his body emanating confidence and satisfaction. "Now we know that his name is Muiredach."

WE WERE all sitting in the day room, listening to Cathal speak. Not only had we learned our enemy's name, we also had a general description of how he looked—a mythborn with a lean body, marble-white skin, amber eyes, and golden hair—and that was enough to spot him in a crowd. Aengus's interrogators had also managed to learn of several locations across Dublin that Muiredach used as meeting and supply points. Cathal doubted we'd find him there, so he allowed the Court to handle clearing out those places.

"What is most important is that he's not invisible anymore," Cathal said. "He can hide, but now we know who to look for, and we will find him in whatever shadows he lurks."

Others nodded, determination clear on their faces. Now that the Scáthanna had a real target, it was only a matter of time to them.

I, on the other hand, had more doubts. It felt like ever since this whole mess had started, we'd made hardly any progress, and celebrating that we finally knew who our enemy was—after all those efforts, and after three of our members died—felt almost... pathetic. Like we were desperate to find any achievement worth mentioning to avoid slipping into hopelessness.

My feelings must have sneaked into my expression, because Cathal looked at me with curiosity. "You don't seem convinced."

Of course, all heads turned to me, so I had no choice but to speak my mind. "It all feels too little and too late. Like we haven't done enough for those who died. We have no victory to claim. No revenge for them."

In the silence that fell after my words, I felt a pang of regret. They'd been through so much and lost close and dear friends, and I was taking away what little comfort they might have found in finally making real progress, no matter how small it was.

Yet, to my surprise, Cathal smiled.

"Enemies will always be out there, known and unknown. Team members will die, and we will mourn them. We will avenge them when the opportunity arises. So, yes, what we learned tonight is little, and perhaps unworthy of a celebration. But there's something else we're celebrating tonight." He looked me in the eye. "We have a new member, and after today's events, everyone here is certain they can trust her. Now we know she would risk her own wellbeing, risk death or torture, for the good of the team. Since she joined, she's proven that she won't question my orders or go off on her own, and that's more than she gave even the Trinitians. So yes, we have reasons to celebrate today."

I looked around, finding in their expressions confirmation of what Cathal had said. I had no doubt that I still had much to learn, but it wasn't about my weapon skills or even knowing all about how the team went about doing, well, pretty much everything. What he'd pointed out was the change in my mindset. Some time between our first conversation—when his offer was little more than a means of getting away from Eithne—and tonight's ambush, I had truly embraced that I was one of them.

Ever since the war had ended and all the members of my squad had parted ways, I'd been a loner. At first, I tried to find a place for myself in Trinity, especially as I hoped for something more with Albert, but I had never fit in. Even when I worked with Trinitians, I didn't feel like a part of something bigger. Then, after I moved out to focus on my information-gathering work, I'd never developed close ties with anyone. With the affliction foretelling my death, I'd convinced myself it wasn't worth the time and the pain those I'd eventually leave behind would suffer. I made myself believe that I didn't long for something more. I had friends, acquaintances, and business contacts, but I hadn't belonged anywhere... until now.

Of course, being a part of something had its consequences too: less freedom and privacy, people always being around whether I wanted their company or not, and all the anxiety that came with caring for them and their safety—but I was willing to pay that price.

Besides, they had their own price to pay as well. They had to deal with a myth-touched unused to their ways, and if that wasn't annoying enough, I could eavesdrop on every single one of their conversations if I wanted to.

So, all in all, it was a fair trade for all of us.

"I think that's enough for one night," Cathal said. "As much as I want to make plans and keep pushing, so that Muiredach feels surrounded and out of options, we all deserve some rest first. I allowed Aengus to oversee the interrogations and handle any minor information, but he knows that if his people stumble upon something solid, we're going to take over." He looked straight at me. "When the right time comes, we will have a proper celebration for you. But until then, I wanted to make sure you know you're acknowledged."

He turned and walked out. Sadb and Faolan soon followed, and I was alone with Riagán. He was smiling.

"Shower?" he asked.

"With you? Always," I replied.

Sadb and Faolan would likely be in there too, washing off blood and tiredness, but I cared little about it. It wasn't like I wanted to keep my relationship with Riagán secret from anyone, especially from them. And, in the end, we were not going to do anything but shower together. The very thought, though, brought warmth and lightness to my heart.

"We won't take long," he added, leading me to the door.

"We won't?" That was new.

So far, Riagán had been taking my request for "taking it slow" seriously, but he did enjoy the closeness and intimacy, understanding that this was what would build a solid foundation for our relationship and let us decide if we wanted one to begin with—but, truth to be told, I was certain that by now we were both past the decision stage.

"We made promises last night," he said with unusual seriousness, "and I believe I was supposed to tell you something next week. Now that we're done with the ambush, I see no reason to wait longer. But I'd also rather not make any serious confessions with an audience consisting of Sadb and Faolan. Their comments and cheering would likely ruin the mood," he added in a lighthearted way.

I stopped mid-step and turned to face him. "Riagán, I... I didn't mean to force anything on you." I should have known he'd take my remark seriously.

He put a finger to my lips with a gentle hushing sound. "Ruining the mood is Sadb's and Faolan's job," he whispered. "Come, let's wash off the stench of death and move to a more pleasant part of the night."

There was a promise in his words, and I stopped thinking that I should offer him a way out. If he wanted one, he'd never have made that offer to begin with.

"And what if I decide to run?" I teased as we resumed down the corridor.

Riagán grinned. "The Scáthanna never hide nor run in the face of danger," he repeated the words he'd said to me once already. "And you *are* one of us."

One of them—and a part of a family.

I liked the sound of it.

THANK YOU FOR READING!

Thank you for reading! If you enjoyed the book, please
consider leaving a review.
Kaja's adventures continue in
Snakebitten

Sign up for the author's newsletter and receive your
complimentary copy of Scourges, Spells, and Serenades – a
collection of fantasy short stories:
authorjm.com

ABOUT THE AUTHOR

Joanna might be a bit too cautious to do anything even remotely daring or dangerous herself, so she writes about daring adventures and dangerous magic instead. Yet, she found enough courage to abandon her life in Poland and move to Ireland, and then some years later, she abandoned her life in Ireland to move over to the US. She's determined to settle there, once she finally chooses which state to reside in.

When she's not writing or thinking about writing, she plays video games or makes amateur art. She lives the happy life of a recluse, surrounded by her husband, a stuffed red monkey, and a small collection of books she insisted on hauling across two continents.

You can find the full list of her publications and more about her at:

http://authorjm.com

and connect with her via social media:

facebook.com/AuthorJMac

instagram.com/authorjmac

indiepocalypse.social/@AuthorJMac

bsky.app/profile/authorjmac.bsky.social

threads.net/@authorjmac

x.com/AuthorJMac

goodreads.com/authorjmac

bookbub.com/authors/joanna-maciejewska